P9-AGF-149

Destined for You

Books by Tracie Peterson

Destined for You

TRACIE PETERSON

BETHANYHOUSE

a division of Baker Publishing Group
Minneapolis, Minnesota

© 2021 by Peterson Ink, Inc.

Published by Bethany House Publishers
11400 Hampshire Avenue South
Bloomington, Minnesota 55438
www.bethanyhouse.com

Bethany House Publishers is a division of
Baker Publishing Group, Grand Rapids, Michigan

Printed in the United States of America

All rights reserved. No part of this publication may be reproduced, stored in a retrieval system, or transmitted in any form or by any means—for example, electronic, photocopy, recording—without the prior written permission of the publisher. The only exception is brief quotations in printed reviews.

Library of Congress Cataloging-in-Publication Data
Names: Peterson, Tracie, author.
Title: Destined for you / Tracie Peterson.
Description: Minneapolis, Minnesota : Bethany House, a division of Baker
    Publishing Group, [2021] | Series: Ladies of the lake
Identifiers: LCCN 2020042361 | ISBN 9780764232343 (trade paperback) |
    ISBN 9780764232350 (cloth) | ISBN 9780764232367 (large print) | ISBN
    9781493429790 (ebook)
Subjects: GSAFD: Historical fiction.
Classification: LCC PS3566.E7717 D47 2021 | DDC 813/.54—dc23
LC record available at https://lccn.loc.gov/2020042361

Scripture quotations are from the King James Version of the Bible.

This is a work of historical reconstruction; the appearances of certain historical figures are therefore inevitable. All other characters, however, are products of the author's imagination, and any resemblance to actual persons, living or dead, is coincidental.

Cover design by Paul Higdon and Peter Gloege/LOOK Design Studio
Woman on cover by Magdalena Russocka / Trevillion Images
Lake Superior cover scene by Matt Anderson Photography / Getty Images

21 22 23 24 25 26 27   7 6 5 4 3 2 1

Chapter 1

Gloriana Womack was not one to brook nonsense. If her twenty-five years had taught her anything, it was that eight-year-old boys were constantly in motion. And that motion often took them to places that guaranteed the need for a bath. But with the school bell set to ring in less than ten minutes, Gloriana barely had time to get her brother, JT, into a clean shirt.

"I told you not to go outside until it was time to leave for school."

"Aw, Glory. I just wanted to see if Papa was still here." The curly-headed boy let her dress him but kept straining to see out the window.

"Papa told you he'd be back to walk you

to school. He's not going to leave before he does that. Remember, he's not fishing today. He has business to tend to."

"I don't know why I have to go to school anyway. When I get big, I'm gonna catch fish like Papa does. He didn't go to school."

"Which is exactly why he wants you to. There are a lot of things that are limited for Papa because he didn't get an education. Even taking care of bank business requires someone to go with him. Mama used to read for him, but now I do it."

"Mr. Carson went with him today," JT said.

"Yes, he did. Mr. Carson is very helpful in these things." She had nothing but fond thoughts for the sweet young couple next door. Scott and Sally Carson had become like family.

Gloriana finished the last button on her brother's shirt and had just straightened when their father bounded into the house with a grin.

"There's my family. Are you ready, JT?"

The boy shoved his shirt into his waistband and pulled up his suspender straps. "I am now. Come on, or the bell is going to ring and I'll be late. Don't forget we have to get all the way up the hill." JT gave Gloriana a hug, then went running to his father, who bent over just as the boy approached. JT jumped on his back and gave a whooping cry. "To school!"

Gloriana laughed. JT had more energy than any other boys she knew. "Be good, JT." She handed her father a cloth bag with the drawstring pulled tight. "Here's his lunch."

With the men of the house gone, Gloriana began her daily routine of housework. She threw JT's dirty shirt into the pile of laundry she would have to tackle later. For now, she would get the breakfast mess cleaned up. They'd had flapjacks, and it seemed JT had tracked stickiness everywhere.

She took a dish towel that was already damp and dipped it in a pan of hot water that she'd readied for the dishes. The table, a hardy pine creation that had been gifted to her mother and father when they married, was soon decluttered and cleaned to Gloriana's standards. She finished tidying up the kitchen and then went to work on the dishes. When everything was finally washed, dried, and put away, she stood back and surveyed her handiwork. Nothing was quite so satisfying as a clean kitchen.

Now to mop.

A knock interrupted her plan. Gloriana dried her hands on her apron and untied the strings. She hung it up on a peg by the back door and went to receive her guest.

A petite brunette stood on the other side of the door. Gloriana smiled.

"I figured since Papa and Scott got back from town, you would be busy with your husband," Gloriana said.

Sally Carson patted her ever-rounding belly. "The baby has other plans. I've been having some pains."

"Is it time?" Gloriana asked, alarmed.

Sally shook her head. "The midwife said it's false labor, but the real thing will come soon enough. Scott is busy trying to make sure everything is ready. He's making some repairs to the house that he and your father talked about. I just came over to borrow some white thread. I'm finishing up the last few diapers."

"Of course. Come in and have a seat. Don't wear yourself out." Gloriana went to her sewing basket. "It's going to be so much fun to have a baby around. I remember when JT was born. Actually, I remember when Tabby and Aaron were born as well, but that seems like a long time ago now." For a moment Gloriana found herself thinking back to those happier days when the family had all been together. Before sickness had robbed her of a mother and two siblings.

"How long has it been since . . . well, since they . . ." Sally let her voice fade to silence.

Gloriana returned with a spool of white thread. "Three years since Mama and Aaron and Tabitha died from scarlet fever. It seems like forever at times, and other days it feels like it was just last week."

"I'm so sorry. I didn't mean to bring up painful thoughts."

Gloriana dropped into her father's chair by the fireplace. "You didn't bring up anything that wasn't already there. I miss them so much that they are never far from my thoughts."

"I wish I could have been here for you. You've been such a dear friend to me since Scott and I arrived last spring. I don't know what we would have done if you weren't here. Why, we wouldn't even have a place to live if not for your father renting us the little house next door."

"Papa is that way. Always so generous and kind. I think your arrival helped him as much as it did me. I think we were both lost in our sadness." Gloriana tried not to think about how much she missed her family. Scarlet fever had come like a thief without warning. Only a handful of the families who lived nearby had suffered from the sickness. Everyone else had recovered, but not the Womack family. The doctor said their cases had been more severe.

Gloriana pushed aside the memories. "Papa said Scott ordered a new rug. That will be so nice for the baby."

"For me too. I get so cold. When the wind comes down from the north, I just about freeze."

"And you haven't even experienced winter yet. You'll appreciate the extra effort the men put into getting the firewood stocked up. Having it stacked around the outside of the house adds extra insulation and makes it easy to bring inside. We'll get by just fine. You'll see."

"I do worry about Scott." Sally shook her head. "He works so hard."

"Yes, but when the harbor closes in January, he'll be here with you and the baby. There's still work to be done, making repairs and getting ready for the next fishing season, but having the men home is always nice."

"But the storms between now and January are yet to be endured. I've heard so many horrible stories."

Gloriana nodded and reached out to pat Sally's hand in reassurance. "They are bad, to be sure, but being afraid won't change things."

"I know, but just seeing some of the storms this summer was enough. I don't like to think of what's to come. How can a person live through such things?"

Gloriana wished she could say something comforting, but she knew as well as every other person in town that Lake Superior was extremely unforgiving at times. Papa said the lake was like a wild animal. You could never hope to tame it, and to ignore it could easily spell your doom.

"Sally, just remember that God is in charge, and He knows the lake because He created it. We can trust Him to watch over us and guard us."

"Yes, but people die out there all the time."

"They do, but you can't live your life in fear. People die logging the woods. People die from sickness, like my mama and brother and sister."

"Or in childbirth," Sally murmured.

"Goodness, just listen to how morose we've managed to get. This is a beautiful day, and you are soon to deliver a much-desired baby. We need to think on that and other good things."

"I know you're right. I need to get back home. Do you still want us to come for supper at five?"

"Yes. Papa wants to get to bed early so he can get out on the lake early. At least they're sticking close and just heading over to the Apostle Islands. He said they'd haul in whatever the pound nets have caught and then take up the nets before the weather turns bad. We always retrieve them before October."

Sally nodded and squared her shoulders, as if determining to be brave. "I know they'll have their hands full. Oh, I almost forgot. Could I borrow some cinnamon too? I want to make the men some cookies to have as a snack tomorrow." She scooted to the edge of the seat and struggled to her feet.

"Of course." Gloriana went to the kitchen and pulled out a drawer in her spice container. She pulled a stick of cinnamon from a small glass jar. "Here you go."

"Thanks, Gloriana. You always make me feel so much better." Sally's large brown eyes were edged with tears. "I don't mean to always be so afraid, but our life has been rough. Since my mother died, I don't know what I would have done without Scott. I had nobody else."

"Well, you have us now." Gloriana hugged her friend close, as she might have done JT. "Now, try to enjoy the day."

"I will. I promise."

Gloriana had a few minutes to herself before JT returned home from school. Papa was off seeing to something for the boat, and the house was clean and supper was already baking in the oven. She settled down at the kitchen table with her Bible and had just started to read when another knock sounded on the front door. It was unusual to have more than one visitor in a day. With a sigh, Gloriana closed the Bible and went to see who it was.

"Mr. Nelson," she said, surprised to see the schoolmaster. Beside him, a downcast JT stood digging his toe in the dirt.

"Miss Womack, is your father home?" The severe-looking man had been the subject of many of her brother Aaron's pantomimes, and the cause of the utter desolation of JT.

"I'm afraid you'll have to deal with me for the time being."

JT looked up with a pleading expression. Gloriana could only imagine his crime.

"Jeremiah Thomas carved his initials on his school desk, and I have come to deliver him home for punishment from his father. I have already delivered three well-placed swats and commanded that he repair the damage immediately."

"JT, is this true?" Gloriana asked in as stern a voice as she could muster.

"It's true. He swatted me real hard," JT confirmed.

"I meant did you carve on the desk."

He nodded, then looked at the ground again. "I'm sorry."

Mr. Nelson pushed his glasses up the bridge of his nose. "Unfortunately, I believe your brother is only sorrowful for getting caught."

"I will see that our father learns of what happened. I'm sure JT will be happy to repair the desk."

Mr. Nelson looked at her for a long moment. "Very well. I shall leave him to your care."

He turned with the precision of a soldier and marched away. Gloriana might have laughed at his formality but for JT. The boy would see her amusement as something to capitalize on. Already she could see him relax his shoulders as he gave a sigh.

"I'll have your pocketknife," she said.

"Mr. Nelson took it. Mean old bear."

"JT, that is not to be tolerated. Mr. Nelson is your elder and teacher. He is your authority at school, and you have dishonored yourself today."

Her brother's lower lip jutted out and quivered. Tears were soon to follow.

Gloriana gave him a brief hug. "Go to your room and wait for Papa."

JT said nothing more but hung his head and moved toward his bedroom. Part of her wanted to run after him and tell him everything was forgiven and there would be no further punishment, but another part knew he'd never learn if he didn't have to face the consequences of his actions. It was just so hard to be an eight-year-old boy in a world full of rules.

Norman Womack looked at his son and shook his head. "I'm very disappointed in you, JT. What got into your head that made you think it was all right to destroy someone else's property?"

"I don't know." JT kept his gaze on the floor. "I guess I didn't think."

"No. You sure didn't. I can't understand what got into you. I'm disappointed, son. Very disappointed."

JT bit his lower lip and braved a glance at his father's face. Gloriana wanted to step in and save her brother from further pain and discomfort, but Papa had made it clear after Mama died that Gloriana could no longer play the role of sympathetic sister. She would be JT's disciplinarian in their father's absence, and it was crucial that she understood how important that role was. Children without discipline grew up to believe they could do whatever they wanted. Papa had told her that it wasn't easy to be so firm with JT, but it might very well keep him from making bad choices in the future. Gloriana knew her father's words were true, but she hated seeing JT so upset.

"So what do you have to say for yourself, Jeremiah Thomas?"

JT knew that when his full name was used, there was severe punishment coming his way. "I don't know. I didn't mean to hurt the desk, but when I started, it was just fun and I couldn't stop."

"Did you know what you were doing was wrong?"

JT nodded. "Yes, sir."

"There will be other times in life when you might get involved in something that you find fun but know is wrong. You have to fight against those kinds of wrongdoing. They will not only cause you a world of problems but may hurt others as well, like Mr. Nelson."

"Mr. Nelson is mean. I hate him!" JT's expression showed he had surprised himself by making such a strong statement. He wasn't usually one to sass or speak against other people.

"I don't much care if you like him or not. Each man makes his own judgment about such things," Papa declared. "What I do care about is you speakin' your mind when I'm reprimanding you. That will get you a more severe punishment."

JT frowned and fixed his father with a spiteful look. "Then I hate you too."

Gloriana made a move toward her brother, but Papa waved her off. "That is your choice, JT, just as it's my choice to deny you supper. Furthermore, you will not only sand and paint your desk but every desk in that classroom."

"That's not fair! I didn't carve on those other desks."

"You keep sassin' me, and I'll have to spank you as well. Now, go to your room and get ready for bed."

JT's face reddened, but he didn't say another word. He stormed off to the back of the house and slammed his bedroom door.

"I've never seen him like that." Gloriana looked at her father. "What's gotten into him?"

"Hard to tell. Boys can be like that." He shook his head. "You can't hold it against him, Glory. He's let his anger get the best of him. I'll go talk to him about it later. He's not gonna be able to sleep for some time. He knows what he did was wrong—at school and here at home. It'll get to eatin' at his heart, and he'll be filled with remorse. It might take time for him to admit it, but eventually he'll be sorry for what he's said and done."

That evening, just before Papa went to bed, Gloriana heard him talking to her brother once again. She stood outside the door, hoping and praying that all would be resolved. She certainly didn't want Papa leaving without JT apologizing.

But the boy stood firm in his anger. He reiterated that he hated his papa. It was something Gloriana had never heard come out of his mouth. She knew the last few years had been hard on him. Losing their mother had taken joy from all of them. In fact, Gloriana found little joy left in her heart. She hurt at the thought of their loss and couldn't imagine how it must be for a little boy to be without his mother and siblings. He had adored Aaron, who at sixteen surprisingly always found time to play with JT. Tabitha treated JT like her own baby. She had been five when JT came into the world, and she was always at his side. Was all of JT's anger due to that loss?

Gloriana heard her father tell JT good night and reassure him that he was loved despite his wrongdoing. JT said nothing, and Gloriana wanted to go to his bedside and demand he make up with Papa. She was a firm believer in not letting the sun go down on one's anger.

She eased away from the room as her father came out. She gave him a sympathetic shrug, having no idea what else she could do. Papa followed her out to the front room.

"Give him time," he said. "He'll come around."

"I just want to shake him. I'm so troubled by his attitude."

Papa smiled. "You can't let it get you all caught up. Children say things without thinkin', and once he thinks it through, he's going to feel powerfully bad about it. We'll show him forgiveness, though."

"And what about the punishment?"

"That stands. A person must bear the consequences of their actions, or they learn nothin'."

"But there's always the possibility of grace."

Papa gave her a hard look. "Do you think the punishment was too severe?"

"I'm sure I wouldn't know." Gloriana gave a sigh. "I trust your judgment, Papa. I didn't mean to sound like I didn't."

He smiled. "Don't fret. I'll lend a hand in due time and see that those desks get fixed up, but first JT has to accept his punishment and show a willingness to obey."

Gloriana nodded and stretched up on tiptoe to kiss her father's cheek. "I love you, Papa."

"And I love you, Glory. You look more like your mama every day, with your pretty blond curls just like hers and those bright blue eyes. It was her eyes that caught my attention the first time I saw her. Never saw eyes that color of blue."

His expression took on a distant look, and Gloriana clearly saw regret in his eyes. It was regret that matched her soul. Regret over a loss that could never be changed.

Chapter 2

At four the next morning, Gloriana fed her father a hearty breakfast of pickled herring, poached eggs, toast, and her homemade berry jam, with plenty of hot coffee.

"Much obliged, daughter. That will keep me content for a few hours at least."

Gloriana smiled and placed a large sack on the end of the table. "This will help you past that."

"When we get enough whitefish, I'll be back. With it getting close to their time to spawn, we're going to be gradually busier, and I have to get my pound nets in, so we have more than a few things to see to."

She kissed the top of his billed cap. "I know you'll be home when you can, and I'll have something warm for you to eat."

He got up from the table and patted his

belly. "You cook ever' bit as good as your mama. She'd be so proud of you, Glory. She'd be happy you put aside your own desires to take care of me and JT, but as soon as that boy's old enough to do for himself, I want you to reconsider marriage."

"Papa, we've already talked about this, and now really isn't the time to start up a conversation. If God has a man for me, He'll send him our way and make it clear. He'd have to be someone willing to take on all three of us, or he couldn't possibly be the right man." She smiled. "Now, you're going to be late if you don't get a move on."

Papa glanced toward the hall that led to the bedrooms. There was no sign of JT. Not that Gloriana had really expected him. It was a struggle each day just to get him awake in time to go to school.

"I hope he won't give you too hard of a time today."

Gloriana shook her head. "JT will be fine, just like you said. He needs time to rethink things. Now, get on with you, and don't forget your food."

He grabbed up the bag. "I love you, Glory."

"I love you too, Papa. Oh, and don't forget." She beamed him a big smile. "If you face trouble, remember that I'm right about Jesus."

This was something her mother had always said before letting her husband head out onto the lake.

He chuckled. "The good Lord can have me anytime He wants to come get me." He opened the door. "Smells like there might be a rain in our future."

Gloriana followed him outside. It was chilly, and she wished she'd brought her shawl. Instead, she hugged her arms to her body to ward off the nip in the air.

Sally and Scott came out of the little house that Gloriana had once lived in as a girl, back when it was just her and Mama and Papa. "Morning," she said with a wave.

Scott and Sally made their way closer. "Good morning to you," Scott replied. He smiled. He was always smiling. He seemed happier than anyone Gloriana had ever met.

Sally pushed a tin into Scott's hands. "These are for later. Did you get your lunch as well?"

"I did." He leaned down and kissed her. "I'll be back before you know it."

Gloriana and Sally watched the men leave. Within view down the rocky path was the object of their attention, the *Ana Eileen*, a fishing boat named for Gloriana's mother. Neither said good-bye, as that was considered bad luck, and even if Gloriana didn't believe in luck and superstitions, she knew her father did.

She took Sally's hand. "Let's pray for them." She didn't wait for Sally's answer. This was their custom every day the men went fishing.

"Father, we ask Your blessing on the *Ana Eileen* and the men who serve her. Let the catch be plentiful and the weather fair. Bless all those who sail today, Lord. In Jesus' name, amen."

"Amen," Sally whispered.

Gloriana opened her eyes to gaze after her father and Scott. "Did you get your cookies made?"

"Yes." Sally's voice was barely audible. She refused to look away from her husband. "I hate it when he goes away."

"I know." Gloriana put her arm around Sally and said nothing as the sun rose on the horizon in streaks of red and pink. *Red sails in the morning, sailors take warning* was a well-known saying. It was even in the Bible—the sixteenth chapter of Matthew—although the words were a little different.

"I have laundry to do," Gloriana said with a sigh, "and an angry little boy to send off to school."

"Why is he angry?" Sally asked, rubbing her belly.

"He carved on his school desk and was reprimanded by the schoolmaster and his father. I think disappointing Papa was the worst of it." Gloriana gave a sigh. "Last night he was so bitter and angry. I'll wake him up and see how it fares with him this morning."

Sally nodded and began walking toward her little house. "I hope it goes well."

Gloriana cast one more glance toward the *Ana Eileen*. "I do too," she whispered.

Lucas Carson listened as Jay Cooke instructed him on his new job. The financier, who was well known for having raised enormous amounts of capital for the North during the War Between the States, was now heavily invested in railroads and wanted to see his projects pushed ahead without delay.

Having worked for years as an attorney for Jay Cooke's railroad interests, Luke wasn't surprised that today's conversation was centered on the railroad's progress.

"As you know, we are close to breaking ground in Minnesota on the Northern Pacific Railway, and the Lake Superior and Mississippi Railroad is well underway," Mr. Cooke began. "I have a good team of men in St. Paul, as well as a few in Duluth, but I want you there as well. As I understand from your supervisor, you have a brother in Duluth."

Luke nodded. "I do."

Mr. Cooke fixed him with a stern look. "That will help. You will have someone with whom you can stay, and perhaps the solitude won't seem quite so overwhelming. I've had letters from some of my men that speak to their dismay with the isolation of Duluth."

"I'm sure I can adapt, sir. I've never minded wild spaces and isolation."

For a moment Mr. Cooke studied him as if to unearth deceit, but Luke spoke the truth. He'd always enjoyed the unsettled regions of the country whenever he'd had a chance to see them—which, granted, hadn't been often. His father despised such locales. They were a long way from Philadelphia.

"Good. I hope to send you there tomorrow. I know that hardly leaves you much time to put your affairs in order, but while I apologize and sympathize, I cannot alter the date."

"I assure you my affairs are in order, and I will have no trouble leaving tomorrow," Luke assured him.

"Then I will have my secretary give you what you'll need to get up to date on what is happening in Minnesota. There is a great deal to accomplish in order to get the Lake Superior and Mississippi in place by next

August. One thing, however, that I must remind you of is the conflict between the cities of Duluth, Minnesota, and Superior, Wisconsin."

Luke nodded. He knew very well about the rivalry of the two towns. They were located across from each other on St. Louis and Superior Bays. Separated by the Minnesota and Wisconsin Points, the two cities had long fought for the right to be the primary city on the west end of Lake Superior. Superior, Wisconsin, had better shipping access and thus had grown considerably, but Duluth was no quitter, and with the help of men like Mr. Cooke, who had invested heavily in the success of the little town, prosperity came closer every day.

"I considered sending you by ship, but instead I'm sending you to St. Paul first, and that is best accomplished by rail. A group of men there will be making their way north on the track that's been laid, and then from the current terminus, they will venture forth on foot, horse, and wagon. I want you with them, and I want your honest opinion of the route they've chosen. I've heard the area is nothing but swampland and lakes, but we must make do."

"Very well." Luke was still unclear as to what his job would be.

"There is a great deal of trouble brewing between the two cities of Duluth and Superior, and I need to know I have a man there who is loyal not to the city nor the railroad but to me. I also want a man of godly resolve. I know you to be a strong Christian man and believe you will pray and keep God's Word ever present in your heart. This is the kind of man I need in Duluth—the kind of man who will seek God first. Will you be that man for me, Carson?"

Luke had always admired the fact that Jay Cooke was a strong man of God himself. He often opened their meetings in prayer. "Of course, sir. I am happy to go and serve you in this capacity. However, I would like to know exactly what you would have me do while I'm there."

"Your working title will be general manager. The various work gangs each have a boss. In turn, these bosses report to the project managers, and they will report to you. Each team is to document the progress made on the line, as well as detail lists of what new supplies are needed. You will go over all of the requests and note whether they are reasonable or whether something different should be done. You will be my eyes and ears. You will double-check that plans are going ahead as configured by our people and see that no one who is against us interferes. Can you do this?"

"Yes, to the best of my ability. However, if there is a problem between the cities, that concerns me."

"There are reasons for concern. Superior has gone against us every step of the way. They want to force our hand and make their city the railroad terminus. I have bought a considerable amount of property in Duluth, which is why I want the railroad there. That was my risk, but Superior's investors were hardly offering up the kind of money I was. It has created bad blood that will only be perpetuated when the Northern Pacific lays tracks in the spring. You have always seemed like a levelheaded young man. I've heard of you negotiating difficult deals where the other party seemed unwilling to yield even an inch. I feel you are the man for this job."

"I appreciate your confidence," Luke told the older man. "I will do my best for you."

"Good. I will pay you your regular salary." Mr. Cooke paused and ran his hand down his very long beard. "I will also give you a monthly bonus for your trouble and the isolation."

Luke nodded. Whatever was going on in

Duluth, it was to his advantage, and he would get to see Scott again. Poor Scott. He had fallen in love with the kitchen maid and married her shortly after the death of the girl's mother the previous December. They had hoped to keep the marriage from his father, who had no problem with his son having a dalliance with the help but would never accept one as a family member. When it was learned there would be a baby, Scott had found it necessary to confess his actions. Father had not only been upset by the news, he'd become furious and had irreversibly disinherited Scott. They had left Philadelphia in shame and settled in Duluth with financial help from Luke.

"I will expect regular letters from you each week, if possible," Mr. Cooke continued. "I realize the winter months will make this more difficult, so a monthly report during that time will be acceptable."

"I understand and will do what I can to see that you have what information is available."

Mr. Cooke got to his feet, and Luke rose as well. They shook hands, and the financier handed Luke an envelope. "Travel expenses."

Luke placed the envelope in his inside coat pocket. "Thank you. I will be in touch with your report."

Martin Carson looked across the table in disbelief. "You have to be joking. You can't leave Philadelphia for that godforsaken country."

"I'm afraid I must. Mr. Cooke requires it of me, and you've always instructed me to do whatever he commanded." Luke took slices of rare roast beef from the platter offered to him by the footman. He waited as the next servant poured au jus atop the thick pieces. He was starved, and the meat was testing his patience as he waited for all the dishes to be served and his father to begin eating.

"Would you care for me to say grace?" Luke asked, knowing the answer.

"No. I would like you to explain more about this unreasonable demand."

"It wasn't really a demand, and it was certainly not unreasonable. I might have refused, but the job was offered because of the great confidence Mr. Cooke has in me. I thought that might please you. Instead I find you surly and discontented." Luke prayed over his meal silently, then followed his father's lead and sampled the roast. It was nearly tender enough to cut with the fork.

"I am glad to hear that a powerful ally

found my son's work of value, but Duluth is too far away. I need you here in Philadelphia."

"Are you suggesting I give up my position with Mr. Cooke?"

"Of course not!" His father pounded his left fist on the table but never gave a sign of losing his fork out of the other.

They ate in silence for several minutes, and then his father began to pose additional questions. "What, exactly, will you be doing?"

"I've been given the title general manager. Mr. Cooke, as you know, has two railroad projects going on at the same time. Each has a manager, but Mr. Cooke wants someone who will oversee everything. After speaking with his secretary, I learned that involves more than just the two railroad projects. Mr. Cooke has his hand in a lot of other projects as well, including the idea to dig a canal from Lake Superior directly into Duluth's harbor. Right now ships must come by way of the Superior, Wisconsin, entrance, and there has been a lot of disagreement between those two towns. Mr. Cooke has also started building a large hotel, a grand affair for important clientele. There are a dozen other projects, but I won't bore you with them. Suffice it to say, I will oversee these things."

"I suppose you'll see *him*."

"Him who?" Luke raised a brow and waited for his father's answer.

"Your brother." Martin Carson's voice was full of contempt. "And *her*."

"Sally. Yes, I shall see both of them." Luke continued to eat. The food was sumptuous, and there was no sense in letting his father ruin the day, much less the meal. "Mr. Cooke suggested I could stay with them."

"I can't imagine they have proper accommodations, unless you've bought it for them."

"I assure you I have not purchased them a house." Luke refrained from admitting he had sent money so they could rent one when they first arrived. Since then, Scott had found a good job fishing, and the rent was part of his pay.

"They probably live in a hovel."

"Perhaps, but I'm looking forward to seeing them again, especially with the baby being due almost any day. Your first grandchild, I might add."

"You might also bite your tongue. That baby is nothing to me. He or she will no doubt be raised in squalor and poverty."

"It wouldn't have to be that way. You have the means to keep that from being the case."

His father gave a low growl. "I won't go back on my word. Your brother made a grave error in defying me."

"To marry the woman he loved? That hardly seems fair of you, Father. You have no tenderness for your own child."

Luke could see he'd riled his father. "He might have at least remained here so that I might oversee the child's upbringing."

"So you could take the baby away from them, you mean? I remember the offer. You suggested that he might divorce his wife and return home with the baby so you could see it properly reared."

"There was nothing wrong with my offer." Father waved his hand over the linen- and china-covered table. "Just look at what they might have had. I could have given Scott and the child everything. All would have been forgiven with one simple action."

"An action that would deny Scott happiness and refuse the woman he loved. It would have ripped a newborn from the bosom of its mother." Luke shook his head. "I cannot approve. It was cruel."

"It was for the betterment of all. She was nothing more than a scullery maid! My sons could have married royalty. There were offers, as you well know."

Luke remembered a couple of rather homely daughters of a financially strapped duke—a relative to the queen of England. The duke needed to marry his daughters to money to save his estates and in return had assured Father that his sons would receive titles from Queen Victoria herself. Things like that were important to Luke's father, a transplanted Englishman.

"He could have had so much more," Father muttered.

Luke smiled. "But his heart chose Sally. I've never seen two people more in love. I would have thought you'd be happy for them, but instead you turned into a raving lunatic."

"Watch your tongue, boy." His father shook his finger.

"Or what? Will you disinherit me as well?" At one time Luke and his brother would have shared everything, but now his father planned to leave it all to Luke. Little did he know that Luke intended to split the inheritance with his brother anyway. It was the very least he could do. He fixed his father with a stern look. "I will not have you hold it over my head. Either leave me an inheritance or don't, but I will not give up my relationship with Scott."

"I'll hear nothing more of this. I regret that you must leave tomorrow for Duluth. I will look forward to your return." Father refocused his attention on the food while Luke stared at him. How could he just forget Scott so easily?

"You should probably know that I have no idea when that might be," Luke responded. "It could be years. Mr. Cooke wants someone in place who can keep his affairs in order and out of the hands of the people he considers the enemy."

"Years? That's ridiculous. He can hardly expect you to make a life there."

"But he does, and frankly it seems to be an exciting time for Duluth. They have few people presently, but more are moving in daily, and Mr. Cooke has even advertised incentives for folks to relocate. It's the way railroad investors do business. People are needed to ensure settlement and growth."

Father shook his head. "There is plenty to invest in right here. I don't know why he sees the need to send you off to the ends of the earth."

Luke laughed and speared the last piece of his roast. "I have no doubt you would gladly advise him on where he should or shouldn't invest, but for now, I'm off to Minnesota."

Chapter 3

That evening, with a soft rain falling, Gloriana listened to the men talk about their day as the two families shared supper.

"I didn't know for sure that we'd get that last pound net taken up, what with the storm moving in," Papa declared. "I thought we might have to leave it for another day, but the worst of the weather went north, and while the water was rough, we managed it."

"And the fish were plentiful," Scott added.

Papa nodded. "They're definitely starting to spawn."

"I'm just glad you're home safe," Sally said, shaking her head. "I don't think I'm cut out to be a fisherman's wife."

Papa chuckled. "Every woman I know says that. It's a trial for those at home to wait and watch, knowing they can't do a thing to help. I remember one year a fierce storm came up, and ships were tossed about like toys. One of the ships was right off the shore—we could see the men fighting to get to safety as the ship was breaking apart. The lake was terrible, offerin' no mercy. We did our best to render aid, but nothing worked, and within twenty feet of safety, those men perished." He shook his head. "It has always kept me mindful of life's uncertainties."

"That's terrible," Sally said, looking at the others. "Why could no one throw out a lifeline?"

"The storm was too fierce," Gloriana replied. She'd heard the story more than once. "They tried over and over, but just as they threw it out, the storm would spit it back at them. They even tried weighting the line and shooting it out."

"It's true," her father said, nodding. "Everything that could be done was done. Sometimes it's just not enough."

"But to be there on shore and see those men die." Sally shuddered. "I wouldn't be able to bear it if that happened to Scott. I think I'd throw myself into the water as well."

"Let's talk about something more pleasant," Gloriana declared.

The younger woman had paled. She

gripped her husband's hand. "Maybe I should just go fishing with you, and then if anything happened, we'd be together."

Gloriana laughed. "Papa says having a woman on board a ship is bad luck. He'll take a cat with him, but not a daughter."

Papa gave her a wink. "A cat is far less trouble than a daughter, even though there are those who think them just as much bad luck."

"Well, I know I don't have any peace of mind until you walk through the door . . . smelly though you may be," Sally said, looking at Scott.

He leaned over and kissed her cheek. "I have to confess, I love being on the lake. I never felt comfortable in a suit, working in my father's bank. I could never figure out what was wrong. I thought maybe it was working with numbers, but now I know I need to be outside. I love the wind in my hair and the open water. I treasure it."

Gloriana had to smile. She'd heard her father say the same thing. He would always come home and tell her stories when she was little. For the first six years of her life, she had been an only child. She had loved being the center of her father's attention and listened with captive imagination as he described his encounters on the lake.

"Superior is a fickle woman," he would tell her. "Fickle and jealous and given to pure meanness when she's angry. But when she's at peace with ya, there's none more generous. 'Course, you can never trust her. You'll never know for sure which way she'll act until you're out there."

Gloriana had heard this from her father all her life. Everyone in Duluth knew the truth of the Great Lakes. She looked at JT, who had been uncharacteristically silent throughout the meal.

"Are you ill, little brother?" She reached over and felt his forehead under a tousle of curls.

He shook his head. "May I be excused?" He looked at Gloriana, but it was his father who needed to answer.

"You may," Papa said with great tenderness in his voice. "Later, maybe we can have us a talk."

JT said nothing but scooted back from the table and jumped down from the chair. "Good evening, Mr. and Mrs. Carson."

"Good evening, JT."

He left the room, and Gloriana turned to her father. "He was that way this morning and when he came home from school. He's still very angry, and I can't figure out why. I know he hates disappointing you."

"Maybe he misses the others," Sally said. "Especially his mama."

There was dead silence for a moment, and Sally's face reddened.

"You know, Sally, you may be exactly right. I think of my own loss and deal with it as best I can, but that poor boy lost his mama and his brother and sister." Papa looked thoughtful. "I need to be more considerate."

They finished supper with a blueberry crumble Sally had made. Everyone praised her for the delicious dessert, and she shared that it was her mother's recipe and got a little teary.

"I know you miss her very much." Scott patted her hand. "Sally and her mother were very close, and it's been nearly a year since she passed."

"The first year is always the hardest," Gloriana declared.

Papa nodded, but no one really wanted to discuss the matter, so the room went silent again. Finally, when they'd finished eating, Gloriana began to gather the dishes.

"I have a few things I need to tend to before I head to bed," Papa said.

"So do we," Scott replied, helping Sally to her feet. "Thanks again for a delicious meal. But please know we don't always have to come over. If you want privacy, we would understand."

"There's plenty of time for privacy," Papa said. "Besides, I consider it part of your pay."

"Are you sure I can't help you with the dishes?" Sally asked.

"No. Just get home and rest. JT can come and dry if I need help."

"I'm grateful." Sally looked at Papa and then Gloriana. "We never would have survived if not for your kindness and Scott's brother, Luke."

After they'd gone, Gloriana hurried to finish up the dishes. She wanted to work on her knitting before they headed to bed. She was making thick cable sweaters for Papa and JT from a dark, unwashed wool yarn. Gloriana had gotten the idea from Mrs. Sedgwick, the pastor's wife. The unwashed yarn made the sweater more waterproof and thus warmer for long days on the ship. They would make perfect Christmas presents.

She glanced at the small table beside her chair, which held a picture of the entire family. It wasn't very big, but everyone was there, and they looked so happy. She gazed at her mother and smiled. Mama had never been one for fancying herself up, but she had donned a lace collar and a cameo for the occasion. She looked quite ornate.

Gloriana wiped a single tear from her eye. She missed Mama more than she could say but knew there was no sense in crying. If Papa saw her, he'd feel the need to cheer her up, and Gloriana didn't want him to be distracted from his work. He worked so hard.

An hour or so later, she heard her father coming in for the night. She could see he was weary and chilled to the bone.

"Would you like me to heat some water for a bath?"

He smiled but shook his head. "No, that's all right. I cleaned up already. I'll warm up once I get under a few blankets."

"Are you planning to go back to the islands for whitefish tomorrow?"

"You betcha. The numbers are good and getting better. We'll use the gill nets and probably get more than we need for the orders to Peterson's and Jacoby's. I'll bring home plenty to smoke." He yawned. "But there is something I need to tell you before I head to bed." He took a seat in his favorite chair.

Gloriana added more wood to the fire. "What is it, Papa?"

"I just wanted you to know that I know you're right about Jesus." He yawned again and rubbed his eyes. "I know you worry about such things."

She didn't know what to say. Her mother had tried all of Gloriana's life to get her husband to accept the Christian faith as his own and take Jesus as his Lord and Savior.

"Pastor Sedgwick came by tonight when I was tendin' to my nets. He told me I reminded him of the disciple Peter, who was also a fisherman. Peter, I guess, was a hard case like me. He knew Jesus was Lord, but he had some difficulties with his faith." Papa got to his feet. "I told Pastor Sedgwick that I knew Jesus was Lord but wasn't sure I'd ever acknowledged Him as my Lord. We talked a bit more, and I confessed my heart to Pastor. I made sure I was right with God. I guess I just wanted you to know so you could stop worryin' about what would happen to me if I met with trouble."

Gloriana forgot about her knitting and jumped to her feet. She encircled her father in a hug. "Oh, Papa, this makes me so happy. I can just imagine Mama dancing a jig in heaven." She kissed his cheek and pulled back to see his face.

His eyes were damp. "I know she'd be pleased, but I never wanted to do it for that reason. I knew it needed to be between me and God. I couldn't accept the Lord just because she wanted me to."

"I know, Papa. Nor for me."

"No, but I felt His callin' to me, and I came for myself . . . and for Him." He gave her a smile. "Now I know what your mama was talkin' about when she spoke of the peace of God. I feel it too."

Gloriana smiled. "Thank you for telling me, Papa. I will rest easy now, knowing you belong to Jesus."

"I always knew I would," Papa told her. "I was just stubborn."

"Like JT."

He nodded. "That boy is the spittin' image of me at that age." He ran his hand through thick gray-blond curls. "Heart and soul and outward appearance. He's got a tough road ahead, and no one knows that better than me. That's why I'm tough on him. Hopin' to save him some sufferin'."

Gloriana nodded. "I hope he'll soften his heart and understand your love for him."

"In time he will, Glory. In time he will."

Theodore Sedgwick considered his choices. His life had been a waste in so many ways. There were times when he'd felt he had accomplished something good, but they were few and far between. And now, even after twelve years, he still hadn't managed to do the one thing he wanted more than anything else. To see Luke Carson dead.

"There's still time," he muttered, hoping that was true.

He walked to the window of his small apartment. Glancing down at the street below, he saw a wiry older man hurrying down the sidewalk. It was about time he got there. Theodore moved quickly to open the door, even though he knew the man had three flights of stairs to climb before he'd arrive at Theo's place.

From his door, Theo could see the stairs, and when the man's bowler hat came into view, Theo felt a wave of anticipation wash over him. He'd heard rumors, and now finally he'd have them confirmed.

"Mr. Sedgwick," the man said, pausing a moment to catch his breath. "I have that information you wanted."

"Don't speak here in the hall. Come inside." Theo yanked the man into the apartment, then closed the door.

Panting, the older man pulled off his hat and nodded. "It's all true. Mr. Carson is bound for St. Paul and then Duluth. He's going to oversee everything in Duluth for Mr. Cooke."

Theo fished out the five dollars he'd promised the man. "What else do you know?"

"There's a position open that will allow you to work in close proximity to Mr. Carson. That is what you wanted, isn't it?"

"It is." Theo didn't want to give himself away. "My family lives in Duluth, and I've always wanted to make my way back there to be close to them." Half of that was a lie, but this man was none the wiser.

"Well, I heard there are two positions needed in the office that Mr. Carson will have in Duluth. Personal secretary to him, and a clerk."

"And how am I to secure the position as personal secretary?"

"I suppose you would have to interview for it," the man replied.

Theodore didn't like the sound of that. It was always possible Carson might remember his name from twelve years earlier when Theo worked for the elder Carson's bank.

Theo's funds were dwindling, but he knew this man could still prove useful. "If the right man could secure that position for me, I could make it worth his while."

The wiry fellow raised a brow. "I suppose a letter could be sent from Mr. Cooke assigning a particular man the position. For, say, the sum of twenty dollars?"

Theo was incensed by this price. He pretended it didn't bother him, but he didn't have much left of his savings, and losing twenty dollars would put a tremendous dent in the money he needed to get to Duluth.

"Ten dollars, and no one needs to find out how helpful you've been to me."

The man grimaced, then nodded. "Ten it is. I'll have a letter written up for you before morning. It shall be signed and delivered before six."

"See that it is," Theo said, handing the man half of the money up front. "You'll get the other half in the morning. Make sure you aren't late."

The man smiled. "I'll be on time, mark my word." He left as quickly as he'd come.

Theo stood by his open door a moment, contemplating what was about to happen. In the morning, after he got the letter, he'd make his way to St. Paul. Hopefully he could catch up with Lucas Carson there, at the offices for the Lake Superior and Mississippi Railroad. If not, Theo could always find him in Duluth.

After a dozen years of keeping close watch on what Lucas Carson did and said, Theo finally felt he might have a chance to ruin the man. After all, Carson had ruined Theo's life. His actions had brought about the end to both a lavish lifestyle and the life of the only friend and mentor Theo had ever had.

Rafael Clarington had become a friend by chance when Theo had been hired to work for Martin Carson. Well, not exactly for him, but as a teller at his bank in Philadelphia. Theo had just graduated from college with the help of some friends who had managed to get him the answers for his final tests. Theo had paid a pretty penny for them, getting the money from his preacher father. Theo had told his father the money was needed for an increase in his rent, and his father, though skeptical because of the past, gave Theo the money he had carefully saved all his life.

At his new bank job, Theo had met Rafael Clarington, who worked in the audit department. It wasn't long before the two men were the best of friends, despite Clarington's being much older. In time, they devised the perfect scheme to embezzle money. They never took much, lest it be noticed and someone called it to the attention of Mr. Carson. Clarington, it turned out, had quite a history of such *shenanigans*, as he called them. To the older man, it was nothing more than a game. No real harm was ever done, and he benefitted greatly.

After a while, he bought a place and invited Theo to live with him. Those had been good years, until Lucas Carson figured out their arrangement at the bank. Clarington was caught, since he was the one who had fixed the books. He never mentioned Theo to the police or at his trial, and he was found guilty and sentenced to fifteen years of hard labor in prison.

Everything Clarington owned was sold

to recoup the embezzled money. Theo had been dressing for work when men showed up to make an inventory of everything in their home. He had tried to explain that not everything in the house belonged to Clarington, that some of it was his. The men were unimpressed with his pleas. They didn't even ask his name. Instead, they told him he could take whatever he could carry out in the next five minutes. Everything else would be sold.

Thankfully, Theo had thought to stash some money in his room. It hadn't lasted long, however, and he'd had to find another place to live. He despised working at the bank without Clarington, and he struggled to find a new job too. Thinking back on his desperation at that time made Theo all the more driven to make Lucas pay.

Two years after his friend and mentor went to prison, Rafael Clarington had died. No one ever said how, but Theo figured someone had it in for him. Theo had been truly heartbroken. Rafael had been more of a father to him than his own. Now, twelve years after their thievery had been discovered by then eighteen-year-old Lucas Carson, Theo still blamed him for the death of his friend. Theo wanted Carson to pay, and pay big.

For years he had wondered how to get the upper hand. He wanted to kill Carson, but not until he made him suffer in shame just as Theo had suffered when he was forced to leave his home with nothing but what he could carry. The way Rafael had suffered when he'd been sent to prison. He wanted Carson to know the pain of loss. If Theo could get the position as his personal secretary, that would put him in close enough proximity to make a plan and see Carson dead.

It was infuriating to imagine a boy, barely a man, having the ability to figure out what Clarington had done. His father had brought Carson in to work a summer position, hoping Carson would one day take over running the bank. Because Carson did nothing by halves, he dove into the work with gusto, and it wasn't long before he was making changes to improve efficiency. When he started staying late to give the books a thorough audit, Rafael hadn't even batted an eye. He'd assured Theo there were too many safeguards built into his scheme. No one, much less an eighteen-year-old child, would be able to figure it out. But Lucas Carson had done it, and worse yet, he'd done it in less than forty-eight hours.

Rafael had been stunned. He had no warning, but when the Carson men showed up with guards, he had known his scheme was uncovered. He tried to deny it, but in the end, in order to reduce his sentence, he admitted to what he'd done. He also made it clear he had acted alone.

Theodore stroked his chin and smiled. His father had always told him to be patient in life's trials and God would present a solution. Carson was going to Duluth—a place Theo knew quite well, having grown up there. And his folks were still there, which would provide him with free living arrangements. Now, if his luck held, Theo would get the job. Most likely Carson wouldn't remember his name as one of dozens of bank employees so many years ago, but if he did, Theo would simply use it to his advantage, reminding Carson that he had worked for his father and had been highly praised as one of the best employees.

Theo glanced around the hovel that he called home. "Things are finally looking up, Rafael. Soon we'll have our revenge, and Lucas Carson will know what it feels like to truly suffer."

Chapter 4

"Aren't you tired yet of not speaking to Papa?" Gloriana asked her little brother.

"I'm mad at him. He punished me extra hard," JT replied.

The entire ordeal had left a feeling of heaviness over the house, and Gloriana was determined to put an end to it.

"JT, it's Papa's job to correct you when you do wrong. You know it was wrong to carve on that school desk."

"But I didn't carve on all of them, so it's not fair that he's making me work on all of the desks. He's just being mean." JT finished his milk. "I'm ready to go to school now."

Gloriana knelt beside him. "Do you remember how Mama always said we shouldn't let our anger go on and on? You've been angry at Papa for three days now, and it needs to end. The Bible says we need to forgive one another. Papa loves you and has only given you this punishment to teach you not to do it again."

"I didn't need him to punish me. Mr. Nelson whupped me, and that made me figure not to carve on the desk again."

Gloriana brushed back his blond curls. "You're a good boy when you want to be, and you have such a kind heart. I want you to think about making up with Papa when he gets home tonight. Ask God to help you do the right thing. It's really hurting Papa."

"Good, 'cause he really hurt me."

She frowned. "Jeremiah Thomas, I've never heard you talk like this. You're being plain mean-spirited. I think you'd better spend some time praying about your heart." She got to her feet. "I love you, but I certainly don't like the way you're acting."

JT looked upset at this. He jumped off the chair and wrapped his arms around her. "Don't stop likin' me, Glory. You're all I got."

"No, you have Papa too. You're the one who is pushing him away." She hugged him close. "You need to make things right. Do it tonight."

But the opportunity didn't come that day. Instead a strong gale blew up and a thunderstorm moved in, bringing a chilly rain that came in sheets the wind sent sideways. Gloriana had barely managed to get the wash inside before the storm hit. She watched the lake heave huge waves upon the shore and worried about Papa and the others out fishing. Had they gotten to safety in time?

At four o'clock, JT came through the door drenched. He was shivering so much that his teeth chattered. Gloriana stripped him of his wet clothes, wrapped him in a blanket, and put him in the rocking chair by the fireplace. As she dried his hair, he told her about his day.

"I did really good at math. You would have been proud. I know my times tables up to ten."

"You always have been good with numbers. How about your reading?"

He frowned. "I don't like words as much as numbers. There's only ten numbers, and then you just reuse them, but they always mean the same count unless you put them in a different column. There's twenty-six letters, and they don't always sound the same way, so it makes it seem like there are a whole lot more letters than just twenty-six. Then, when you mix them up in words, they make all sorts of different sounds."

"I'd never thought of it that way." Gloriana stepped back. "There, your hair's much drier. Why don't you just sit here and warm up while I get you something hot to drink?"

"Hot cider?" he asked.

She smiled. "Sure. Why not?"

She went to the kitchen and warmed some cider on the stove. Pastor Sedgwick had just brought her several gallons of apple cider in trade for fish her father had given the Sedgwicks. People often made trades in order to have what they needed. Ever since the jugs had arrived, JT wanted to drink it all. He seemed to have a hollow leg when it came to apple cider. Of course, he'd have a bellyache to end them all if he drank as much as he wanted.

When it was sufficiently warm, Gloriana poured JT a cup and took it to him. "Here you go, but no more until after supper."

He reached out from the blanket to take the cup. He immediately put it to his lips and took a drink. "How come we don't make cider, Glory?"

"We would need apple trees. Besides, I really don't need the extra work. We smoke fish and pickle it, we pick berries, and I make all sorts of jam. I think that's plenty of work, don't you?"

He shrugged. "Maybe we could stop doing that other stuff and grow apple trees. I like apples—especially your apple pie."

"Well, once you get warmed up, you should get dressed, and maybe I'll make some apple tarts for supper." She rubbed his head affectionately, then returned to the kitchen. Peering out the window, she could see the waves crashing on the shore. There was no sign that the storm was letting up.

By evening, with no sign of her father or any of the other fishermen, Gloriana started to worry. She knew Sally must be beside herself.

Gloriana pulled the apple tarts from the oven and set them aside. "JT, please come here for a minute."

He wandered into the room with a wooden sword at his side and an eye patch over one eye. Papa had given him these toys and told him stories about pirates, and JT loved to reenact the battles he'd been told about.

"What do you need, Glory? I was just about to kill Blackbeard."

She smiled. "Can he wait just a few minutes? I need to run next door and invite Sally to join us. I don't want her to be alone this evening, especially with the baby so close to being born."

JT straightened and put his hand on the hilt of his sword. "Blackbeard can wait."

"Good. I should be back in just a couple of minutes." She pulled a woolen shawl over her head and wrapped it tight.

The wind seemed to calm a bit as she made her way to the small cottage next door. She remembered from the days when this had been her home that the cottage always seemed cozy and strong against the storms. Her father had built it with the help of a friend, and that alone had made Gloriana feel safe.

She knocked once and was almost immediately greeted by Sally. The petite woman's face was ashen. "I thought maybe you were Scott." She ushered Gloriana inside and closed out the weather. "Do you suppose they're in trouble?"

"I don't know. I think they're probably seeking shelter. They have no way to let us know. Last year we had a whole week of storms that made it impossible for them to get home. Why don't you get your things together and come spend the evening with me? If the men don't come back, you can just stay the night as well."

Sally didn't have to be persuaded. She grabbed a basket and went to her bedroom. Within minutes she was back with her things.

Gloriana grabbed a shawl from the peg by the door. "The wind has died down a little, but it's still raining." She wrapped the shawl around Sally's narrow shoulders, then took her basket. "I'll carry this, and you hold on to me. The ground is pretty slippery from all the water."

The two women made their way back to the Womack house and breathed a heavy sigh once they were safely inside.

"That wind is picking up again." Gloriana pulled the basket out from under her shawl and set it by the stove.

"Mr. Griggs stopped by and said there's a prayer meeting starting at seven," JT announced. Mr. Griggs was their neighbor to the north. Usually, when the pastor called for prayer like this, he would notify a dozen of the church men, and they would spread the word.

Gloriana took off her wet shawl and hung it by the door. "I thought they might call for one." She looked at Sally. "When the weather is bad and a lot of the men are still out on the lake, we usually gather to pray for their safe return. You can stay here if you like, since the walk will be difficult in the wind."

"No," Sally replied, shaking her head. "I want to come too."

"Well, then, let's eat supper quickly, and then we can go to the church."

"I don't think I could eat a bite."

"You're far too thin as it is," Gloriana said, then looked at her brother. "I know you're hungry. You're always hungry."

JT nodded. "And you made apple tarts. I saw them cooling."

Gloriana smiled. "Go get washed up, and we'll eat. I have hot pea soup with big chunks of ham. Oh, and fresh bread." It was one of JT's favorite meals. Their father's too.

The three of them sat down to the meal, and Gloriana said grace. She added a prayer for their loved ones and all the other men who were on the water. When she concluded and looked up, she saw Sally wipe her eyes.

"We have to keep up our strength. This storm could last for days. Our men are smart. My father has been working Lake Superior most of his life. He knows when to take cover." Gloriana didn't bring up the fact that storms sometimes snuck up to betray even the most seasoned fishermen. "Now, eat up." She ladled soup into each bowl, then passed the plate of bread.

After supper, they donned their warm clothes and made their way to church. It was nearly a half-mile walk, which under normal circumstances wasn't at all difficult, but with Sally and the storm, it seemed to take much longer. Gloriana kept a firm hold on one of Sally's arms while JT held the other. They paced themselves to what Sally was able to do, and by the time they reached the church, everyone was wet and completely worn out.

"I'm so glad you came," Mrs. Sedgwick said, embracing Gloriana. "We weren't sure if you would make it."

"Of course. It's important to come together and pray when storms are upon us."

JT saw one of his friends and pulled on Gloriana's shawl. "Can I go sit with Jimmy and his mother?"

She nodded. "We'll all go sit with Jimmy and his mother." She smiled at the pastor's wife. "It won't prevent JT's thoughts of playing instead of praying, but hopefully it will give us all a little comfort, knowing we're in this together."

Mrs. Sedgwick smiled. "I'm sure it will."

More people were arriving, so Gloriana moved Sally toward the pew where JT had already made his presence known. Most people's heads were already bowed in prayer. The pastor had lit candles all over the church, and it gave a welcoming glow, plus added warmth.

Gloriana sat down beside her brother in hopes of keeping him in hand, and Sally sat on her other side. It was hard to see her so upset and fretful. Gloriana had gone through a lot of these worrisome times, but this was new to Sally. She'd experienced the men being away for several days because of their jobs, but this felt different.

Pastor Sedgwick took the pulpit. "I want to welcome you to God's house. Jesus made it clear to us in the Bible that His Father's house was to be a house of prayer, and so we gather here this evening to pray for our loved ones who are on the lake."

Gloriana could remember so many prayer meetings like this. Some ended with joyous returns and others with loss and great sorrow. Just a few years back, they'd had a terrible November storm that destroyed ships and made many a widow. It was an awful thing to face, but it was the way life was on the lake. They lived and died by it.

Pastor Womack urged them to open their Bibles if they'd brought them. "We'll stand and read Psalm 107, starting with verse twenty-one." He waited for the congregation to rise and began.

> "'Oh that men would praise the
> Lord for his goodness, and for his
> wonderful works to the children of
> men!
> "'And let them sacrifice the sacrifices
> of thanksgiving, and declare his
> works with rejoicing.
> "'They that go down to the sea in
> ships, that do business in great
> waters;

"'These see the works of the Lord,
  and his wonders in the deep.
"'For he commandeth, and raiseth
  the stormy wind, which lifteth up
  the waves thereof.
"'They mount up to the heaven, they
  go down again to the depths: their
  soul is melted because of trouble.
"'They reel to and fro, and stagger
  like a drunken man, and are at
  their wit's end.
"'Then they cry unto the Lord in
  their trouble, and he bringeth them
  out of their distresses.
"'He maketh the storm a calm, so
  that the waves thereof are still.
"'Then are they glad because they
  be quiet; so he bringeth them unto
  their desired haven.
"'Oh that men would praise the
  Lord for his goodness, and for his
  wonderful works to the children of
  men!'"

Pastor Sedgwick stepped away from the pulpit and raised his hands. "Let us spend this time in prayer for our loved ones who are on the lake—who battle the stormy seas."

Gloriana bowed her head. She couldn't count the number of times she'd heard that psalm read. Some considered it in part or whole to be the "Sailor's Psalm." It definitely spoke to the perils of the sea.

Lord, You are good to us.

She always liked to begin her prayers in praise. It was something her mother had done, and it seemed only right to continue the tradition.

We put our trust in You because You are faithful and worthy of our trust. Even when bad times come like these, we know Your love is perfect and casts out fear.

JT giggled, and Gloriana nudged him, knowing he and Jimmy were probably not praying.

Father, I know You hold our lives in Your hands. You are with each and every man out there on the water and You know what they need. I pray for safety for each one—safety for them and their ships—safety for us on land.

Gloriana licked her dry lips. A shiver ran down her spine. Each time she faced these moments with her mother, Gloriana had taken strength from her. Now Mama was gone, and poor Sally sat in her place. Sally had faith in God, but she was a new Christian, and that faith had not been tested very much. Sally was terrified, and Gloriana could feel her trembling. Gloriana wished she could offer the younger woman the same strength Mama had given her, but she wasn't sure she had any to spare.

An older man got up to offer his prayer aloud. "O great God of the universe, we humbly bow before You—seeking You. Draw near to us, we pray. Put a guard over our loved ones. Calm the lake and the storms that rage around her. Bring our loved ones home without injury or loss. We commit this to You, great Father—thankful that You hear our prayers." He sat back down and folded his hands in silent prayer.

Gloriana added an "amen" and continued with her own prayers.

The service went on for an hour, with people speaking up from time to time to offer their prayer aloud. It calmed Gloriana's spirit. Unfortunately, it seemed only to bring on tears for Sally. Slipping her arm around the younger woman's shoulders, Gloriana held Sally close.

"Let's head home," Gloriana murmured as folks started to leave. "Maybe we can get a ride from someone."

"I'll go ask Mr. Griggs," JT offered. "I saw he had his wagon."

Gloriana nodded. "Go ahead, JT."

The old man was happy to help, and despite being nearly seventy, he had the strength to lift Sally into the back of the wagon so she didn't have to exert herself.

"Thank you so much, Mr. Griggs,"

Gloriana called above the wind and rain as he dropped them home.

"It's no problem." He helped Sally up the walkway and gave a slight tip of his hat. "I'll be keeping watch through the night and praying."

Gloriana met his gaze. She saw the worry there and looked away, nodding. Things were truly grim.

Chapter 5

Luke felt a great sense of excitement as he and a small party of others boarded the train in St. Paul. There was less than ninety miles of track laid beyond the city, but it gleamed in the autumn sun and promised great things to come. Several of the men on the train talked freely of investments and plans for the future. Luke would do his best to make their acquaintances and see what possibilities they might hold for an association with Mr. Cooke. His employer was always looking for investors and investments, and it served Luke well to keep his ears open for opportunities.

Just as Luke planned to get up and introduce himself, a man appeared in the aisle. This had been perhaps the biggest surprise for Luke. Theodore Sedgwick had introduced himself only moments earlier and presented Luke with a letter from Jay Cooke himself.

Luke had read the letter and then read it again. The words were burned into his memory. *"I believe Mr. Sedgwick will make you a good secretary. He has been carefully chosen from a group of men who had no fear of relocation to Duluth, and who had years of experience in office service. Jay Cooke."*

The idea of not being allowed to choose his own secretary bothered Luke. He had always had a keen sense of his employees and had chosen them himself through what he considered to be God's discernment. Having no say in the matter made him uneasy.

"May I join you, sir?" Sedgwick asked.

Luke put his discomfort aside. He smiled and motioned to the wooden seat opposite him. "Please sit and let us use this time to get better acquainted."

Sedgwick did as invited. Luke studied him for a moment. He was painfully thin and careworn. He was clearly years older than Luke.

"Why don't you tell me about yourself? Did you serve in the war?" For Luke, this was always a telling sign of a man's overall character.

"I did, proudly." Sedgwick smiled. "I was with the Fourth Maryland Volunteer Infantry. We fought for the Union with great pride."

"I was with the Thirty-Second Pennsylvania, Company E. We were known as the De Silver Greys." Luke smiled sadly. "It was a great bunch of fellows. We lost far too many."

"Indeed," Sedgwick replied. "But right prevailed."

"Yes, I believe it did." Luke shook off the sad memories. "Tell me what you've been doing since the war."

"I've worked for a number of powerful men. I have a talent for organization and detail. Many have found me useful for these reasons."

"But you never stayed with just one?"

If the question concerned Sedgwick, he didn't show it. He kept his gaze fixed on Luke. "I'm afraid it had to do with my health. I tried various areas to live, but often it didn't agree with my condition."

"Which is?"

"Trouble with my lungs, I'm afraid. Some areas just seem to irritate them more than others."

"What made you think Duluth would be an acceptable place to live?"

Sedgwick smiled. "Because I grew up there. I had no trouble whatsoever as a boy. In fact, it wasn't until I became an adult and went off to school in the East that I even learned of my condition. I never let my parents know about it for fear of worrying them."

"And who are your parents?"

"Pastor and Mrs. Sedgwick. They oversee a small church that grew with the town. My father was actually a fisherman prior to becoming a pastor. He felt God's call much as Peter the disciple did."

Luke smiled. Knowing Sedgwick came from people of faith put him at ease. "I'm a man of God myself. My faith has always been very important to me. It's seen me through a lot of bad times."

"Oh, to be sure," Sedgwick said, giving an enthusiastic nod. "A man without God cannot hope to make anything of himself."

"So, tell me what you know about Duluth and this railroad," Luke said, changing the subject.

"Duluth is a small community. There are several small villages along Lake Superior, and all are very much in close contact. Duluth has, in fact, absorbed several of those villages, and they now call themselves one. There is an abundance of logging going on, as the forests are vast, and fishing and other businesses related to the lake have sprung up over the years. There are some tremendous boat builders, for example. The railroad coming is the best of all. It will ensure the city grows and survives. Across the bay is the real trouble. Superior, Wisconsin, wants to be the big city of the area, and they feel that with Mr. Cooke bypassing them with the railroad, they have been irreparably snubbed. They are still working to change Mr. Cooke's mind."

"That won't happen. Mr. Cooke has made it quite clear that Duluth is the terminus of his choice for the Lake Superior and Mississippi Railroad. It lines up perfectly with his plans for the Northern Pacific line, which will end in Tacoma in the Territory of Washington. Instead of fighting his decision, perhaps they'd be better off to show how they can work with Duluth."

Sedgwick nodded. "I've often suggested that very thing." He smiled. "Some men will not hear reason."

Luke nodded and turned his attention to the train's jerky movements as it began its forward journey. He had received a detailed map of the line thus far. Their first stop would be White Bear Lake, a favorite picnicking spot for those in St. Paul. The beautiful parklands situated around the crystal lake provided city dwellers with a quiet respite just ten miles north of their homes. Several wealthy people had built small cottages near the lake for longer escapes during the summer months.

Luke turned back to Sedgwick. "I

understand you will be my assistant and stenographer for our business letters and other transactions. I should tell you that I'm a rather private man and am used to taking care of most things for myself. There will be times when I still manage for myself. Mr. Cooke had arranged for us to have a clerk, and if you feel the need for one, we will hire a man. But if not, I'm just as content for it to remain the two of us. I wouldn't wish for you to take offense, however. Nor to be unfairly overworked."

Sedgwick nodded. "I completely understand. There is no need for a clerk. I'm quite capable. I will be here when you wish for my assistance. It was suggested that, with the secrecy we are struggling to maintain due to the rivalry between Duluth and Superior, when it is necessary to send information to St. Paul, I could deliver it in person."

Luke hadn't heard this suggestion until now, but it made sense. "That would be beneficial. I will keep that in mind."

Watching the landscape as the train moved north, Luke continued with his thoughts. "The rivalry sounds like a very delicate situation. As I understand it, Duluth relies on the Superior entry to the lake."

"Yes, it's a very narrow opening, and one of the bigger issues now that the railroad matter has been resolved. Duluth needs a canal to open the lake into their immediate area."

"Jay Cooke is quite interested in the canal, but I've not had a chance to study up on it."

"I'm sure you'll hear a great deal more once you're established in Duluth. The town officials will no doubt wish for Mr. Cooke's help in making the canal a reality."

"No doubt."

Again Luke gazed out the window as the scenery changed from town to countryside. There were beautiful autumn colors everywhere. Oranges of cherry and sugar maple, reds from the northern oak. There were even yellows of goldenrod painting the landscape and leaving little doubt as to the time of year. Someone mentioned they were slated for an early winter and that the beautiful colors were proof.

"Have you arranged a place to stay in Duluth?" Sedgwick asked. "I'm certain my parents would be pleased to extend you a room until you were better situated."

"I have a brother in Duluth. I figure to stay with him and his wife. The baby's due any day now, and I look forward to spoiling my niece or nephew."

The thought of his brother being a father brought a smile to Luke's face. Scott had always been a tenderhearted person. Luke could still recall times when Scott had rescued damaged baby birds or wounded rabbits. He was always seeking to help those in need. When he'd first married Sally, Luke had thought the situation was no different. Sally's mother had been ill, and when it became obvious that she was dying, Scott stepped in to offer comfort. The love born of their time together seemed natural. At least to Luke. Their father saw it as nothing more than a boy's dalliance with his father's servant.

Sedgwick frowned. "I didn't realize you had family in Duluth."

"Well, it's not a bad thing, Sedgwick, so cheer up."

This seemed to startle the older man. "I . . . it wasn't my intention to frown. I suppose I just have a great deal on my mind."

"Are you looking forward to seeing your parents again?"

Theodore nodded. "It's been some time. I do fear, however, that I might find them ill or in a bad way. We haven't kept in touch as I would have liked. My father was distressed that I was unsettled in my youth. I fear I was a disappointment to him, despite my college education and war service."

"I doubt he is that disappointed. Perhaps miscommunication has caused you both unnecessary concern? This will be the perfect opportunity to set matters straight, don't you think?"

Sedgwick nodded. "I do hope that will be the case."

They didn't stay long at White Bear Lake. Once the train had taken on water, they were soon on their way to Forest Lake, where the lake was even bigger and the fall colors even more beautiful, if possible.

Luke noted that the land grant given to the railroad was a perfect route, as far as he could tell. There were already towns sprung up along the way. Some had been there prior to the railroad's arrival, and the path had been chosen because of the settlement. However, usually towns had come into being with the encouragement of the railroad, which offered incentives and free land. There would be even more towns by the time the railroad was complete.

Harvested wheat fields left a carpet of yellow stalks behind, further coloring the landscape. Luke had heard one man in St. Paul boast of getting thirty-five bushels of wheat to the acre. Not being familiar with the growth and harvesting of wheat, Luke could only imagine that was good, as the man seemed quite pleased.

By the time they reached Rush City, fifty miles from St. Paul, Luke was ready to move around a bit. "We will be here for an hour," the conductor announced. "Feel free to enjoy some early supper."

Luke got up and stretched. Sedgwick appeared to have nodded off and seemed completely content in his nap. That suited Luke just fine. He'd prefer a little time to himself. He was still dealing with the surprise of this stranger being his secretary.

He walked through the train car to the platform between cars. It was now late afternoon, and the warm air had turned cold.

"There's been quite a storm blowing through up north," an older gentleman commented as Luke stepped down from the train. "We're going to have an early winter, it would seem. Lucky for us, the storm is moving east rather than south."

Luke nodded and pulled up his coat collar. The damp cold seemed to permeate the wool as if it were nothing more than a dressing coat.

The older man pressed a printed flyer into Luke's hands. "I hear you're bound north to Duluth. I wouldn't want to be on the big lake this day," he declared and headed toward another group of men as they exited the train. "Old Gitche Gumee will be roiling like a witch's caldron."

Frowning, Luke couldn't help but wonder

if his brother would be fishing despite the change in weather. He glanced down at the handbill.

Enjoy hearty beef stew and our world-famous blueberry pie.
Come to Turner's across from the depot.

It was only then that Luke realized he was hungry. He had originally intended to eat when they reached their overnight destination. It wasn't that much farther, but given the delay of an hour at this station, he figured he might as well have something now.

The small town was surprisingly well-developed. The tracks had only been in place for a year, but in that time, they had attracted plenty of attention. There was a post office and a flour mill, as well as a grain elevator and plenty of houses.

Turner's was a small restaurant situated between a dry goods store and a cobbler. Luke made his way inside and found the place warm and homey.

"You want to eat, mister?" a young woman asked.

He turned and found a girl who couldn't have been more than thirteen or fourteen looking him up and down. "Yes. I'd like a table."

She led the way and put down a small chalked menu. "We don't serve a lot of different things, but what we have is really good, and our blueberry pie is world-famous."

Luke smiled. "How did that happen?"

She frowned. "Well, folks talked it up. Folks in other countries." She shrugged.

He glanced down at the menu and fought to keep from laughing out loud. "I'll have the beef stew—a large portion, please. And, of course, a piece of the world-famous blueberry pie."

"You want some coffee too?"

Luke nodded. "That would suit me just fine."

She took back the chalkboard and made her way to the kitchen. Luke looked around the room and found that several of the other men from the train had wandered in. The same young girl came and took them to tables.

Luke rubbed his eyes and thought again of Scott awaiting him at the end of the journey. It felt like years since they'd seen each other rather than just months.

"Pardon me, but are you Mr. Carson?"

The warm baritone voice of the stranger made Luke smile as he looked up. "I am."

"Name is Rowland. Archibald Rowland, but most folks call me Archie," the broad-shouldered, balding man declared. "I'm the line manager out of Duluth. We'll be seeing a lot of each other."

Luke stood and shook his hand. "Luke Carson, as you guessed. Will you join me?"

"Certainly." They sat, and it was only a moment before the young waitress came around.

"Hello, Mr. Rowland. You want the usual?"

"I surely do. Bring it nice and hot. It's getting pretty cold out there."

She nodded. "Everyone is telling me there's signs of an early winter."

Rowland grinned. "Did they tell you the Indians were packing in grain and smoking extra fish?"

"Yeah, I heard that. And Granny says the geese are headin' south fast."

She headed back to the kitchen, and Rowland turned to Luke. "The Indians are usually right about the seasons. Geese too."

Luke shook his head. "I wouldn't know, but it seems worthy of consideration, since both have been here longer than I have."

"Fact is, winter is coming, and we'd best be ready."

The girl returned with coffee for them both as well as a small pitcher of cream. "I know you like to milk yours down, Mr. Rowland."

He chuckled and poured a generous amount of cream into his cup. "I guess I'm pretty well-known along the line."

Luke drank his coffee black and relished the warmth. "So what are your thoughts about the route? Are we on schedule?"

"We're doing just fine. We'll work as long as we dare and then stop 'til spring. There's been some interference here and there from the Superior folks. Nothing too difficult to handle and totally expected."

"That doesn't sound good."

"It's really nothing we didn't anticipate. They're still working to get the track rerouted to Superior. They feel that as long as we aren't building out much from Duluth yet, there's still a chance."

"Then maybe we need to get to laying track faster out of Duluth. Mr. Cooke still expects the line to be complete by next August."

"We have been modest with our movements out of Duluth only because of the problems we've run into here and there along the line. Occasionally the surveyed route has had issues and we've been obliged to alter it a bit. We don't want to lay out too much from Duluth and then find we need a huge alteration to join up with the line coming from the south."

"I suppose I can understand that."

The girl returned with two big bowls of stew and a platter of bread and butter. She didn't even speak after depositing everything on the table, as another group of men came into the restaurant in search of food.

Luke smiled. "Do you mind if I offer grace?"

"If you hadn't, I would have."

They both bowed their heads, and Luke blessed the food and asked God for better weather.

"Amen," Rowland said, reaching for the bread. "But you can't let the weather bother you. It's just a part of this region. What with us being so far north and Superior sitting just over from Duluth, we're going to be at the mercy of it all. I've been up here three years now, and one thing has always been the same."

"What's that?"

"Ain't nothin' the same. It changes all the time up here." He laughed, and Luke joined in.

"What a comfort." Luke sampled the stew and was pleasantly surprised. He'd expected a bland combination of meat and vegetables, but someone here truly understood the technique of blending flavors. This stew was the best he'd ever had. Was that a hint of burgundy he tasted?

"Good, huh?" Archie asked.

"It is. It's marvelous. I would never have expected to get something this masterful out here."

"Jessie, that's the gal who waited on us, her mama is quite the cook. She married a Frenchman who was a chef at a fancy restaurant in Montreal. He died, but not before teaching her a thing or two about cooking. Wait until you taste her blueberry pie."

"Don't you mean the 'world-famous' blueberry pie?"

Archie chuckled. "I see Jessie set you straight, but it truly is world-famous. One of those German princes was over here hunting and demanded the recipe one year. The next year, we had a couple of gentlemen from Switzerland who had eaten it while visiting the prince, and when they asked for the recipe, he told them he wasn't at liberty to give it and they would have to request it from the cook herself and told them about Rush City. So you see, it truly has caused a sensation all the way to Europe."

"Well, the moniker seems truly earned. I look forward to sampling this delectable pie."

They finished the stew and let Jessie refill their coffee as they continued to discuss the future of the railroad.

"What takes the longest," Archie began,

"are the trees and the water. They're every-where, and it's a job to work around them. We're getting there, though, and both are necessary for the line, so I can't bring my-self to curse them. Building a higher founda-tion for the track has been the trick. In places where the water saturates the ground, we lay a bed of gravel and build up from there. It's working to make a solid foundation. We've got a lot of good wood from the trees. Some is great for ties, but a lot of that fine oak would probably make a fella some good money if sold to the furniture makers back east."

Luke had never considered such a thing. "Seems it would be easy enough to ship the wood by train. I'll let Mr. Cooke know about it and see what he thinks."

Jessie returned and placed a plate of pie in front of each man. The pieces were huge, and blueberry filling oozed out from some of the flakiest crust Luke had ever seen.

"I didn't bring you extra cream because it looked like you still had plenty," Jessie de-clared. "Besides, some folks don't like cream on their pie." She shrugged and walked away, as if the thought was too much to discuss.

Luke chuckled and picked up his fork. "Well, here goes. I'll try it without cream first and then with."

Archie waited for him to try the pie before

sampling his own. Luke didn't even attempt to hide the smile that formed on his face.

"It's good, huh?" Archie said, pouring cream over his pie.

Luke shook his head. "Good doesn't begin to describe it. This really should be world-famous."

Archie handed him the pitcher of cream. "She bakes 'em every day, and there's never a piece left over."

"I can see why. Say, Archie, I have an idea. Why don't we terminus the railroad right here in Rush City? Once Mr. Cooke tastes this pie, I think he'd understand and approve."

Archie roared with laughter, causing most of the other customers to glance their way. Luke just shrugged and returned his attention to the pie. There was no sense delaying his enjoyment by having to explain.

Chapter 6

The next afternoon the storm had moved out, leaving behind gusty winds that were far more manageable. Gloriana felt her hope renewed as some of the ships returned to Duluth. They looked worse for the wear, clearly having endured damage, but they were otherwise whole, and that gave her a sense of relief.

"See there, I'm sure Scott and Papa will be here before we know it," she told Sally.

"I'm going to head home and make sure everything is ready for Scott." Sally heaved a sigh. "I'm so happy to see the storm has finally passed." She kissed Gloriana's cheek and hurried as best she could for the door. "Thank you for everything."

"Of course. We're family."

Gloriana closed the door behind Sally. The Carsons really had become like family.

The men were often doing various house projects together, and Sally and Gloriana constantly shared recipes and sewing tips. Truth be told, Gloriana was looking forward to the baby's birth as much as Sally. She was anxious to play auntie to the little one, since she doubted she'd ever have children of her own.

Gloriana went to tidy up her father's room, where Sally had been staying. She replaced the sheets and took the blanket outside to hang on the line for a while. Papa would find everything fresh and clean when he returned home.

With most of her chores done already, thanks to Sally's help, Gloriana went ahead and washed out the sheet and pillowcase and got them on the line as well. She could iron them later that night when Papa had gone to bed. He always went to bed early after enduring a storm, and she couldn't blame him. He'd no doubt been constantly at full attention for the last forty-eight hours. He'd be exhausted.

She glanced at the clock. It was nearly two. It wouldn't be long before JT was home, and there was no telling about Papa. She pulled out a drawer in the pantry and placed six potatoes in her apron. Thinking about Scott and Sally, she added two more. The men would also be hungrier than usual. No one got to eat much during stormy seas.

After depositing the potatoes on the table, Gloriana went for her paring knife and a bowl. She had already decided to make fish stew. It would be hearty and filling, and she had made fresh bread earlier that morning. She'd figure out something for Papa's sweet tooth as she worked on the stew.

A knock on the door startled her. She wiped off her hands and undid her apron strings. Her mother had taught her never to answer the door wearing an apron.

Gloriana pulled open the door with a smile. "Yes?"

It was Orrin Johnson, one of her father's dearest friends. He looked stern, almost upset. "Gloriana." He tipped his cap. "Could I come in for a minute?"

She nodded. "Of course." She stepped back. "Papa isn't back just yet."

He nodded and took off his cap. "I know. That's why I'm here."

It dawned on her the reason for the look on his face. His discomfort. She reached for a chair to steady herself. "What happened?"

"Sit down, and I'll tell you all I know."

She felt her knees weaken and did as he asked. If Captain Johnson himself had come, the news couldn't be good.

"Is Papa . . . is he . . ." She couldn't bring herself to ask the only question that mattered.

"I'm sorry, Gloriana."

"You're sorry. Is he . . ."

"He went down with the ship." The words were matter-of-fact and to the point.

She heard her own sharp intake of breath but felt as if it lacked all oxygen. "No!"

"I'm sorry, Gloriana. I did what I could. The storm came on so quickly that we didn't have time to get to land or the safety of a cove. We had headed out to deliver fish to the North Shore, and the storm was too much. We fought for hours, but everything went wrong. I was barely keeping my own ship afloat when I saw your father's break in two and go down. I saw him right to the point that the water swallowed him and the others. Against my better judgment, I tried to search for survivors, but there were none. The waves were twenty to thirty feet high. No one could have survived. The *Ana Eileen* is on the bottom of the lake with her crew."

Gloriana stared at him, not knowing what to say. She had always known the possibility of something like this. Her mother had talked to her about it from the time she was a child. She'd attended dozens of services for those lost on the water. It was the way of life in a lake town like Duluth.

"I'm sure sorry, Gloriana. I don't know what else to say."

"I'll have to tell the families," she murmured. "Sally was so fearful of this very thing."

"I'll tell the families. You take care of Mrs. Carson, and I'll see to the others. It's the least I can do. They'll want to talk to someone who saw them last."

Gloriana was still too shocked to think clearly. "Thank you. I'll tell Sally." But what in the world could she say to the poor woman?

Captain Johnson covered her hand with his own. "I'm here for you, should you need a friend. You know all of us captains are. Our families too. We take care of our own."

Gloriana felt his hand on hers. It was icy cold. Like her father's now was, no doubt.

She jerked away, then apologized. "I'm sorry. I'm just . . . I'm not myself. I can't think clearly."

He nodded. "You don't have to apologize, Gloriana. You've been dealt a blow. I can stay for a time, if you need me to. Or I can send Mrs. Johnson."

"No." She got to her feet. "The others need to know. Sally needs to know, and then when school lets out, I'll have to break the news to JT." At this, tears came to her eyes. He would be devastated.

The captain rose. "I understand. Just know we're all here for you. You won't ever be alone."

She forced herself to meet his kindly gaze. "Thank you."

He nodded and secured his hat, then walked out the door with his head hung low. Gloriana prayed Sally wouldn't see him. The last thing either the captain or the young mother-to-be needed was that encounter. Sally would need the privacy of her house to receive the news. She would need Gloriana to deliver it, not some rough seaman.

Gloriana knew she didn't have time to process her own grief. There were too many others who needed her to be strong. She glanced heavenward.

"I don't know why You allowed this, but somehow I must find a way to go on."

A cold shiver went through her as her words seemed to bounce back to slap her in the face. Maybe God no longer cared. Maybe there were too many others asking why and He didn't have time for her thoughts. Whatever it was, Gloriana had never felt so distant from God.

She drew a deep breath and went to the kitchen to rinse her face. There was no time to worry about God. She patted her cheeks and eyes dry, then put on her shawl. There was no sense in delaying.

The walk to the smaller cottage seemed twice as long as usual. A gust of wind whipped up and nearly knocked her to the ground. Not that it would take much. Gloriana steadied herself, still trying to think of how to break the news. No matter what she did to soften the blow, Sally's heart would shatter into a million pieces. She supposed getting to the heart of the matter quickly was the best way, just as Captain Johnson had done.

Gloriana knocked on the cottage door and waited. She'd already decided to invite Sally to live with them. The girl had no other relatives. No one to care whether she lived or died.

Sally opened the door. "Are they back?" she asked with great hope. She strained to look beyond Gloriana, then frowned. "Where are they?"

Gloriana motioned her friend inside and followed after. "We need to talk. Captain Johnson just left my house."

Sally didn't comprehend the situation and nodded. "What's going on?"

Gloriana pulled her to the small rocker and pressed her to sit down. "I'm afraid there's bad news." She pulled up a straight-back chair from the kitchen table, then sat and tried to gather her thoughts. "Captain Johnson told me, and now I must tell you. You must be strong and brave."

Sally's face went ashen, and she sank back into the rocker. "Tell me."

"He saw the *Ana Eileen* go down. She broke apart in the storm. Papa and the crew weren't able to get to safety, as the storm came upon them too quickly. Captain Johnson saw the men in the water, but the waves were twenty to thirty feet high." She paused to make sure Sally was comprehending the news. Her eyes were wide with fear. "Captain Johnson tried to rescue the men at great risk to his own ship and crew, but . . . but . . ." She couldn't seem to force out the words. "They're gone. They're all gone."

Sally shook her head. "No. It's not true. They just went into the water. They'll swim to safety. They'll come home."

Gloriana wished it might be so but knew better. "I'm sorry, Sally. It doesn't work that way in a storm on Lake Superior. Even the strongest swimmer would drown."

The silence that fell over the room was deafening. Gloriana watched as Sally continued to shake her head. Finally the young woman opened her mouth to speak, but all that came out was a moan that quickly became a wail.

Gloriana didn't know what to do. She remembered times when her mother held the wives and sisters, daughters and mothers of men who had died. She wanted to embrace Sally, but it was impossible with her friend in the rocker, and in Sally's delicate state, Gloriana wasn't about to force her to her feet. So she sat and waited to see what Sally would do next.

The wail quickly became a screaming cry. Gloriana reached out and took Sally's hand. "Remember your baby. You mustn't fret so."

Sally didn't even seem to realize Gloriana was there. She continued to scream, leaving Gloriana to wonder how many other wives were screaming across the town.

Gloriana sat with Sally for as long as she could. Seeing it would soon be time for JT to come home, she did the only thing she could think of.

"Why don't you come home with me?"

Sally shook her head. "I have . . . I have to be here. Scott might . . . he might have . . . he could have . . ." She began to cry again.

The sound tore at Gloriana's already wounded heart. "Look, I have to go home. JT will be there soon, and I have to tell him."

Her words caught in her throat. She felt like wailing alongside Sally but knew she didn't have that luxury. Why was she always the one who had to be strong?

"Why don't you join us for supper?" Gloriana knew none of them were going to feel like eating, but it seemed the reasonable thing to say. She got to her feet and placed her hand on Sally's shaking shoulder. "I'm so sorry. We never know when something like this will happen, and it leaves us so torn apart. I wish I could make this easier on you, but I know nothing can."

Sally glanced up but said nothing. She buried her face in her hands and continued to cry. There was nothing Gloriana could do. It was best to let Sally have time to mourn.

Taking up her shawl, Gloriana didn't even bother to wrap it around her body. Instead she made her way home through the cold wind and wondered how it would go with JT.

She didn't have long to wait. JT came through the door in his usual energetic way. He'd already learned that some ships had gone down, but apparently it hadn't dawned on him that his father's boat might be one of them.

"Did you hear about the *Pride of Bisbee*? It ran aground off Bark Point. They said it was something to behold. Can we maybe go see it?"

Gloriana saw his hopeful expression and wished she could keep him from the coming sorrow.

"JT, I need you to come sit down with me. I have to give you some news."

"Am I in trouble again?" he asked, his countenance falling.

"No, of course not." She took him by the hand and led him to the sofa. When they were both seated, she continued. "You know, the storm was very bad. I'm sure other ships ran aground, and I know some . . . well, some sank."

JT's expression fell. "Did Papa's ship run aground?"

"No, but something bad happened." She waited a moment to let the reality sink in.

"Really bad?" he barely whispered.

"Yes. I'm afraid Papa and the others weren't able to keep the ship together, and it broke apart."

"Did they die?"

She bit her lower lip and nodded. JT sat stoically, although there was unmistakable dampness in his eyes.

"It's all my fault. I was mean to Papa. It's all my fault."

She put her arm around his shoulders. "No, it wasn't anyone's fault. It was a bad storm, and these things just happen. It wasn't your fault."

"But I was mean to him. I didn't talk to him." JT's voice was starting to take on a hysterical edge. Gone was the fixed look, and panic was setting in. "If I had been nice to him—if I had told him that I loved him when he came to say good-bye, it wouldn't have happened. It's my fault."

"That's not true. Please listen to me. Life doesn't work that way. God isn't that way. You were angry at Papa, but he understood. He told me so. He didn't hold it against you."

"But maybe God did. Maybe God is punishing me."

Gloriana had wondered at God's part in it herself. Why had He allowed this to happen?

"No." She forced the word out. Even if she knew it to be true, she was angry at God herself. It wasn't fair that Papa was gone—that they were orphaned. That Sally had no husband—no father for her baby.

JT broke into tears. "Maybe he's not really dead, Glory. Maybe he washed up on shore. Maybe he doesn't know who he is anymore, and he's lost. We should go look for him." The voice grew hopeful.

"Captain Johnson saw him go down into the water, JT. Captain Johnson wouldn't lie about something like that. Papa is gone."

"It's not fair." He pushed her away and ran from the room. "It's not fair!" His door slammed.

Gloriana drew a deep breath. "No, it isn't at all fair."

She walked to the kitchen and saw the potatoes she'd left on the table. She put them back in the pantry. No one was going to want chowder tonight. She thought about the laundry on the lines outside and, hearing the wind pick up again, decided it would be best to bring it in. She made her way outside, trying to think of what she should do next. How was she supposed to manage things? There wasn't that much money in their savings. The property was paid for, but there would be taxes due eventually. Food to buy. What was she supposed to do now?

She looked out across the water. The cursed water. Her father's burial ground. With his blanket in hand, she walked toward the edge of the ridge and looked down on the rocks below. The wind whipped up and unfurled the blanket like a flag. Gloriana let it ripple in the wind and then released it. The gust snatched it up, taking it out over the water. Then, without warning, the blanket dropped to the waves and floated on top for several moments.

It was a fitting farewell. Papa would sleep forever in the deep.

The blanket grew soggy and disappeared under the waves. Gloriana watched until it was completely out of sight before returning to the clothesline for the sheet and pillowcase.

The wind died down once again, as if its job were done.

She hugged the laundry close and glanced back at the waters. "Where were You, God?"

There was only the sound of the waves on the rocks and the occasional sound of wagons. God wasn't offering any answers. Maybe He never would again.

"I made sure I was right with God. I guess I just wanted you to know so you could stop worryin' about what would happen to me if I met with trouble." Gloriana could almost hear her father speaking the words again.

"He got right with You, Lord, and then You took him from us. It's not right. It will never be right."

She made her way into the house and threw the laundry into a chair, not caring one bit that her mother would never have allowed such a thing. She too was gone. They were all gone except for her and JT.

The light was growing dim, but Gloriana couldn't compel herself to light the lamp. She felt empty inside. Hollow and hopeless. Why bother with light? She sat down at the table and stared at the box of matches by the lamp. The light would help nothing. There was no light where her father's body rested.

"What about the light of God?" a voice from somewhere deep inside her seemed to whisper.

Gloriana ignored it.

A knock came again on the door. Who would it be this time? Pastor Sedgwick making the rounds to attend his grieving flock? A neighbor or friend come to see what they could do? She took her time and lit the lamp before rising to see who had come. She had no desire to see anyone.

She opened the door and found Sally clutching her abdomen.

"It's . . . the baby!"

Chapter 7

Gloriana sent JT for the midwife after she put Sally to bed. The young woman was in immense pain. No doubt the shock of losing her husband had brought on labor, but the baby was due any day, so things should go well. At least that was what Gloriana kept telling herself.

When JT returned with Abigail Lindquist, one of the local midwives, Gloriana breathed a sigh of relief and waited for instruction.

"We'll need plenty of towels and hot water," Abigail instructed. Being mother to eight of her own children, she tended to be someone folks listened to without question, and Gloriana was no exception.

Thankfully, there were plenty of clean towels, and it was easy enough to put a large pot of water on the stove. Gloriana checked the wood supply. It was good. They had plenty to keep them through the night.

But this started her down another path of thought. Would they have enough wood for the winter? There was so much that would fall to her now. Things her father had previously arranged for or taken care of himself were now her responsibility. She could hardly go into the woods and cut down winter fuel, as her father had done. She'd heard him making plans with Scott to do that very thing in the coming weeks. Now they were both dead. Who would cut their wood? She couldn't do it, and neither could JT. She supposed they'd need to hire it done or beg help from one of the other fishermen when they went to cut their own. Captain Johnson might know someone, or perhaps he could arrange for each family to donate a bit. It wouldn't be unlike other arrangements she'd heard of. But even that couldn't go on forever.

Abigail appeared. "She's doing just fine, but she's a long time from delivering. This being her first, she may very well labor all night and into tomorrow. I'm going to head home, but I'll be back in a few hours. I would try to get some rest and tell her to do the same. I told her if things progress faster than I thought and she feels the need to push, she should send someone for me right away." She patted Gloriana's arm. "I heard about your father. I am so very sorry. Don't fret about anything. We ladies will gather up some supplies for you, and our men will discuss how to help you settle in for the winter."

"Thank you." Gloriana clutched at the older woman's hand. "I was just wondering what I was going to do. JT is devastated, and I really don't know the state of things as well as I should."

Abigail nodded and squeezed Gloriana's hand. "That's the way of it when something like this happens. There's so much shock and disbelief. In a few weeks you'll finally under-stand the truth of it and how your world has been completely turned upside down. Don't be afraid to let folks help you. Don't be afraid to tell us what you need."

With that, Abigail left Gloriana with her sorrow and fears, as well as her worry about how they would manage. Two women, a boy, and a newborn. It was almost too much to consider.

Luke had been impressed with the final miles of the route. They walked or rode by wagon as they progressed ever closer to Duluth, and along the way Archie had told Luke about the plans they had for the line.

They left Fond du Lac by river steamer for the last twenty miles of the journey, and Luke found he was more than ready to arrive in Duluth, no matter how small and uncivilized it was. All along the route he had been regaled with stories of the place by either Theodore or Archie, and he was ready to form his own opinion. Jay Cooke had visited once three years earlier. There had been even less of a town back then, but he had been able to see great potential. Men like him were visionaries, and Luke often wished he could be like them. Even so, there was a thrill attached to his travel and job.

Mr. Cooke believed in Luke's capabilities, and that encouraged him. Maybe as a visionary, Mr. Cooke was able to see something in Luke that he couldn't see for himself.

The late hour kept Luke from being able to see much after leaving Fond du Lac, but as they neared Duluth, he spied lights dotting the blackness here and there. Scott had written a couple of letters describing how beautiful the area was and how he and Sally liked the people. It would be good to see his brother again and declare his journey at an end.

The temperature had dropped into the forties, making Luke more than a little chilled. As they drew closer to the big lake, he knew that the damp air was the reason. He felt colder than he ever had back in Philadelphia. It seemed strange to him, given there was plenty of humidity there as well, but something about it was different here, and he'd just have to get used to it.

"Brought you a cup of coffee," Archie said, handing a mug to Luke. "I've been talking with some of the crew. It sounds like it's warming up."

"This is warmer, eh? I'm sure glad for this fire." Luke held his hands out to warm them. "My fingers are frozen."

"You need better gloves. A better coat too. You'll be able to buy them in Duluth. Back in the old days, before much of anybody moved north to Minnesota, they were always advised to bring warm clothes. Some folks didn't take it seriously. They'd arrive in the summer heat and swat mosquitos as big as birds, and laugh about being hale and hardy enough to endure the Minnesota winter. Then winter came, and they were scrambling."

"Philadelphia gets plenty cold. I guess I just didn't take into account that you are much farther north and situated on a large body of water. Philadelphia was near water too, but I obviously misjudged."

"You'll learn, as we all did. They've

built—or I guess I should say, are building—a nice-sized hotel in Duluth. It's called the Clark House, but it's not yet ready for us, so you'll probably be directed to the Jefferson House."

"I know about the Clark House. It's part of what I'll be overseeing." Luke strained his eyes at the lights in the east. Would they ever get there?

Theodore Sedgwick showed up with another cup of coffee for Luke. "Oh, I see you already found the coffee." He frowned in the glow of the firelight.

"Archie here was good enough to bring me one, but thank you."

"Are you two discussing the railroad?" Sedgwick asked, looking for a place to set one of the mugs. He finally settled on a nearby deck stand.

"We were talking about the Clark House," Luke replied, then took a long drink of the hot black liquid. It was perfect and gave him a momentary warmth that had been missing.

"Ah, the new hotel Mr. Cooke arranged."

"Yes. I was just about to tell Archie that I won't be staying at the boardinghouse with the others, but rather at my brother's house. He lives near the lake, as he is a fisherman."

"I just heard the storms of the last few days claimed many a boat and crew," Sedgwick said. "I pray your brother was not among the lost."

Luke frowned. He'd heard rumors about the storm, but no one had mentioned deaths. "I didn't realize things were as bad as that."

"Yes." Sedgwick nodded and sloshed his coffee over the side of the mug. He ignored the mess and continued. "A few dozen boats were lost, as I understand it. The storm came up quickly. I think it was maybe three days ago. Many of the men were caught out on the water with miles to go before reaching safety."

Luke nodded. "I suppose we shall know soon enough what has happened."

He left the fire and walked to the deck rail to gaze out across the water of the St. Louis River. From the look of the lights glowing across the water, it appeared that Duluth sat on the left, down by the water's edge. It then rose up the hills behind. Scott had told him it was a sort of terrace town, and the lights seemed to prove this true. To the right was Superior, Wisconsin. It was very close, and in that moment, Luke finally understood the rivalry. They were truly sister cities, separated only by a small opening of water.

As they slipped from the St. Louis River into St. Louis Bay, Luke strained to see out into the darkness. Reaching out from the Duluth side, Luke had been told, was Minnesota Point—a long bar of land, at the end of which sat the lighthouse. This natural breakwater not only offered protection but stood ready as a permanent gatekeeper into Superior Bay. Jutting out from the opposite side was another bar of land called Wisconsin Point. Each state had made a stand, declaring their territory, it seemed.

The steamer slipped ever closer and passed from St. Louis Bay into Superior Bay. Beyond Minnesota Point lay the lake, although the thin strip of breakwater offered little division from the miles of vast blackness that lay beyond. Lake Superior—the great lady herself.

The water looked like a void, an endless blackness that threatened to swallow anyone who dared to cross her. Luke had seen the ocean before and even crossed it several times, but there was something surprisingly eerie about this lake. Maybe it was all the stories he'd heard. From those familiar with it, it sounded as if the lake were a haunted entity who held grudges against those it found wanting.

"There's our welcoming committee," Archie said, motioning him to the other side of the boat. "I think you'll be pleasantly surprised to see how many have turned out."

Luke could see a large number of people

gathered on the dock. Once the steamer was secured, they disembarked to be greeted by those who represented their housing and care, as well as others who simply wanted to celebrate their arrival.

"We're very glad to welcome representatives of the Lake Superior and Mississippi Railroad. And especially happy to have you with us, Mr. Carson," the mayor declared. "However, with the lateness of the hour, we will take pity on you all and allow you to head off to your various places of rest."

There was a bit of upheaval as all that was sorted out. Many of the men on board were going to stay with individual families who had opened their homes to strangers. Several were heading for Jefferson House, a boardinghouse that had the good manners to send a wagon for the luggage. Otherwise, people were instructed to retrieve their things and follow the locals on a march up the wharf and into town.

"There's hardly a carriage to be had here, although there are numerous lumber and farm wagons," Archie explained. "However, you're in luck. I know a fellow who will drive us over to where your brother lives. But first, let's arrange for your trunks to be delivered."

They grabbed their bags, and Archie waited while Luke found the freight man and arranged for the many trunks he'd brought. Some of it was business, but most was personal, and he was beginning to question the sanity of hauling so much stuff along. When the freight man learned that Luke was Jay Cooke's associate, he gave every assurance that the trunks would be delivered before midnight.

Satisfied that he'd done all he could, Luke caught up to Archie, and they made their way north and then east. It wasn't long before Luke was introduced to Samuel Griggs. The sleepy old man greeted them in a gruff, groggy manner. It seemed to Luke that perhaps the old man had been drinking.

Nevertheless, Griggs hitched his team and headed onto the road with Luke and Archie on board. He said nothing and offered no explanation of where they were going. Luke wondered at the old man's attitude but figured it wasn't good to rile him with questions. After all, he was doing them a favor.

Griggs soon brought the wagon to a stop and motioned to the smaller of two houses. "That's the house. The little one. That's where you'll find the missus."

"This is where I'll bid you farewell until later," Archie said, reaching out to shake Luke's hand. "It's been great getting to know you, and I'm sure we will do good work together."

"As am I." Luke hopped down and grabbed his luggage off the back of the wagon. "What do I owe you?" he asked, coming up to the front where Griggs sat.

"Nothin'," the man said. He slapped the lines and started the horses back down the road.

What a strange man. Luke watched for a moment, then turned back toward the houses. The little cottage was dark. It was late, and perhaps they'd all gone to bed. There was nothing to do, however, but wake them up. Then it dawned on Luke that Griggs had said this was where he'd find the missus. Perhaps Scott was away on some extended fishing venture.

"She knows me. It's not like I'm a stranger," Luke mused aloud. But it would hardly be appropriate for him to stay with Sally if Scott wasn't there. Perhaps she'd have an idea where to send him for a room.

Luke walked down to the cottage, wishing it was daylight so he could see by more than what little light the larger house provided. Whoever those folks were, they hadn't yet gone to bed, and for that he was grateful. The lamplight shining out of several rooms kept him from tripping over his feet.

When he reached the door to the small cottage, Luke knocked. To his surprise, the door creaked open. He made his way inside.

"Scott? Sally?"

There was no reply, and darkness made it hard to see where he might find a lamp or matches. Luke put down his case and let his eyes adjust to the dark. He thought he could see the outline of a table and made his way carefully to its edge.

He gently felt around until his fingers touched the smooth glass base of a lamp. Upon further inspection, he found a box of matches and struck one. He held it up to allow him to see exactly what he was dealing with. In a quick minute, he had the lamp lit and the glass chimney back in place.

The cottage was small. There was the combined living room and kitchen area and nothing more. On the far end of the room was a fireplace. He went to investigate and found there had been a fire, but it had been allowed to die out. He saw the wood stacked to the left and decided it was cold enough to warrant rebuilding the fire.

He had no idea where Scott and Sally might be. Perhaps the baby had come, and she was at the doctor's house or hospital. But did Duluth even have a hospital? Did women go to the hospital to have a baby? They hadn't when Scott was born. Most women had their children at home in the comfort of their own beds.

The wood responded quickly to Luke's attempts and soon blazed with an abundance of light and heat. Luke stood and gave the room a better look. It was impeccably neat. Everything was in its place. Sally had always seemed good at organizing and cleaning.

Spying two doors, Luke picked up the lamp and went to see what might be in those rooms. The first was a bedroom that had been converted to a washroom and storage. He spied the monogrammed luggage Scott had taken from home, so at least he knew he was in the right house. He would have hated to be milling about in a stranger's home.

Continuing his tour, he found a second bedroom behind the other door. There was a small cradle in one corner and a trunk. On the other side, a neatly made bed was pressed against the wall. At the end of this, someone had strung a rope from one side of the corner wall to the other, and there were several articles of clothing hanging there. Behind these was a small stand with a wash basin. Another trunk sat at the end of the bed.

The room was sparse but clean. Luke couldn't imagine how hard the adjustment must have been, however. Carson servants lived better than this. How could Scott have found such poverty to be acceptable? How could he have managed without more?

"Because he loves Sally. Nothing else matters," Luke said to no one.

He had always wanted that kind of love for himself, but it had never come.

"Hello? Who's in here?" a feminine voice called from the other room. Her tone sounded accusing.

Luke left the bedroom and came face-to-face with a young woman. She looked to be in her twenties and had an abundance of windblown blond curls that even now she was fighting back into place.

She eyed him with suspicion. "What are you doing in here?"

"I'm sorry. I hope I didn't startle you. I'm Lucas Carson. I'm Scott's brother. I just arrived," he hurried to explain. "Mr. Griggs brought me here."

The woman's tight expression relaxed. "I see."

"And you are?"

"Gloriana. Gloriana Womack. My father owned this cottage and rented it to your brother and Sally."

Luke gave her a broad smile. "Then at least I'm in the right place. Do you by any chance know where my brother and his wife might be?"

At this, the woman looked away and bit her lower lip. She said nothing for several long moments. Luke was surprised by her attitude but waited patiently.

Finally she spoke, motioning to the two chairs at the kitchen table. "You'd better sit down."

Chapter 8

"Dead?" Luke shook his head.

"Yes, I'm sorry." Gloriana had tried to figure out an easier way to share the news, but in the end had found herself blurting out the truth. "They were crossing to the North Shore to deliver fish, and the storm came up out of nowhere. They were all caught off guard. Sometimes storms do that. My father didn't usually have that trouble. He always seemed to have an intuition about storms, but this time apparently it failed him."

It was obvious the poor man was having trouble reconciling the news. Who could blame him? Gloriana was still struggling to reconcile it, and it had been two days since she'd learned the truth.

"Sally is next door. She's in labor, but the midwife says she's lost the will to live. A doctor has been sent for, and he may well have to cut the baby from her."

"I want to see her."

Gloriana nodded. "I'll take you to my house, but first, do you have any questions? I don't want to talk about this in front of Sally. She can't bear it."

"I don't think I have questions. Scott went fishing with your father and his crew, and the storm came up and the ship sank."

The way he said it seemed so matter-of-fact that it made Gloriana angry. "Yes, and eight men lost their lives. Perhaps you weren't that fond of your brother, but I was, and I loved the rest of the crew as well."

Luke's brow furrowed as confusion filled his expression. He shook his head. "I didn't mean to sound callous, honestly. I loved my brother deeply."

Gloriana forced herself to calm down. She could see the hurt in his eyes. "And I didn't mean to sound so angry. But I am angry. I'm angry at the loss, and I'm angry at trying to figure out the future. My eight-year-old brother is blaming himself for his father's death, and now he has no one but me to rely on."

"I am sorry."

Gloriana barely heard him. "Most of all I'm angry at God. He took my brother and sister and mother three years ago, and now my father and your brother. They were good men. They were good friends—in fact, Scott was like a son to my father. He loved him. We loved Scott and Sally." She got up and began to pace. "And now they're gone, and Sally will most likely die as well. It makes no sense. God is cruel."

"He gives and takes away, but still we must say, 'Blessed be the name of the Lord.'"

She turned on her heel and fixed Luke with a hard look. "How can you say that?"

"What else shall I say? I'm hurting just as much as you are, but I cannot see that blaming God will help any more than you blaming yourself."

"Oh, I don't blame myself. I had nothing to do with this. God who controls the world—the seas and storms—He is the one who could have done something, yet He stood by idle." A sob broke from her throat. She was losing control in front of this stranger, and it only furthered her frustration. "I've lost everything and have no idea how I'm going to face the future, and yet God is silent." Tears streamed down her cheeks. "It's a terrible burden to bear, and I would think you feel it as well."

"I do. I can hardly comprehend my brother being gone. I just had a letter from him, and his happiness was spelled out across the pages. He loved fishing." Luke shook his head. "I can hardly imagine coming from our background of wealth and enjoying manual labor, but that was Scott. He was always full of surprises."

"I know he loved it." Gloriana wiped her cheeks with her sleeve. "He loved Sally and the coming baby as well. Now he'll never see that child. It's not right." She buried her face in her hands and let go of her tears.

To her surprise, she wasn't alone for long. Luke came to her and put his arms around her. Pulling her close, he offered words of comfort. "I'm so sorry. My heart is broken for you and for Sally. Theirs was a truer love than most I've ever seen."

He held her while she cried, and Gloriana let him. She wanted to pull away and stand strong, but there was nothing left to give. She had watched Sally slipping away for two days and knew the young woman would soon be dead. She had no idea if the baby would live. The midwife wasn't very hopeful.

The thought of the baby dying made Gloriana cry all the more. She cried for all of them. The sweet family she had come to love, the hope of playing auntie to the babe. She cried for all of it.

Luke patted her intermittently but never once suggested she stop crying. Gloriana had never known such compassion from a stranger. It was as if God had known she needed a friend and had sent him.

But if God were truly that kind, He could have just kept the tragedy from happening in the first place.

That thought brought her back to anger, and she pushed Luke away without warning and headed to the door. "This isn't doing any good. Come next door, and I'll take you to Sally."

If Luke was shocked by her attitude and action, he didn't say so. Instead he nodded and looked around as if searching for something. Then he reached for his head. "I was looking for my hat, but I see I completely forgot to even remove it. Forgive me."

Gloriana shook her head. "There's nothing to forgive."

She led the way to her house, wondering the whole time what he must think of her falling apart in his arms. She was embarrassed at how she'd sobbed. Such weakness was not a pleasant thing to witness, especially from a stranger.

Opening the door, she found the midwife gathering a stack of towels. "I think the baby has finally decided to come," Abigail said. "He's moved down the birthing canal, and I can just see his head."

"Mrs. Lindquist, this is Lucas Carson, the uncle. His brother was married to Sally."

The older woman nodded. "I must return to Sally. You should be able to see the baby soon. Gloriana, come and help me."

Gloriana nodded and took up an additional stack of towels. "I'm right behind you."

They entered her father's room, and immediately Sally moaned. "The baby. The baby is coming."

"Yes, dear. I know. Just go ahead and let him come. I'm here to help." Abigail deposited all but one towel and placed it under Sally's legs.

"Is the doctor coming?" Gloriana asked. She placed her stack of towels beside Abigail at the end of the bed.

"No. He was out on another call. His wife promised to send him, but thought he might be some time. I believe we'll be just fine now, however. The baby is moving well and should be with us momentarily."

Of course, that didn't answer the unspoken question of whether or not the child would be alive. Gloriana didn't know whether to hope that, if Sally died, the child would as well. That seemed cruel, but on the other hand, what would a newborn do without his or her mother?

"There now, here we go." Abigail's gentle

words did little to soothe Gloriana's concerns. "Just push him on out. Or her. You might have a wee girl here."

Sally said nothing. She had fallen back against the pillow, as white as the sheets beneath her.

Gloriana went to her and wiped her face with a wet cloth. "Sally, you're nearly done. Keep going. The baby will be here soon."

"It doesn't matter," Sally whispered so softly that Gloriana thought she'd misheard. "Nothing matters without Scott."

"Of course it does. This baby needs you." Gloriana dampened the cloth again and wiped the younger woman's face. "You must live for the baby."

Sally shook her head. "Not without Scott. I can't. He was my strength."

"God is your strength, child," Abigail declared. "Scott might be gone, but God will never leave or forsake you."

Gloriana fought back a bitter retort. She didn't want to make matters worse. Sally must find the will to live, and Gloriana wasn't about to let her anger at the Almighty interfere with that.

The baby slid out, and Abigail rejoiced. "A girl! You have a sweet little daughter."

She hung the baby upside down and stuck her finger in the baby's mouth to clear it of mucus. When the baby began to cry good and hard, Abigail handed her to Gloriana.

"Get a towel and rub her off, then wash her in that basin I prepared. She won't like it, but it will aid her health."

The baby was wailing something fierce, but there didn't appear to be any real tears. Gloriana marveled at the tiny infant. Their gazes met, and for a moment, Gloriana felt a wave of guilt. The baby should be greeting her mother, not a stranger.

She whisked the baby to the basin Abigail had prepared and did her best to wash the newborn. The infant was slippery, and Gloriana feared she'd lose her hold. It had been a long time since she'd washed a baby. She forced herself to focus on the task at hand, making sure the newborn was completely clean. The bath was brief, and as soon as Gloriana finished, Abigail instructed her to wrap the baby in swaddling.

"Bring her to Sally," Abigail commanded when Gloriana was done. "Sally Carson, wake up and see your baby."

Sally opened her eyes as Gloriana bent to show her the baby. "She's beautiful, Sally. You must see her."

The exhausted mother lifted her hand to touch the baby's cheek. "She is lovely."

"She's also going to be quite hungry.

That's why you must recover so you can feed and nourish her," Abigail declared.

Gloriana tucked the baby in the crook of Sally's arm. "She needs you, Sally. You cannot leave us."

"May I come in?" Lucas Carson asked from the door.

Abigail quickly wrapped the afterbirth in a towel. "Let me pull over the covers." She hurried to make Sally presentable.

Luke came cautiously into the room.

Sally opened her eyes again and looked at the man who stood at the side of her bed. "Hello, Luke. I'm glad you've come."

"So am I." He looked at the baby. "She's beautiful. Congratulations. I know Scott would be very proud."

She gave a weak nod. "You know about him?"

"Yes. This young woman told me when she found me exploring your little house."

"This is Gloriana. She's my dearest friend in the world."

"Yes. We met briefly, and she told me of all our sorrow."

Gloriana liked the way he included them all. It truly wasn't just one person's sadness, but an entire community's.

He touched Sally's cheek. "I'm here to help you now."

"Do I get to see the baby?" JT asked from the doorway. He yawned and then scratched his head. Apparently all the noise had woken him.

Lucas rose and glanced at Gloriana.

"This is my little brother, JT." She turned back to the boy. "Yes, take a quick peek, and then back to bed with you," Gloriana instructed. "Sally needs to feed her baby girl, and then both of them will need a lot of rest."

JT came to Gloriana's side and stared up at Lucas. "Who are you?"

He smiled. "I'm Scott's brother, Luke."

JT frowned as he looked at his sister. "Does he know?"

Gloriana nodded. "Yes. I told him."

"Gloriana." Sally's weak voice barely registered.

"I'm here."

If possible, Sally looked worse, and Gloriana feared the truth. She was dying.

"Luke?"

He came to stand beside Gloriana. "I'm here too."

Sally lifted the baby ever so slightly. "Take her, Gloriana."

Gloriana accepted the baby, not wanting to argue the point that the child needed to nurse. The baby fussed for a few seconds but calmed, as if understanding the need for quiet.

"I want you and Luke to . . . to look after her. She needs you now."

"She needs you, Sally. You alone. She's already lost her father. Don't deny her a mother as well."

Sally met Gloriana's eyes. "I . . . can't. I don't want to be here . . . without him."

"But Scott wouldn't want you to leave the baby," Luke replied. "Sally, please try."

She gave a faint smile. "Promise you'll both . . . care for her?"

"Of course," Luke promised.

Sally looked to Gloriana. "Promise?"

"I will. I'll love her as my own." Tears came to Gloriana's eyes. How could Sally leave them now? How could she desert the baby she had so wanted?

The baby began to fuss and then cry in earnest. Gloriana held her tighter and rocked back and forth. Still the infant refused to be comforted. It was as if she knew her mother was passing.

Abigail reached up to touch the center of Sally's chest. She leaned her head against Sally's breast and then shook her head. "She's gone."

Gloriana drew in a sharp breath that was racked with sorrow. She shifted the baby to her shoulder and pressed her face against the tiny head. She couldn't believe this was happening. "Poor babe."

After they'd sat in silence for a few minutes, Gloriana realized they had some decisions to make.

"I'd like to call her Sally Marie after her mother and Scott's," Luke said.

"That sounds nice." Gloriana barely managed to speak. It was all too heartbreaking.

"I know an Ojibwe Métis woman who can nurse the babe. She won't charge much," Abigail said, pulling the cover up over Sally's face.

Luke fished out several bills. "Get her. Pay her whatever she asks. The child must survive."

Abigail nodded. "I'll have her here soon. I'll leave my things, Gloriana, and come back to get them when I bring the wet nurse."

"That's fine. I'm sure we'll all be awake."

JT had come to Gloriana's side and he wrapped his arms around her waist. "What are we going to do now? Who will care for the baby?" It was all so much to think about.

"We will," Lucas Carson replied. "We promised."

Gloriana nodded. "Yes. We promised."

"Will baby Sally live here with us? Will Mr. Carson live here too?"

Gloriana looked to Luke. "I . . . well, I hadn't thought that far ahead."

"She should probably remain with you. I

know nothing about babies." Scott's brother gave her a smile. "But if I could stay in the cottage next door, then I can be nearby to offer my assistance."

"Of course." Gloriana had already considered renting the place out so they'd have money to pay the bills. Would Lucas Carson be willing to pay rent? It was too much to think on just now.

"I'm glad we get to have her stay here," JT said. "Then we won't be so sad."

Gloriana glanced down at Sally's covered body. "We'll have to make arrangements for her."

"Don't worry. I'll take care of everything," Luke replied. "You just see to the babe. I'll manage the funeral."

"There's going to be a big memorial service for all of the men who died at sea. Perhaps we can arrange something around the same time with Pastor Sedgwick."

"You know him?"

"Of course. He's our pastor." Gloriana shook her head. "Why? Do you know him?"

"I met his son Theodore on the way to Duluth. He's to be my personal secretary and assistant."

"Oh." Gloriana looked away, lest her lack of enthusiasm give her away. It didn't work.

"Do you know Theodore Sedgwick?"

"Not well. I know of him from his mother. He has been a great source of grief, but I suppose it's unkind of me to say so." She turned back to Luke. "Please forgive me and forget I mentioned it. We have far too many other important things to figure out. First and foremost is Sally and, of course, the baby. I'll need the cradle brought here from next door."

"Of course. Anything else?"

Gloriana looked down at the fussy infant. "There's a trunk of baby things that Sally and I made. It's near the cradle. Eventually I'll need that as well."

"I'll bring them both."

Gloriana allowed her gaze to meet his. She honestly didn't know what she would have done if Luke hadn't shown up when he did. "Thank you."

Chapter 9

Theodore didn't bother to knock on his parents' door, but instead opened it and let himself in. He had little nostalgia for the house where he'd spent his childhood. Life in Duluth had been bitter and filled with troubles. He wanted nothing of it but to take back what it had stolen from him.

"Who's there?" his father called, coming down the hall.

When their gazes met, Theodore could see the contempt in his father's eyes. He was just as unhappy to see Theodore as Theodore was to see him. Theodore forced a smile nevertheless.

"What do you want?" his father asked.

"It's good to see you too, Father." Theodore removed his hat and tossed it onto the receiving table.

"We weren't expecting you."

"No, I'm sure you weren't. Believe me, I didn't expect to be here. However, in an effort to reclaim my good name and turn my life around, I felt I had to come." He began to remove his gloves. "And I knew I had to start with you. So I've come to beg your forgiveness."

His father's eyes narrowed, and the look on his face was guarded. "You've come to beg my forgiveness for what?"

"For the trouble I caused. For the problems I created that threatened to destroy your good name and community standing." Theodore hoped he sounded and looked sincere. He'd practiced long and hard. Hours of staring at himself in the mirror and forcing the lie.

The older man crossed his arms. "What, if I may ask, has brought about this desire for reformation?"

Theodore had been ready for this question. "I have resolved to rectify my soul with the teachings you instilled. My heart has struggled for some time regarding my relationship with God, as well as our relationship. I can see now the error of my ways and desire to right the wrongs of the past."

Father's expression softened a bit, but the doubt was still fixed in his eyes. "To what purpose?"

"That I might stand ready on Judgment Day with a clear conscience where God is concerned. And as for us, that we might re-make our relationship and renew the love that once bound us as father and son."

"Did such love ever truly exist?" his father questioned. "From your first breath it seems you've been against me."

Theodore hated him for the response. They *had* been at odds since the day Theodore was born. All he remembered of his father were rules and regulations. Long boring sermons at church and at home. Discipline that bordered on the edge of cruelty.

"I like to think it did," Theodore forced himself to say.

"What I remember is rebellion and difficulty—a full-out rejection of the God I served and loved."

"When I was a child, I thought as a child. The Bible allows for that, so why shouldn't you?" Theodore fought to keep his voice gentle. "I come seeking forgiveness. Your God says that you must give it, lest you not receive it from Him."

"My God? I thought you were claiming an association for yourself?"

Theo wanted to scream in frustration at his mistake, but instead he shrugged. "This is still new for me. For years you acted as though He were yours alone—that no one in this family could come to Him except through you. But even that I cast aside as my own misconception and hold you to no account." He paused and gave a pleading look. "Will you let your anger at me estrange you from God Himself by refusing forgiveness?"

The last of his father's wall seem to crumble. "Of course you have my forgiveness. I wouldn't refuse any man that. I've only ever wished good for you, Theodore. I don't know why you would think otherwise. What does it merit me to pray down condemnation on my own child?"

Theodore had often wondered that himself, but now wasn't the time to question it. If he forced the issue and insisted that had been his father's heart all these years, he wouldn't be able to move forward and accomplish what he desired to do—which ultimately was to ruin this man and his precious Duluth once and for all.

Theodore smiled. "So may we start again? Would you perhaps extend a welcome and allow me to stay here with you while I begin work for my position with Mr. Jay Cooke?"

"You've been hired by Mr. Cooke?" His father's arms relaxed to his side.

"I have. I'm assigned to Cooke's representative in Duluth, Mr. Lucas Carson. I believe he has a brother, Scott Carson, who works as a fisherman here."

Father's expression grew grim. "He had a brother. The poor man was lost in the last storm. His ship, the *Ana Eileen*, went down."

"The Womack fishing boat?"

"Yes. It's gone, along with several others and the crews that manned them. I'm afraid you've joined us at a grievous time."

"I heard voices. What's going on?" a female voice intruded.

Theodore saw his mother look out from her room down the hall. "Mother!"

"Teddy?" She tied her robe as she hurried to join them. "It is you!" She wrapped her arms around him. There was no love so forgiving as a mother's.

"I've come home."

She hugged him close, then pulled back and looked at her husband. She was still taking her cues from him, and Theodore hated her for it.

"I have asked Father for forgiveness and now am asking you as well. I have come to an understanding of my wicked past and have made myself right with God," he said.

"Oh, Teddy, that is good news," she said, not waiting for her husband's reply.

"I wondered if I might stay in my old room for a time. I've just arrived and will be working with Lucas Carson, Mr. Jay Cooke's representative. I will, of course, look for other furnishings on the morrow, but for now . . ."

"Of course you may stay with us." She looked at his father.

"Yes. Yes, you may stay with us, Theodore."

Theodore could see that his father wanted to add something to his agreement, but instead he remained silent. No doubt a list of rules and regulations would follow at another date, but for now Theodore had what he wanted. The pretense of peace with his parents and a place to live. The rest would be arranged in time.

It seemed all of Duluth turned out for the memorial service for those who'd died in the storm. Gloriana donned her best clothes and made sure to have two handkerchiefs in her reticule. She had arranged with Pastor Sedgwick to offer a small private burial for Sally just after the larger service, and she knew there would be tears aplenty.

JT had been terse all morning, not wishing to attend. He was still convinced that his bitterness was the cause of his father's death, and he begged Gloriana to let him stay home.

She went to his room and found him lying on his bed. Without a word she slipped off her shoes, slid onto the narrow mattress, and pulled him close, as she'd often done after their mother died.

"JT, you know in your heart that only God gives or takes a life. We have no power over such things. Your anger at being punished did not cause the storm. We do not believe in such superstition, and Papa would be disappointed in you if you started such nonsense now."

"But I was so bad."

"It doesn't matter. You're forgiven. Papa forgave you before you even acted that way."

"How could he?"

"Because that's what papas do." She tried not to think about God and her own ongoing war. "Papa knew before you were born that you wouldn't always do things right, but he loved and wanted you more than anything. Without even needing to speak a word, it was understood that he would love you even when you were naughty and did things you shouldn't do. Can you honestly imagine those silly school desks being more important to him than you were?"

"No, but he told me I'd shamed him."

"So do the right thing now and bring him honor. Come to the memorial and tell people what a wonderful papa he was. Tell them how much he loved you and me. How good he was to us and how much we will miss him."

"We will miss him for a long, long time, Glory. I still miss Mama and Tabby and Aaron."

"I do too." Gloriana fought back her tears. "We will always miss them, JT. That's because we will always love them."

"I don't want them to be gone. Not even Scott and Sally. Poor baby Sally won't ever know her mama and papa."

"That's why we must care for her. As she grows up, we will teach her about them. I'll need you to help me with that, because you knew Scott so much better than I did."

"Luke knew him even better than me," JT said.

"Yes, but baby Sally will need all of us."

"Is she going to the church too?" JT sat up.

Gloriana did likewise and nodded. "She is."

"She won't remember it."

"No."

JT thought for a moment. "Then I'll remember it for her and tell her about it. I can do that for her."

Gloriana smiled as her eyes dampened with tears. "That would be a very kind thing."

A half hour later, they sat in the church as a family. Luke sat at the end of the pew on Gloriana's right, while JT sat on her left. She held the sleeping baby, thinking back on the evening Sally Marie had been born. Born into despair and sorrow. Would her life be bound up in such things?

The church was the largest building in town, although it was small by the standards of what was needed. The new St. Paul's Episcopal Church, being funded in part by Jay Cooke, was still weeks from being finished. It was hoped that their first service would be on Christmas Day. But today, the mourners gathered in the old church, with the family members of those who were lost let inside first, and then the townspeople filling in. Mourners even spilled out into the churchyard. The windows of the building were opened so they could hear what was being said as best they could. Thankfully, it was a calm and pleasant day.

Pastor Sedgwick opened them in prayer and then song. "We will sing 'Rock of Ages,'" he announced. The pianist played the introduction.

Without benefit of hymnals, the congregation joined in.

> Rock of ages, cleft for me,
> Let me hide myself in Thee;
> Let the water and the blood,
> From Thy wounded side which
>   flowed,
> Be of sin the double cure;
> Save from wrath and make me pure.

Gloriana hugged Sally close as the baby began to stir. The congregation continued to sing. Sally opened her eyes as if to acknowledge the music's purpose. Gloriana smiled at her and gave her cheek a tender touch. A baby of sorrow.

The words of the song trickled through her thoughts, and Gloriana wished she could take comfort in them, but none was found.

> Not the labor of my hands,
> Can fulfill Thy law's demands;
> Could my zeal no respite know,
> Could my tears forever flow?
> All for sin could not atone;
> Thou must save, and Thou alone.

The congregation continued to sing, but while there was no solace in their words,

Gloriana was caught by the rich baritone voice of the man at her side . . . and by his tears.

The weeks passed, and Gloriana found herself growing quite attached to baby Sally. Having helped her mother with her siblings, especially JT, Gloriana wasn't a stranger to the care and upkeep of an infant. She couldn't feed Sally from her own body, but the wet nurse supplied that need, coming every four hours night and day to help.

Luke paid the wet nurse generously, but after weeks of service, she announced she was expecting another child of her own and had to resign her position. Gloriana was devastated, not knowing how they would get by. The midwife mentioned glass bottles that were proving to be useful to other women. But when Gloriana tried them, the baby refused to take them. She seemed to despise cow's milk, be it fresh or canned. As the baby grew hungrier, Gloriana was at her wits' end.

"I don't know what to do for you, sweet Sally," she said, rocking the baby by the fireplace. The infant fussed, unsatisfied with words and warmth.

The front door opened, and JT and Luke blew in.

"It's the witch of November," JT declared. "She's come early and is churnin' things up something fierce." He sounded just like their father. Would he one day follow in those footsteps and risk his life on the water too?

"I'm glad you're back from town," she said. "What were you able to accomplish?"

Luke held up a jar of what appeared to be milk. "The midwife said to try goat's milk. She said it might sit easier on Sally's stomach." He placed the jar on the table, along with a burlap bag. "I got the other things you asked for." Next he saw to his dripping coat and hat.

JT had already hung up his coat and hat and was crowding in next to Gloriana at the fire. "I'm so cold."

"Well, pull up your stool and sit." She looked back at Luke. "Would you please put some of the milk in one of the bottles? I'm not convinced it will help, but we must try. She seems determined to starve herself. I wish we could get the wet nurse back for just a little while."

"Abigail said she'd try to find us someone else, but . . . well, she made another suggestion."

Gloriana shook her head. "What? Anything to help."

Luke flushed. "She suggested . . . well, that you could, um . . ."

"Out with it." Gloriana grew more frustrated, and as she did, so did Sally.

He turned away and poured the milk in one of the bottles. "She said to try putting the bottle under your arm, very close as if . . . as if you were feeding her from . . . your . . . ah . . ."

Gloriana caught on. "I see." She looked at the baby and then at her breast. "I hadn't considered trying to fool her."

"Abigail said the warmth of your skin against the baby's face might also help, so you could open your . . . well, you know how it would need to be." Luke brought her the bottle, capped with a leather nipple.

"At least we got rid of that nasty-tasting rubber," Gloriana said, looking at the bottle and then the baby. "Do you want to say hello?"

Luke took the swaddled baby and held her up to his face. "Hello, Sally. How's my darling girl?"

Gloriana got to her feet. "I think this will work better if I feed her alone. You and JT stay out here, and I'll go to my room and see what I can do to hide the bottle close to my body. Supper's in the oven, so you might check it in a few minutes, and then when I'm done with Sally, we can eat."

"What am I checking for?" Luke asked, his expression confused.

Laughing, Gloriana reached for Sally. "That it isn't burning. If something looks too brown or smells burnt, take it out of the oven, please."

Luke handed her the baby, and Gloriana made her way to the solitude of her bedroom. She placed Sally on the bed long enough to unbutton the front of her dress and unfasten the ties on her corset cover. This wouldn't be easy, but if it helped the baby feel more comfortable and actually eat, it would be worth any amount of trouble.

Gloriana unhooked the top of her corset and hid the bottle under her arm, then tucked her corset cover around it. Next she lifted Sally in her arms and maneuvered her to the bottle. At first the baby protested, but finally she latched on to the leather nipple and sampled the goat's milk. Gloriana waited to see whether the baby would like the offering. She hadn't even thought to warm it up, but thankfully, it didn't feel all that cold. Luke had no doubt kept it close to his body, and that had warmed it some.

Sally continued to feed, pausing now and then to look at Gloriana as if to question this new arrangement. She finally seemed to accept the situation and ate her fill, falling asleep as she fed.

Gloriana breathed a sigh of relief. Finally, they had figured out something that worked.

"I wasn't expecting to find you here," Pastor Sedgwick said to Luke as he greeted him at the door with JT.

"Luke eats with us all the time. He helps with the baby too," JT explained. "But he lives next door because he can't stay here. That wouldn't be . . . wouldn't be . . ." He struggled for the right word and then blurted it out without warning. "Proper!"

"No, indeed," Pastor Sedgwick replied. "How are you today, Mister Womack?"

"I'm okay. Gloriana's feeding the baby, and then we're gonna have supper. I'll bet Gloriana would let you eat with us too."

"I would imagine you're right, but alas, I promised Mrs. Sedgwick that I'd be home for supper, and I don't want to disappoint her."

JT nodded. "Well, you can still sit down."

Pastor Sedgwick laughed. "Thank you very much for the invitation. I shall do exactly that. Maybe you can tell me how you're doing. Is there anything I can help you with?"

The curly-headed boy considered this a

moment. "I don't know. Glory just makes everything work out. I go to school and she does everything else. She's really good at everything."

"I agree, she is," Luke said, enjoying JT's ease as he spoke to another grown-up. The boy never seemed to be at a loss for words. Perhaps because he was the youngest, and there was never anyone for him to speak to but adults.

"Oh, I forgot. I'm supposed to get my boots cleaned before supper." JT jumped up and went racing for the door. "Excuse me."

Luke chuckled and motioned for the pastor to join him by the fireplace. "Come sit. I haven't had a chance to talk to you much. I believe you know that your son is working for me."

The pastor took a chair, and his expression seemed to sober. "Yes. Theodore told me."

"He's doing quite well, although I admit it's hard to get used to working with a stranger. I had a secretary back in Philadelphia. We'd worked together for several years. Trying on a new secretary hasn't been without its challenges, but I have to say that your son works hard to please."

Pastor Sedgwick gazed into the fire. "I'm glad to hear that. He has struggled a bit to find where he belongs."

"I suppose we have all done that."

"Oh, certainly. I used to be a fisherman before becoming a preacher. Our family was here prior to the Panic of '57, when so many people pulled out. We're members of the 'Ancient and Honorable Order of the Fish Eaters.'"

Luke chuckled. "I'm afraid that's an order with which I'm unfamiliar."

"We're the ones who remained. There was a big boom here prior to the crash. A lot of people came up here, hearing about prosperity. There were eleven incorporated townships and a combined population of fifteen hundred. We had sawmills and flour mills, boat builders and farmers. And then it all came to an end."

"I remember the crash well," Luke admitted. "My father is in banking, and it wasn't pretty. Problems started abroad in England. My family is originally from London, and we heard about the issues early on. As soon as the prime minister circumvented having gold reserves to back their currency, we knew there were going to be major problems and took steps to do what we could to protect our fortune. Still, we lost a good amount of money."

"It spelled doom for us here. The towns dissolved with the evacuation of the people.

We had to get our supplies from Superior, which was better situated and established. Those of us who were left found our main food supply in the lake. Hence we were called fish eaters." He smiled. "We still are. It's a sort of rite of passage."

"So what happened?"

"Your Mr. Cooke happened. Of course, there was also a little thing called the War of Northern Aggression."

Luke gave him a curious raise of a brow. "I've only heard Southerners call it that."

Pastor Sedgwick laughed. "Yes, well, I had a lot of dear family in the South. But that aside, I did not feel we were wrong to take our stand against slavery. After the crash, my faith was challenged, and I began to study God's Word with more interest. As I studied, I felt a calling to share what I learned, and before long, I found I was doing more preaching than fishing. It started with simple discussions amongst other fishermen. Then folks started coming to me with their questions. One day they asked if maybe I could just have a little gathering on Sunday, since most of the preachers had gone and those who'd stayed weren't to their liking.

"I think my family was surprised by my decision to become a full-time pastor to a flock of starving, scared people down on their luck, but as the church flourished, I believe they saw God's hand in it. My wife, Greta, always understood. She'd say to me, 'Christopher, I will not even attempt to interfere with the Almighty. Should He call you to perform on street corners, I will stand by your side.'"

"What a wonderful wife. To have such support must have truly blessed you."

"It did and always has."

"And what of your children? Is Theodore the only one?"

Pastor Sedgwick shook his head. "No, although he is the eldest. I have four, and all are married with children save Theodore. Three sons and a daughter."

"And the others moved away from Duluth?"

"Yes. They chose homes elsewhere, and they are dearly missed. We hardly have a chance to know our grandchildren, although we get occasional letters." He shrugged. "But we act as grandparents to a good number here. Especially the ones who've lost their fathers and grandfathers, uncles and brothers. The lake can be especially cruel, but she calls to them and employs them, and they have no ability to ward her off."

"And Theodore is now returned." Luke wanted so much to ask for information but knew it wasn't right. The best he could do was give the pastor openings for comment. Whether or not he took them was entirely another matter.

"Yes. He's returned." Pastor Sedgwick looked as if he might say something else, then stopped. "I hope he finds his place with this new job."

"Pastor Sedgwick, I didn't know you were here," Gloriana said, coming to join them. "I was just feeding the baby and getting her settled."

"And I was just getting to know this young man a little better," the pastor said, rising in greeting. "But alas, I must return home. I promised Greta I would be there for supper." He smiled at Gloriana, then turned back to Luke. "I wish you the best, Mr. Carson."

"Luke. Please call me Luke."

Pastor Sedgwick nodded. "I would be honored."

Chapter 10

"What do you know about Theodore Sedgwick?" Luke asked Gloriana after supper that evening.

She gave him a quizzical glance, then shrugged. "Rumors mostly, although his mother has spoken at times of her concern for him. He's twenty years my senior and was long gone before I started taking notice of the men in town."

Luke chuckled. "And when did you start taking notice?"

She smiled as she stacked the dishes. "I suppose about the time most girls do—when I was fifteen or so. Of course, up here most of the eligible ladies had chosen their mates by that age."

"But none of the beaus suited you?"

"There were a couple I thought rather

promising, but they didn't have the same interest in me. And those who did had Papa to contend with." She smiled. "He was quite particular."

"And who could blame him? When I think of someone wanting to date Sally, I get very protective."

Gloriana laughed. "Let's give her a few years, please."

"So did you and your father entertain the idea of any of the gentlemen of Duluth?"

"I suppose there were a couple he had his eye on. But we were in no hurry. Mama needed my help at home, and I was in no hurry to leave." Her voice softened. "Then, when Mama died, I felt obligated to forget about such things and take care of JT and Papa. I knew that if God wanted me married, He would send me a man who would love Papa and my brother, and we could all live together as one big happy family. I didn't get my hopes up, however." She looked a little sad. "Now it doesn't matter. Papa isn't here."

"Let's not dwell on that. I'm really hoping to better understand my associate. I got the feeling there was something Mr. Sedgwick's father wanted to say about him, but he held back. You wouldn't know about some past conflict or trouble, would you?"

Gloriana grew thoughtful. "I remember

hearing his mother mention something that happened when he was much younger. This would have been before he left town. Probably when I was just a little girl. I don't know much about it, but she said he had shamed them— risked his father's good name. It cost the pastor a great deal of money, but I can't tell you why. Then he moved to Philadelphia to go to college, and eventually started work at a bank." She shrugged. "His mother had brief letters over the years. I know he fought for the North in the war. His folks were pleased he'd done at least that much, but I get the impression he's mostly been a disappointment to them." She put her hand to her mouth. "I shouldn't have said that. I don't want to be a gossip."

"I'm sorry for pressing you for the information. It's just that I know nothing about him. He works well enough, but he seems cloaked in mystery." Luke shrugged. "I can't put my finger on it. He's willing enough to do what I ask of him, however, so I suppose I should just put aside my concerns and let him work."

Gloriana got to her feet. "I don't know. Mama used to say those feelings were there for a reason. She believed it was God's prodding."

"But you don't?"

She didn't even look at him. "I don't know what I believe anymore."

Gloriana hadn't meant to speak the words aloud, but she ignored them and gathered up the supper dishes. She poured heated water into the basin and chipped off pieces of soap to melt in the water.

"I suppose I'll be going, but first can I help you by drying the dishes?" Luke asked.

"That's fine, if you like. JT is working on some homework from school."

"How's he doing with all this?"

She frowned, remembering how late JT had been getting home throughout the week. "I think he's keeping things tight inside. He's been late from school most every night, but when I try to question him about it, he tells me not to worry so much."

"Sometimes boys need time to process their thoughts."

"Girls do too." She smiled. "It's just never been like him to keep things from me."

"Maybe he needs the time to think. I can't imagine being a boy of eight and losing my father. My mother died when I was just three. She died in childbirth, and I was too young to remember much. My father remarried the next year to Scott's mother. She was a good stepmother and loved me like her own. She's gone now too."

"Did she die when you were young?"

"No." Luke picked up a dish towel. "When I was twenty. About ten years ago. I mourned her passing greatly. Scott was devastated. She was all kindness and generosity. Where my father failed to have feeling, she more than made up for it."

"She sounds like my mother. Although my father never failed to have feeling. He was such a good man. He was generous to all. If anyone ever needed help, my father was the first to volunteer. Mama used to say he loved mightily." She smiled at the memory. She pushed the thought aside. "Speaking of fathers, have you heard from yours regarding Scott's death?"

"Not yet. I sent him a letter giving as much information as I could. I didn't say anything about the baby and Sally, however. It was enough that he had to deal with the death of his son. It didn't feel fair to add to that grief."

"Still, he'll have to be told."

"Yes." Luke looked as though a heavy burden had just been placed upon his shoulders. For a short time, no one spoke.

Gloriana wasn't sure what was bothering him regarding telling his father of Sally's passing and the new baby, but she decided against pressing him on it. "I want to thank you for the new rug. It has warmed the front room considerably, and I'm sure Sally will enjoy crawling on it when she's older."

Luke smiled and glanced over his shoulder at the beautiful piece. "Scott had ordered it for the cottage, but there's no sense putting it in there." He continued drying the dishes but seemed out of sorts. However, he seemed to push that aside and gave Gloriana a start with his next comment.

"I'd like to help give you all a happy Christmas. I know it hasn't been long since our loss, but I'd like to do something for JT's sake."

"I'm listening." She continued washing dishes. She was deeply touched by all that Luke had done for them. She only wished she could figure out how to do for herself in the future.

"I thought maybe when the time comes, we could go cut down a tree and decorate it. Then, Christmas morning, I'll come and fix you both breakfast and bring gifts."

"I'm sure JT would enjoy almost anything, but I can't have you spending a lot of money on him for Christmas. We've always kept things very simple. We read the Christmas story and talk about the truth of the celebration. We usually go to church and then come home, and if there are gifts, we share them then."

A big smile broke across Luke's face. "It sounds perfect. Do we eat before or after church?"

"After." She couldn't help but giggle. She felt like a young, carefree girl. For just a moment.

"Then plan on it." He took a newly rinsed dish from her hands. "Now I need to figure out some ideas for gifts."

"Well, I think for now you should probably head home. That's the last of the dishes, and I have some mending to tend to before I go to bed."

Luke looked regretful but nodded. He hung the dish towel on the handle of the oven door. "I'll see you first thing in the morning for church."

Gloriana shook her head. "No, the weather is too harsh for Sally."

"Are you sure the weather is the reason? You didn't go last week either."

"I'm trying to be mindful of sickness. It killed my mother, brother, and sister. I would think you'd want me to be extremely cautious with your niece."

"I appreciate that you're careful with her, but I think you really need to deal with the conflicted feelings you're having toward God."

She could hardly believe he'd said that as if it were no more difficult than cleaning a cabbage. "I don't want to talk about it."

Luke nodded. "I know. But sooner or later you're going to have to."

~⁓~

"I'm all done with my homework," JT said, yawning as he came into the living room. He stood beside Gloriana, who was mending one of his shirts.

"I'm glad. Pretty soon we'll need to head to bed. I'm sorry you haven't had any time for playing."

"That's all right." He plopped down on the sofa.

"You want to tell me why you've been so late getting home from school? Did you stop off to play first? Is that why you don't seem too put out about missing out on playing?"

"I'm not being bad, if that's got you worried."

She looked at him, surprised by his sass. "That was rather disrespectful, JT. I just like to know where you are. You have chores to do here, and I need to keep on top of your schoolwork. If you don't show up until supper, it makes you late like you are tonight.

You had to wolf down your dinner and then hurry off to finish your work. Now you'll be heading to bed, and we've had no time to enjoy each other's company."

"We did at supper. You cooked real good, Gloriana." He turned on the charm. "Papa said you could make bread even better than Mama." He frowned. "But I don't remember."

"I'm sorry you don't. Her bread was amazing, and I'm sure if Papa said that, he was just teasing. Mama taught me, after all."

"I miss her. Aaron and Tabby too. And Papa." Tears came to his eyes. "I don't know why they all had to go away."

Gloriana put aside her sewing and patted her lap. JT crawled up and rested his head on her shoulder. "I don't either."

"Pastor said sometimes these things happen, and we never get to know why, but that in heaven we'll understand."

A lot of good that did an eight-year-old boy now. Gloriana said nothing despite her thoughts. Instead she hugged him close and hummed a little tune.

"That's pretty. I like it."

"Mama used to sing it all the time when we were babies. I found myself singing it to Sally."

"Baby Sally is lucky she has us, isn't she?"

"She is. Because we love her and want to take care of her. Not everyone has someone to love them."

He leaned up to meet her eyes. "Will you always love me, Glory? Even when I'm naughty?"

"Have you been naughty lately?" she asked, still wondering at his late arrivals home.

"No, but I'm bound to mess up. I keep trying to do what I know is right, but sometimes I might not know whether it's right or wrong. I can't know everything, Glory."

She smiled and ran her fingers through his curls. "You're a very smart boy, and I think if you pay attention to your heart, you'll know."

"Because God will tell me?" He looked at her with his huge blue eyes.

Gloriana wasn't about to bring her spiritual troubles down on him. "Yes. I'm sure God will tell you what to do."

She could feel confident on his behalf, so why couldn't she trust that God was still doing the same for her? Why couldn't she trust that God was listening and still the same caring God she had believed in prior to the death of her father? Even her mother's death and that of her siblings hadn't shaken her so.

"I love you, Glory." JT hugged her neck.

"I'll tell you real soon why I've been late. But it's nothing bad. You gotta trust me."

She smiled. "I will. Go get your sleep gown on, and I'll come tuck you in. It sounds like that wind is picking up again, so you might want to wear long socks."

He got down from her lap and yawned. As she watched him march off, she couldn't help but think about the future again. What were they going to do? Luke was only here until summer, when the railroad reached completion. Sally was his niece, and despite her mother asking them both to raise the child, that was hardly possible. Especially if he took her back to Philadelphia.

Then there was the obvious issue of finances. What little money her father had put aside was nearly gone, and the help from others, while still generous, couldn't go on forever. Gloriana would have to get a job. There was no other way.

She considered the possibility of working at a dress shop. She was good with a needle, and the railroad was bringing in more and more families. There would be wealthier folks coming to live in town, and Gloriana was confident she could replicate some of the gowns she saw in *Godey's Lady's Book*. They were the height of fashion.

With a sigh, she gazed into the fire. Then

there were her thoughts about Lucas Carson.
She liked him very much. He had been such
a help and was so kindhearted and generous.
He was the kind of man Gloriana could have
given her heart to, spent the rest of her life
with, raised a family with. She'd found great
comfort in Luke's playing the role of man of
the house. She didn't care that folks in town
might be talking about their closeness.

But Luke was from Philadelphia and had
no intention of remaining in Duluth. He often
talked about his home in the bigger city and
of the job he did there for Mr. Jay Cooke. He
had shared about his childhood and youth
and even told her a few things about the social life he'd known. The only thing he didn't
speak about was the war. Nobody liked to talk
about the war.

She could see his handsome face as the
flames danced in the hearth. She admired
him so much. What man devoted himself so
completely to his dead brother's child? Anyone else would have found the baby a nurse
and sent her back to Philadelphia, but Luke
wanted Sally here with him.

He'd also been so encouraging in Gloriana's loss. He had helped JT with his sadness.
Just a couple of days ago, she had overheard
him comforting the boy when JT broke down
over his father's death. He and Luke talked

about how much they missed Papa and Scott. Luke had asked JT to tell him about Papa and listened as JT shared all of the things that were so important to a boy about his father. Things Gloriana hadn't thought of in a long time, like when Papa had taught JT to fish off one of the river docks. He had carefully instructed JT how to handle the fishing rod and line, but when the time came to cast, JT wasn't able to coordinate his actions and followed the line right into the river. Thankfully, he already knew how to swim. The memory made Gloriana smile, as she still remembered her father announcing that he hadn't caught any fish, but he had caught one ornery little boy.

But the time was coming when Luke would go away. She had to remember this and not allow herself or JT to get too attached. How could they possibly bear another loss? Yet even as she considered that question, she knew it would rip her heart apart when Luke took Sally away.

She shook her head and then buried her face in her hands. Why did loving someone have to hurt so much?

Chapter 11

The last person she wanted to see was Pastor Sedgwick, but there he stood at her front door, a big smile on his face and a basket of his wife's delicious berry muffins in hand.

"Good morning, Gloriana. Greta asked me to bring these to you. She knows how much JT enjoys them and thought you might like to have them."

"Thank you." She forced a smile and a welcoming invitation. "Won't you come inside? It's quite cold today."

"That's November for you," he declared. "Blustery and damp. Chills a man to the bone."

"Get warm by the fire if you like." She took the basket and placed it on the table. "I have a little coffee. Would you like some?" She had a cup or two left over from breakfast with Luke, but if Pastor Sedgwick wanted more than that, she wasn't sure what she could do. They were out, and there simply wasn't money for more. She knew the time had come that she had to talk to Luke.

"No, I'm fine." The pastor smiled. "I'm not going to stay long. I know you're busy."

As if on cue, Sally began to cry. Gloriana nodded. "Hold on. I'll get her."

She returned with baby Sally in hand. It was amazing how much she had grown in just two months. Gloriana cradled her in a blanket and showed her off for the pastor to see.

"She's gotten big," he said.

"Well, once we figured out that she preferred goat's milk, it made all the difference."

He took hold of the baby's tiny hand. "Precious child. Just precious. You've done some good work in taking care of her, Gloriana. You have fulfilled the Bible's command about taking care of widows and orphans."

"It's been my pleasure. I'm sure when summer comes and Luke takes her back to Philadelphia, I may question my choice to help, but for now she gets me through the days."

"Did Luke say he intends to return to Philadelphia? I'd heard nothing of it."

"I just presume, since that's where his home is, that he will probably want to. But no.

He's not said anything about it." She jostled the baby as she began to fuss again. "Sally has been such a blessing to me and JT both. She helps us reflect on life rather than death."

"It's funny how God often does that. Sends us something to reclaim our focus in times of grief and pain." He paused. "I know this hasn't been easy for you, Gloriana. I know you may be struggling with questions of why God allowed this to happen."

"You mean why God has left us without hope for our future, without the love of our good father? You see, JT and I are orphans too. Of course I would help the fatherless. I am one of them."

"But you mustn't allow it to divide you from the heavenly Father," Pastor Sedgwick replied. "I know it seems like He has been cruel to you—heartless—and perhaps you're thinking that He no longer cares. But, Gloriana, He does."

"He has a strange way of showing it." She frowned. "I have a little brother who often cries long into the night for his loss. I try to comfort him, but my tears are just as plentiful. We have each other, at least, I tell myself, but it serves little purpose."

Another interruption sounded at the door. Gloriana was relieved. She opened the door to find Luke holding a small sack. "Sweets for JT," he said, raising them aloft. "If that's all right with you."

She smiled and took the bag. "As long as I get my share. Come on in. Pastor Sedgwick just stopped by."

"And I'm heading off again," the pastor said. "I was just making my rounds. Gloriana, are you sure there's nothing I can do for you?"

"Nothing," she replied. She knew from his patient smile that he understood, but it offered little consolation. She drew a deep breath. "Thank you for coming by. It means a lot." She didn't really mean the words, but she saw their effect and knew saying them had been the right thing to do. Pastor Sedgwick felt reaffirmed, and that was all that mattered.

"Then I'll bid you both good-bye for now. We hope to see all of you in church on Sunday."

"Hopefully my new carriage will come on the next ship," Luke declared. "I have a nice team of horses but no carriage to put them with."

"And no decent road to drive them on," Pastor replied.

"Yes, but I must protect my little family from the elements," Luke replied.

Gloriana had never heard him refer to

them as his little family. Of course, maybe he only meant Sally. It was impossible to tell.

"Well, I hope to see you all in church no matter how you get there. We miss you." The pastor fixed his gaze on Gloriana. "Greta wanted me to make sure I expressed that."

Gloriana was glad Luke took the initiative to show Pastor Sedgwick out. When he finally closed the door, Gloriana was already at the fireside with the baby.

"Is she dry and safe for handling?" Luke asked, joining them.

Gloriana laughed. "Well, for the moment. As you know, that can change at any time." She handed him the baby, who immediately reached for his face. It would seem Sally knew her Uncle Luke very well. "I have a little coffee left. Would you like me to heat it up?"

"No, come and sit with me. I have some things we should discuss."

Gloriana decided the time had come to tell him of her situation. "I'm happy to do that but must beg to be allowed to go first."

His eyes narrowed. "Of course." He looked momentarily troubled. "Is something wrong?"

"Well, yes and no." She sighed. "It's simply something that must be resolved."

She took the rocking chair while Luke sat

with Sally in Gloriana's mother's old chair. "Please tell me everything."

She nodded. "I need to find work. The truth of the matter is that Papa didn't leave us fixed all that well. We have the rental property, of course." She paused, hoping Luke would think about the fact that he was living there rent-free. "And he had a little savings, but that's mostly gone now from buying food and shoes for JT. I'm going to have to find a way to earn wages so I can continue to support my brother. That, of course, means I won't be available to take care of Sally."

Luke seemed confused, and then it was as if he suddenly found a secret stash of gold. "Oh, my goodness! I never thought. I've been so blind."

Gloriana was taken aback. "What do you mean?"

"I am so dense. I'm sorry, Gloriana. Here you've been allowing me to stay in the cottage without paying my fair share. You've been feeding me and washing my clothes, and I've done nothing but bring an occasional treat to the house." He shook his head and gazed toward the ceiling. "God forgive me." He refocused on her. "Why didn't you speak sooner?"

"I . . . well, everything had been all right, but when I ran out of coffee this morning and knew there wasn't money for more . . . well, I guess I just realized I couldn't put it off anymore."

"Gloriana, this is all my fault. I'm so sorry. I'll pay back rent on the cottage, and let's discuss this situation of a job. You've been nursemaid to my niece for two months. I owe you wages at least for that, not to mention that you've acted as a housekeeper and cook for me. I owe you a great deal, and I'm sorry for not having been considerate enough to realize you couldn't possibly have had the money to pay for all the food you've fed me."

"I don't expect you to pay me for anything, especially not for caring for Sally. I made her mother a promise. I just need to get a job so I can continue to pay for JT and myself." Her heart beat a little faster at the compassionate look he was giving her. "I . . . it was my pleasure having you join us for meals. I just can't make everything work without money."

"Gloriana, if not you, I would have to pay someone else. Sally has known you from her birth. You are every bit a mother to her, and that comforts me greatly. You have loved her, not just cared for her as a nurse might. I don't want her to leave your care. I will pay you back wages and rent, but I will also pay you going forward. Don't consider it pay for caring for Sally—maybe just consider it pay for taking care of me." He laughed. "As you know, I can be rather a mess."

He propped the baby in the crook of one arm and reached into his coat. He pulled out a large leather wallet. Gloriana tried not to look surprised as he handed her more than fifty dollars.

"This should cover the last two months. I'll set up accounts in any stores you ask me to so that you can just go there and shop for what you need. If I might continue to eat my meals with you in the morning and evening, that would greatly bless me." He smiled.

"I wouldn't have it any other way. JT would be angry at me if I sent you away. He's come to see you as a big brother. You've been a blessing to our family, Luke. There's no denying that."

"I'm glad. I'm just sorry for the worry you must have felt over your future. Put it all aside now and worry no more. I will see that you're paid fairly. What else should I arrange? I know the church men have provided firewood, but should I order more?"

"No, we're fine. Papa and Scott had already cut some, and with the extra . . . well, I think we'll be all right for a while."

Gloriana allowed relief to wash over her. Luke was right. She had earned the money in her hand, but at the same time, she'd enjoyed having him with the family. He had helped her from growing too sad. He had regaled them with stories of the world. He had been a good friend.

"Let's speak no more of it. This money will take me far," Gloriana admitted. "I'll put it away to replace what Papa had set aside for emergencies."

"I never thought to ask, Gloriana, but did your father have any life insurance or insurance on the boat?"

She shook her head. "I doubt it. Who had money for that kind of thing? Papa prided himself on owning the house and boat free and clear of financial obligations. He had once put a lien on the property when he built us this new house, but as soon as it was built, he rented out the cottage, and everything he made went to pay off that loan. I remember my folks celebrating when the bill was paid."

"A simple joy, to be sure. Remaining free of debts is the only way to live without fear. Debts bring a kind of shame that no one wants to bear. It's far wiser to save for those things we cannot afford and to learn patience in waiting for them."

"I agree. Papa once told me that saving for something made it all the more precious in the receiving. And he was right." She folded the money. "I must put this away lest I lose it."

"Well, as soon as I get to the bank, I shall have more for you." Luke smiled. "I intend to see you and Master JT properly cared for."

For the next few weeks, Luke continued to berate himself for having been so stupid. How could he not have realized how difficult Gloriana had it? He'd lived in her cottage without paying a penny and had eaten her food—most of which had been provided by others in the small town. It had been so completely heartless of him—not at all the good Christian he wanted to be. When he thought of the sleepless nights she might have had, it bothered him all the more. He'd lived such a spoiled life of abundance. Never once had he needed to worry about whether there would be enough food for the next day.

"God forgive me."

When Luke thought of Gloriana and JT's home, he found himself wanting only to do more. He wanted to build them a bigger house. They could live in the better part of town and rent their current property out in full. There was always a new family coming to town to help with the railroad or one of the other new industries. It would give Gloriana a solid bit of money to live on in addition to what Luke intended to pay her for Sally's care. If Luke worked it out right, they could all live close together as they did now.

Of course, other ideas for caring for Gloriana and JT, as well as Sally, constantly came to mind. Luke was finding himself rather enraptured by Gloriana. He hadn't considered himself looking for a wife, but the more time he spent with her, the more he found himself pondering just that possibility. Maybe the house he built would be one for a bride?

"Here are those maps you asked for," Theodore Sedgwick said, coming into Luke's office. "I'm afraid the route along Moose Lake required some changes, and Mr. Rowland is overseeing those."

"That's not a problem." Luke took the rolled maps and spread them out on his desk. "I will need a full report on the finished work prior to Christmas. Would you see to that? I figure you can go to St. Paul to deliver the updates and reports and see that they get forwarded to Mr. Cooke. Then, on your way back, you can get the updated information on where we're halting the line work until spring." He smiled. "You might even take an extra day on us and do some shopping for the holidays. I have a few things I'd like you to pick up for me as well."

Sedgwick gave a nod. "I will do whatever you need me to do. When shall I leave?"

"Well, Christmas is less than two weeks away. I think you must go soon. Even tomorrow, if that is convenient."

"Of course."

Sedgwick had been nothing but cooperative and good to work with. Luke needed to put aside his uneasiness. He pulled some money from his wallet, then picked up a list from the desk. "Do you think you could obtain these things for me?"

Theodore looked at the list. "I do."

"Do you believe this will be enough money?"

Theodore looked at the bills in his hand, his eyes rather wide. "More than enough."

Luke smiled. "Good. Oh, and I have something for you." He reached into his desk and pulled out an envelope. "A Christmas bonus for a job well done."

Theodore's surprised expression was more than enough to please Luke. Clearly his secretary had not expected such a gift.

"Merry Christmas."

The older man took the envelope and nodded. "Merry Christmas to you. Thank . . . thank you." Theodore put it in his pocket without bothering to look inside. He was a strange little man, but Luke wanted very much to work amicably with him.

"All right, then. Speak with Archie Rowland

about your transportation. They will make every opportunity for you to travel quickly and return in time to share Christmas with your family."

Sedgwick nodded again. "Thank you. I'll return as soon as possible."

He left, and Luke could only smile. Giving surprise gifts was something he enjoyed. It was going to be a lot of fun seeing how Gloriana and JT responded at Christmas. He had great surprises in store. But for now, he needed to make one more arrangement, and that was for a tree. He wanted very much to have an entire day of fun searching for a tree and perhaps eating at one of those Swedish bakery shops.

Then another thing came to mind. He'd been wrestling all day with how to tell his father about baby Sally. The baby was the last connection his father would have to Scott, but Luke worried about his father's ideas for the child. He would never agree to let Gloriana and JT be a part of her life. Once he knew about the child, he would want her for his own, and that thought caused great trepidation. His father could be very cruel and demanding. He would want to raise Sally as a china doll—secret her away, change her name, and wipe away every memory of her mother being a scullery maid. Luke couldn't allow that to happen. He'd been considering what to do ever since Sally had died. He had honestly considered lying and telling his father that the baby had died too, but he knew God would never honor that.

"Lord, I know I have to tell him, but what can I do to protect her?"

He thought again of that horrible night when his sister-in-law lay dying, her will to live gone. She had begged Gloriana and Luke to raise her child. There had been a witness to this deathbed request: Abigail Lindquist. The midwife had heard the entire matter. She could offer testimony. But for what purpose?

Adoption.

The thought came clearly, and Luke almost whooped for joy. Adoption. Of course. He could start the proceedings and adopt Sally Marie Carson before his father could alter the course. He would start the arrangement immediately. What was the name of that judge he'd met at church?

❧

"It's so cold out. Do you really think we ought to expose Sally?" Gloriana asked, her tone full of concern.

"I think she'll be fine," Luke replied. "You've buried her under five blankets. It's a wonder she can breathe."

"She's breathing without any trouble," Gloriana replied, but double-checked the child even as she spoke.

"Come on. I have the wagon ready. We'll drop Sally off with Mrs. Sedgwick and then be on our way. Don't disappoint me."

"Or me," JT said in an annoyed voice. "I've been looking forward to this all week, Glory."

Luke gave her a grin. "What's it going to be? Are you going to keep your word or not?"

"Of course I'm keeping my word. I just want to be sure Sally will be well cared for."

When they reached the Sedgwicks' place, they nearly had the entire conversation again. Finally Luke took the baby out of Gloriana's arms and thrust her at the pastor's wife. "We'll be back by five. Is that good?"

"Very good."

"She needs to be burped after she eats, and remember, only goat's milk. And don't forget to keep her dry," Gloriana fussed. "She has a tendency toward rash if you don't keep her dry."

"Gloriana Womack, I raised four children without your help. I think I can master a day with little Sally," Mrs. Sedgwick declared, sounding firm, though her expression was amused.

"I'm sorry." Gloriana looked forlorn and displaced.

Luke took that as his cue. He handed Pastor Sedgwick a basket. "There's extra goat's milk in bottles here. Should be plenty for the day. There are also lots of flannels for the other end." He laughed and jumped up on the wagon.

"You all have fun. We'll be just fine," the pastor said.

Luke nodded and put the team in motion.

Gloriana was still not satisfied. "Do you think she'll be all right? What if she thinks we've abandoned her?"

"I think that a two-month-old has too many other things to think about. After all, it's nearly Christmas."

"She's three months old."

"Three months or two, I seriously doubt she's all that concerned with much more than eating and sleeping and the occasional bounce on the knee." He nudged JT, who sat between them. "Unlike a certain boy I know who is always thinking about hundreds of things and so busy I can hardly keep up with him."

JT snorted a laugh. "I've just got a lot to do."

"Indeed." Luke laughed with him. "Speaking of which, I understand there's a

Christmas program at the school. Am I invited?"

"You are most assuredly invited," JT said in a very grown-up manner. "All of our family is supposed to come, and I consider you family now. You're like my big brother."

Luke's gaze met Gloriana's over the top of the boy's head. He liked the way that sounded. He was a part of their family.

To his surprise, once they were away from the town proper and found a place to focus on getting their tree, Gloriana lost track of the time and became caught up in their objective.

"I like this one," JT said, standing beside a tall pine. "But it's too big."

"Indeed it is," Gloriana replied. "We couldn't even get it through the front door."

"What about this little one?" Luke asked, pointing out a much smaller tree.

JT frowned and shook his head. "It's too little to put even a few ornaments on it."

Luke grinned as he played the game. "I see your point."

They finally settled on a beautiful balsam fir. It was about as tall as Luke and, as JT pointed out, had soft branches that wouldn't hurt Sally.

The boys cut it down and loaded it on the back of the wagon, looking like a couple of lumberjacks. Gloriana laughed at their antics, which was the purpose for them in the first place. Luke wanted more than anything to see her happy and carefree.

By the time they drove back to town, they were all famished. Luke pulled up to a Swedish bakery he'd tried several days earlier. Gloriana protested, declaring they should just get the baby and head home, where she could reward their efforts, but he insisted.

"They have the most amazing Swedish doughnuts here. They are full and heavy, yet light at the same time. I can't describe them. You really just have to try them."

Luke ordered a pot of hot chocolate and three cups, as well as a dozen doughnuts.

"We'll never eat a dozen doughnuts," Gloriana protested.

"Speak for yourself. JT and I are hungry. We worked hard today and got very cold."

JT nodded, his mop of curls springing out around his face. "We did."

"I need to trim your hair. Goodness, when did it get so long? I just cut it before the . . . memorial." Her voice faded and she looked away.

Luke reached over and squeezed her hand. "That was three months ago, as you pointed out earlier. Time has a way of moving on, even when we aren't ready."

Gloriana looked at Luke and nodded.

"That's very true. I can scarcely believe it's almost 1870. It seemed just yesterday that we were celebrating 1869's coming. Now it's nearly Christmas, and then it will be the New Year, and before we know it, the harbor will be open again."

The doughnuts and chocolate arrived. Luke announced that while the chocolate was good for drinking, it was also very good for dunking doughnuts. Everyone gave it a try and found it to be true. They talked about their day and shared the food until it was gone. Gloriana marveled that JT had eaten three doughnuts and then announced that she'd had two. That meant Luke had eaten seven by himself.

He patted his stomach. "When a man works hard, he has to eat plenty."

She rolled her eyes but said nothing.

After Luke paid the check, they picked up a sleeping Sally, who looked no worse for the wear. The day had turned out exactly as Luke had hoped it would. Now, if they could manage the evening as well, it would be the perfect day.

Gloriana looked at Luke and frowned. "Christmas ornaments? Well, we have some homemade ones."

"Perfect. Where are they? I'll fetch them."

She worried her lip for a moment. "I believe they're in the attic. We usually string cranberries and popcorn for the garland."

"Wonderful. Do you have some of those?"

Gloriana nodded. "I can pop some corn in the fireplace. Just let me put Sally down to bed first. JT can show you how to reach the attic."

She took the baby and moved to the kitchen, where she already had a bottle warming on the stove. Sally was hungry and fussy but never all that much trouble. While Gloriana tested the temperature of the milk, the baby wiggled and squirmed but issued only the faintest cries from time to time. It was as if she wanted to remind Gloriana of her situation but didn't want to be rude. It made Gloriana smile.

"You really are the very best baby in the world."

She took the baby to the bedroom where she usually fed her. Even though these days she didn't have to hide the bottle from Sally anymore, Gloriana found it such a peaceful respite. Her mother used to say there was nothing more calming than feeding her babies. She would sit back and put the child to her breast, and it seemed as if all the cares of the day faded away as the infant latched on.

Gloriana wondered if she'd ever know that feeling. She wanted children of her own very much. She had helped care for her siblings and now Sally, but it wasn't the same. There was no doubt a difference. Wasn't there? Or was it that when you loved someone, it didn't matter?

Sally drifted off to sleep. Gloriana wiped the baby's mouth and burped her, relishing the fresh scent of her hair. Mrs. Sedgwick had bathed her, no doubt. Gloriana wrapped Sally up and placed her in the cradle. For a moment all she could do was gaze down in wonder. No, she didn't think it mattered. Love was love. She would give her life for this child. Nothing was stronger than that.

She made her way to the living room and found the boys hard at work.

"I'm glad you've rejoined us. I was just describing to JT some of the Christmas ornaments I grew up with and how I like yours much better."

"Well, they are definitely nothing fancy." Gloriana picked up one that had been made from a tree branch sawed crosswise to make little wooden discs. Her father had cut one for each family member, drilled a small hole in the top, and Mama had strung it with red ribbon. Then each member of the family had decorated their piece of wood with something special that would remind everyone else of them. This ornament had belonged to Tabby, who had made several small bows with excess ribbon because she liked to wear bows in her hair. Mama had even helped her cut a curl of her hair and tie it with ribbon to paste on the ornament. Her hair had been just as blond as that of Gloriana and the boys.

Aaron was always going fishing, so his ornament had a fishing hook and a coiled piece of fishing line attached to a small twig pole. Mama had decorated one with little pieces of material and a needle and thread, and Papa had used six smooth stones in a circle to represent the members of his family. Then over these he had glued a twig cross to show that all were under the protection of God, because even though he didn't see a need for God in his life, he knew it would please his wife. Mama had helped JT make his by carving and inking an etching of a dog. That had been the year JT had nagged everyone for a dog, but their father told him no. Not until he could prove himself to be responsible enough to care for such a creature.

Last of all was Gloriana's piece. She picked up the ornament and smiled. She had laughed that all she wanted for Christmas was time to read a book uninterrupted. On the ornament was her own rendition of several books. She'd made the pages out of newspaper, then covered them with starched cloth for the covers. On these she carefully penned the names of tomes she had received but never had time to read. She still had those books safely tucked in her hope chest.

"These are too marvelous. I love them," Luke declared. "They show who each person in your family was or even is now."

"Luke had glass ornaments that had been made for the queen of England," JT said in awe. "They were all different colors and cost a lot of money."

"They did indeed," Luke declared, "but not one represented the love that are in these." His gaze met Gloriana's, and her heart skipped a beat.

She smiled and nodded. "It was our last Christmas all together." She felt the weight of her loss once again. "JT never did get his dog."

Chapter 12

"We have to get them to change the line. There is still time," a man Theodore knew as Mr. Gillette declared. "We can offer so much more. We have direct access to the lake, and we will see that the city agrees to build magnificent facilities at the docks."

Theodore nodded and made notes. He knew the desperation of the city of Superior, Wisconsin. They had long held the focus of shipping in the area. The railroad was imperative.

"We've already got people working against Duluth's notion of building a canal into Superior Bay. We won't allow for it. It would spell our utter doom."

"And would probably alter our shipping area as well. Who knows what a canal would do to the natural breakwater?" another man said.

Theodore didn't believe the man was worried about the breakwater so much as his profit margins. The canal, while worrisome, wasn't nearly the problem the railroad had become. The future was dependent upon the railroad. Farmers would bring their grain crops to ship across the lake to buyers back east. Ore and wood would be a huge commodity as well. There would no doubt still be plenty of shipping work for both ports, but greed was a powerful master.

"I will be speaking directly with those men from the railroad who support your cause," Theodore assured them. "None of them were originally supportive of a Duluth terminus. I have their ear, as they believe me to be the closest thing they have to speaking to Lucas Carson in Duluth." He chuckled. "And they aren't wrong. I've made myself indispensable for your sakes."

"And don't think we don't appreciate that," another man named Collins announced. "We cannot allow that railroad to terminate in Duluth. It must be Superior. Let them have their northern route to the Pacific, but on Lake Superior, we must be the ones who control the shipping."

Theodore smiled. These men knew what

it took to sway others to their thinking. "You know that money is what will convince those here in St. Paul to make changes. If properly motivated, they will convince Jay Cooke for us, and our work will be minimal. We will come out looking like nothing more than helpful bystanders. The point is to make it worth their while."

Collins nodded. "We have put together a sizable donation to this cause. You will take it and disburse it wherever it will do the most good. Even to your Mr. Carson, if you think he can be swayed to help us."

"No. I feel we must say nothing to him. He is a good friend to Mr. Cooke, and I don't think they would appreciate knowing that we are paying bribes to alter the terminus. Just trust me to bring you the best possible result." Theodore smiled and tugged on the sleeve of his suit coat. "I have experience in this area and won't let you down."

"Then it will make our uncomfortable trip to St. Paul worth it," Mr. Collins replied, getting to his feet. He pushed an envelope toward Theodore. "Use it where it will garner us the most help, but we will expect an accounting."

Theodore smiled. "Of course," he assured them, knowing it would be used for his own benefit. He wasn't going to waste money helping these ninnies, but he would let them think that was exactly what he was doing.

The meeting ended, and Theodore made his way to the hotel. He had accomplished everything he'd wanted to with the Superior, Wisconsin, men, and now he had some work to do on the maps he'd brought with him to St. Paul.

Rafael would be so proud of him. He'd come up with the brilliant idea to hire a man to reorganize the track route. He'd lied and told the man that problems with the route had been noted and the railroad needed an alternative route. The man had no way of knowing that any route he made would be worse than the one already in place. He wouldn't know that the railroad had spent over a year trying to find the best way to deal with the boggy land. With any luck at all, these new numbers would spell doom for Duluth and give Superior the upper hand.

Theodore checked with the front desk clerk for messages, then made his way to his room. He doffed his outer coat and hat and threw them onto a nearby chair. He'd be going out again for a luncheon meeting, so he saw no need to do more. Taking up the first map, he spread it on the table and used whatever was available to hold it in place. He then took the papers he'd received from his surveyor and began to work at altering figures. The work was tedious. He had to make certain that his marks looked natural. It was all a matter of taking his time and being diligent. Thankfully, he'd always had a bit of artistic bent to his nature. It had served him well enough when he worked for the Carson bank, and it would help him now.

Thinking of his days working for Luke's father's bank, Theodore couldn't help but remember the man who had changed his life. Rafael was dead and gone now many years, but his influence had made Theodore a better man. Or at least a more knowledgeable one. Learning to adjust the books to help themselves to hundreds of thousands of dollars had enriched Theodore's life in more than one way. Of course, it had robbed him of a friend when Rafael had been found out.

He truly missed Rafael, and he couldn't say that of any other person in his life. Being reunited with his parents had only proven that he'd been wise to leave in the first place. Although, to his credit, he had given them a perfect performance. Father had even laughed at one of Theodore's stories a few nights earlier. But no one had ever shown such complete acceptance of Theodore as Rafael Clarington, and none probably ever would. His friend had taken their secret arrangements to the grave and saved Theo from a life in prison. Who could ask for a better friend?

"And Lucas Carson is the reason you're gone," Theodore muttered. If not for Luke's prying and seemingly magical ability to look at a book of numbers and see errors, Rafael would never have been caught.

Theodore frowned. Lucas Carson had caused him more grief than he even knew. He'd lost his home and felt the need to leave a good job, all because of that man. Worse still, he'd lost a good friend. It was all Carson's fault, and Theodore would see to it that he paid for it. When these new numbers wreaked havoc on the rail line—perhaps even caused deadly accidents—Lucas Carson's reputation would be ruined. Especially when Theodore willingly testified that Lucas had altered the drawings.

He would build a network of good support in the Superior men and win their railroad for them. Then, if all else failed, they would at least be in his debt. He smiled. "I like the sound of that. Don't you, Rafael?"

⁓

The next day after Luke left for work, JT posed a question. "Glory, what are we gonna get Luke for Christmas?"

She stopped drying the dishes and turned

to her little brother. "I've been thinking about that, but I'm not sure. I don't have time to make him anything, unless I make some candy."

"What about a compass? I know they cost money, but they're really important. I remember when Papa gave me my first compass and taught me how to use it."

Gloriana nodded. "I've heard it said, 'A man needs only a Bible and a compass to always go the right direction.'"

"Well, Luke's got a Bible, so now he just needs a compass."

"A compass might be a very good gift for Luke. I don't know what they cost, but I'll look when I'm out shopping."

JT seemed pleased with himself. "It's going to be a good Christmas, isn't it, Gloriana?"

It touched her that he could be so positive. It would be their first without Papa, and she hadn't been looking forward to it. In the back of her mind, she worried about it all hitting JT on Christmas morning. He often wept over the loss, but he said very little, and it worried Gloriana that he might feel he couldn't talk about it.

"I believe it will be, but you know, little brother, you can always talk to me about anything."

He smiled. "You can talk to me about anything too."

Gloriana thought about that a moment and nodded. "I know I can. So maybe, if you don't mind—and since you don't have school this morning—you would talk with me."

"Sure. What do you want to know?" He leaned back in his chair like a lawyer with a client.

She might have laughed but was afraid it would hurt his feelings. Instead, she took the chair opposite him at the table. "I guess I just feel a little sad. This will be our first Christmas without Papa."

He nodded. "It makes me sad too. I miss him so much, but Luke said that was all right. He misses his brother a lot. They were really close. Did you know that?"

Gloriana nodded and pretended to pick lint off the tablecloth. "I know you and Aaron were close brothers as well."

"Yup. Aaron said I was a nuisance, but he was always willing to help me when I needed him. And Tabby always talked to me and let me help her roll the stockings and socks on laundry day, so she was good too."

A memory of Tabby and JT rolling clean stockings and socks together flitted through her memory. Those were the little things that were slipping away, even though it had only been three years. Time was cruel in robbing a soul of those details.

"I'm sure they are all so happy in heaven and want us to be happy here on earth."

"I think so too, Glory. Luke told me that there's no more tears in heaven. No sadness or sickness neither." He shrugged. "Sounds like a really good place to go. I wonder if you still get to fish. Papa and Aaron would be sad if they couldn't fish, so they must be able to fish in heaven."

"I don't know the answer to that question, but I agree with you. Heaven will be a wonderful place where nothing will ever go wrong again."

The wind picked up, causing the drafty little house to moan. Papa had always commented on how he was going to fix that one day. Now it was a rather endearing sound that reminded Gloriana of the past.

"You know, while we're here and the baby is sleeping, I think I'll trim your hair. You want to look your best for the Christmas program."

JT nodded. "I don't like haircuts, but I do want to make you proud."

She touched his cheek. "You make me proud every day. I'm really lucky to have you as my little brother."

"Well, tomorrow night at the Christmas

program, I'll have a surprise for you. It's not a present," he said and frowned. "It's a good thing, but it's not a real present."

"You don't need to worry about getting me a present. I'll be just fine without one."

"Oh, I have a Christmas present for you. Luke took me shopping a while back, and I picked out a doozy."

She shook her head at the idea of Luke helping JT shop for her. Was there no end to his generosity? "Well, I wasn't worried about getting a present, but I shall cherish whatever you have arranged." She got up and went to retrieve the scissors and a comb. "Now hold still, and we'll have this done in a quick minute."

Gloriana was grateful that JT was busy the next day with preparations for the school program. It gave her time to visit the stores and figure out a gift that she and JT could give Luke. The idea of a compass was absolutely perfect, but the cost was worrisome. Still, she had the money Luke had given her, and it seemed reasonable that she should spend at least some of it on Luke.

"You might try Mr. Blakely. He does trades and loans all the time on a variety of goods," one of the store clerks reminded her.

"I'll bet you could get a good deal on a used compass."

She nodded. It was a good idea. She made her way to Mr. Blakely's secondhand store. The sign out front stated, *I will buy your quality pieces.*

Making her way into the store, Gloriana marveled at all the things that lined the shelves and aisles. It seemed there was nothing a person wouldn't part with for extra cash.

"Hello, Gloriana. I never thought to see you in here. Have you come to sell me something?"

"No. I came to see if you might have a nice compass I could purchase for a gift. The brand-new ones are a little expensive."

The balding man nodded. "That they are. I believe you might find just what you need in this case at the end." He led the way and reached down to pull out a tray. "This is one of the best. It's made by a quality company in London."

"That's a ship's compass," she said as he handed her the open wooden box. "I only meant to get a small pocket compass."

"This would make a nice accessory for a man's office or library. If I might be so bold, I presume you want this gift for Lucas Carson."

She flushed. What must the town be

saying? "It is very nice, but I doubt I could afford it."

"I knew your father very well," Mr. Blakely said with a kind smile. "I owed him so much. He gave me the money to start my business. Did you know that?"

She shook her head. "I knew Papa was much loved, but no."

"After the crash your father was so good to those of us who remained. Your mother too. They did wonderful little things for everyone." His eyes dampened with tears. "I was devastated to hear I'd lost my dear friend."

"Oh, Mr. Blakely, I'm so sorry." Gloriana reached out to touch his hand. "I had no idea. I'm afraid we've been a bit lost in our own sorrow."

"Of course you have, and well you should be, child." He drew out a handkerchief and unashamedly wiped his eyes and blew his nose. "Norman not only helped me get this business started, he helped others too. Your father was one of the good ones, Gloriana."

She sniffed back tears. "Yes. Yes, he was."

Blakely wrapped the compass in brown paper and handed it to her. "Just take this for your young man. If he's half the man your father was, you'll be blessed."

"I can't give him something that cost me

nothing." Gloriana smiled. "Didn't David himself say that of giving to God? I must pay my fair share."

"One dollar. I will take no more," he replied.

She considered arguing that she knew the piece cost him more than that, but instead she pushed across a dollar's worth of coins. "Thank you, Mr. Blakely. I have only one more request."

"Anything for you." He smiled.

"One day, will you please tell my brother the stories you have about Papa? As the years go by, he won't remember as clearly from his own collection of memories. He'll need friends like you to remind him."

Mr. Blakely straightened as if coming to attention. "I would be proud to do so."

"Thank you. I know I would enjoy hearing them as well."

She left the little shop feeling uplifted and encouraged, and all because someone had bothered to take time to share with her a story of love. She tucked the compass into her bag, knowing Mr. Blakely had probably lost considerably on the deal. It really was, however, the perfect gift for Luke. She could imagine him keeping it in his office. No doubt JT would instruct him exactly where it should go.

Luke led them outside. "Okay, you can look. What do you think?"

Gloriana and JT had been made to keep their gazes on the walkway until they reached Luke's new carriage. Now they stood in awe at the sight of it.

"It's beautiful," Gloriana said. "And enclosed. How marvelous."

"I figure there are more cold months here than hot, not to mention the annoyance of the bugs in summer. Maybe the enclosed carriage will keep them to a minimum." He smiled and opened the door. "Blankets await you."

The ride to the school was bumpy, but so much better than walking the mile uphill. The strong team Luke had secured made short work of it, and when they came to a halt outside the building, it seemed to Gloriana that they had just gotten comfortable.

"I have to go," JT declared, scampering off to join his friends before Gloriana could protest.

Luke came and took Sally in hand, then reached up to offer his assistance to Gloriana. She felt like a fine lady and noticed that the carriage drew more than a few stares. Several church ladies came over to greet her.

"Such a beautiful carriage," one commented.

Another leaned in for Gloriana's ears only. "Has he proposed yet?"

Gloriana felt her face heat despite the cold. She and Luke had only known each other for three months and had spent that time in mourning and trying to figure out how to take care of JT and Sally's needs.

Luke saved her from having to answer. "We'd best get inside, ladies. The weather might cause harm to your delicate constitutions."

The ladies giggled like schoolgirls. It was probable that no one had ever worried about their constitutions. Not only that, but women in Duluth were hardly likely to be delicate.

The schoolhouse had chairs arranged at the back for the parents, while the children's desks had been moved closer to the front of the room. Gloriana could see JT's curly head bobbing back and forth while he chatted with the boys on either side of him. Finally, the schoolmaster appeared and started the festivities off with a blessing.

"Lord our God, King of the universe, we give glory and honor to You and You alone. You have given us great hope and love in the gift of Your Son, Jesus. We thank You for Him and all that He has done on our behalf.

Let our words be of thanksgiving at all times. In Jesus' name, amen."

Several voices affirmed the *amen* before Mr. Nelson continued by introducing the youngest of his charges.

Gloriana sat beside Luke while they listened to the children sing and speak about Christmas. Mr. Nelson had put together a lively program focused on enjoying the time of celebration but not forgetting that it was to honor the birth of Christ.

Sally seemed particularly to enjoy the music. She perked up from her nap when the children began to sing and watched with wonder from Gloriana's lap. When the music ended, the baby seemed perplexed.

Mr. Nelson got up and began to speak about the school year. "I have a special presentation to make this year to one particular young man. He gave of himself in a way that went above and beyond anything he was required to do. Many of you might have noticed how nice the school desks look. That is in thanks to Master Womack."

The severe-looking schoolmaster motioned JT to the front of the room. "JT refinished each of the desks for us. He stayed after school and sanded them and then stained them. They look new again, and we are very grateful. In consideration of that, I created a new award—an award of service. And this one goes to Jeremiah Thomas Womack."

Gloriana remembered all of JT's late nights arriving home. He had asked her to trust him and promised he wasn't being naughty. Tears came, and she let them flow without shame. Her little brother had made her so proud.

"Did you know about this?" Luke whispered.

"No, did you?"

His gaze met hers. "No. He's quite the young man."

JT received his certificate and smiled a toothy grin out at the audience before Mr. Nelson let him reclaim his seat with the other children. Gloriana was grateful he made no mention of JT's carving on his desk in the first place. There was no need to shame the boy and then honor him.

When the program concluded, JT rushed over to Gloriana and Luke, waving his certificate. "Now you know my surprise," he declared. "But I didn't know I was going to get an award. Just look! I've never had an award."

"We'll have to get it framed," Luke declared.

"I'm so very proud of you, JT. I have no words. You are the best little brother that ever was or will be." Gloriana hugged him close, and Sally immediately thrust her hands into his hair.

"Ow, Sally. That hurts," JT complained, but he didn't try to force her to let go.

Luke took care of freeing him. "I am very proud of you, JT. You never said a word about it, so I'm equally surprised."

JT looked up once the baby had been loosed from his hair. "I wanted to do it for Papa. Do you think he knows? Do you think he's proud?"

Luke squatted down. "I think he's very proud."

"He told me I needed to fix the desk I ruined and also fix the others. I was really mad at him for that punishment. It seemed like he just wanted to be mean to me. But then I got to thinking about how it was the last thing I could do to honor him."

Luke shook his head. "No. It's not the last. Growing up to be a trustworthy and honest man will be a lasting memorial of honor to your father. You bear his name—Womack. Wear it proudly and do it no harm. That will make him very, very proud."

JT nodded, his expression solemn. "I want him to be proud of me."

"Oh, JT. He always was." Gloriana bent to kiss his head. "He always was."

"I'll be over here bright and early tomorrow to accompany you to church," Luke said.

"It's terribly cold," Gloriana began.

He shook his head. "I will not take no for an answer. It's Christmas and we will be in church. Then we will come home, and I will cook for you and amaze you with my skills."

"And there will be presents?" JT asked.

"Absolutely. I give you my word there will be presents."

JT clapped. "Then I'm going to bed right now." He jumped up on his stool in order to reach Gloriana's face. He gave her a quick kiss, then hopped down and gave Luke a hug. "I'm so excited. I hope I can sleep fast."

"I'll be there to tuck you in shortly," Gloriana said. When JT was gone, she looked at Luke and shook her head. "Just look what you've done now. He probably won't sleep a wink."

"He will, don't worry." He surprised her by taking her hand. "And you will too, Gloriana."

She felt her hand tremble and wondered if he knew the effect he had on her. When he closed his other hand over hers, she knew he must.

"I know these months have been hard on you. I know you've suffered doubly because you feel God betrayed your trust in Him. But, Gloriana—He hasn't betrayed you, nor did He betray your father. He was there on the *Ana Eileen* with my brother and your father and the others. He never left them for a moment, and when that ship went down, God met them in the depths and welcomed them home."

She tried to swallow the lump in her throat and pull away, but Luke held her fast.

"Don't let the devil have a hold on your heart," he continued. "You have so much love to give. I see you with Sally and JT, and I know there is such kindness and joy in you. Your loss—my loss . . . they are hard to bear and will continue to be for some time. But we aren't alone in this. God is not some cruel prankster playing a game with us. He is the sovereign God of the universe—the Maker of all creation, and yet He knows our every tear, our pain, our loss."

She couldn't look away from Luke's loving gaze. He spoke to her from the intimate depth of his soul. How could she doubt the truth of what he shared?

He touched her cheek, and it was nearly Gloriana's undoing. She shook her head and lowered her gaze. "I should be so grateful for all I have, and I know I need to be cheerful for JT—and strong for him. But I have so little strength. I think the wall I've put up between myself and God has caused me to lose all hope. I just can't seem to tear down the bricks. They are firmly in place, put there by anger, accusation, and bitterness."

"Just talk to Him, Gloriana. Just tell God what you're feeling and thinking. He can hear through the bricks. He already knows what you'll say, but it will do your soul good to tell Him." Luke kissed her forehead.

Gloriana wished it had been her lips he kissed, but she knew that until she resolved matters with God, she was no good to anyone.

Luke left after that, and Gloriana stood for a long time in front of the fire, pondering her soul and the sadness she felt. Could God even forgive her for her anger? She had failed His test of faith—she had denied Him three times at least.

She sank into her mother's soft old chair and wept.

Chapter 13

Gloriana awoke Christmas morning and realized by the silence in the house that no one else was yet stirring. It seemed strange that the baby still slept, but she decided to enjoy these moments of solitude and ponder the day.

Stretching, she snuggled deeper into the covers. She had dreaded the coming of Christmas each year since losing her mother. Mama was the one who had always made Christmas a special time. Now that job fell to Gloriana, and she felt woefully inadequate. Especially this year.

She thought of all the Christmases she'd enjoyed as a child. Waking up on Christmas morning, the first sensation was always the blended aroma of so many wonderful things to eat. Mama would get cinnamon rolls in the oven before church and pull them out to cool just before the family headed out to worship. There was the scent of coffee and other delicious smells in the air, and Gloriana could hardly contain her excitement.

The weeks before Christmas, she and her mother would make candy and cookies, if money and supplies permitted. It was difficult to get supplies in Duluth during the winter months. Often her father and other fishermen would put on snowshoes and trek to Superior or even farther for much-needed medicines or food. Because of all the stories of these long journeys, Gloriana thought they must surely live at the very top of the world. She remembered seeing a map when she finally went to school. They weren't at the very top, but they weren't that far either.

She remembered the celebration they had when Minnesota became an official territory in 1849 and then a state in 1858. She had thought it a grand thing, although some people resented the restrictions and new laws it put on the land. Her father told her that coming under the authority of the United States offered them protection, rather like she was protected as his daughter. It made her feel safe.

Gloriana pushed back the covers and swung her legs over the side of the bed.

Stretching again, she lit a candle. The soft glow of light was adequate without being intrusive. She grabbed her robe and glanced into the cradle. Sally's lips pursed and sucked, but she slept on. The sight made Gloriana smile. What a precious creation. She marveled at how God had sculpted tiny fingers and toes, little ears and mouth. It dawned on her that she was thinking of God's amazing creation, and she reflected on the ongoing war she'd been having with her emotions and heart. There was just so much pain to overcome.

She knew Pastor Sedgwick and Luke would both suggest she give that pain over to God—let Him take her burden and bear it for her. Still, Gloriana felt her anger rise up. If God loved her so much, then why hadn't He saved her father? Why had He allowed her mother to get sick and die? Why had he taken Tabby and Aaron? How could that possibly equate to love?

Sally stirred and began to wake up. Gloriana took the candle and hurried from the room to warm a bottle. There was hardly any warmth left at all in the stove, so she placed a few sticks of wood inside and got them lit. Another task her mother had always overseen. Papa would see to the fireplace, building up a nice big fire to warm the entire front of the house, but Mother managed the kitchen. It was her domain, and everyone knew it.

The memory made Gloriana smile. As the stove's warmth began to build, she could remember her mother telling Gloriana that the kitchen was the heart of any home. Gloriana could see and understand that even at a young age. The kitchen was the gathering place. Many a time her father's friends or crew had met there. Visitors were often directed there, where Mama would lay out a spread of goodies and coffee, or even full meals. Heartaches were shared at the table over coffee or milk and cookies. Every important decision her folks had ever made had been made in the kitchen, it seemed.

Gloriana fed the fire a few more pieces of wood, then got the goat's milk from the window icebox her father had made. The window opened to reveal a box tacked onto the house. On the outside there was a hatch for increasing or decreasing its exposure to the cold. It was convenient and perfect for keeping their food chilled in the winter. Even in the summer, it served a purpose. Her father would pack insulation around it and slip a large piece of ice inside, making it an official icebox.

With the bottle warming, Gloriana went to the living room to tend to the fireplace.

There wasn't much in the way of live embers, but just enough that with a few wood shavings and some kindling, she had a small fire going in minutes. Papa had taught them all how to make a fire.

"Sometimes you have to coax it to life," he'd say. "And other times it will take off without your even trying. It's deadly and must be carefully tended. Many a house or life has been lost due to careless fires."

His warning had never been far from her thoughts. In that moment and so many others, he had been such a good teacher. His absence left a hole that could not be filled.

Gloriana added larger pieces of wood and finally logs, and it wasn't long before there was a roaring fire. She sat on JT's stool and warmed herself while gazing into the flames. What did life hold in store for their future? She sighed. Would anything ever feel normal again? Safe? Would they ever truly be happy?

After losing Mama and the others, Papa had once told her that sometimes just getting through the day was a good enough accomplishment. Endurance was often an overlooked blessing. She sighed.

Remembering the bottle, Gloriana made her way back to the stove. She tested the milk and found it sufficiently warm just as Sally began to offer up her morning protests of having an empty stomach. Gloriana grabbed a cleaning cloth and dipped it into the warm water around the bottle, then took it with her to greet Sally.

"Good morning, darling girl," Gloriana declared, lifting Sally from the cradle. The baby calmed immediately. "Let's get you washed up and into some dry clothes."

She unwrapped the baby from her blankets and swaddling. Sally kicked her legs and flailed her arms a bit, happy for the freedom she'd suddenly achieved. The room was chilly, though, so Gloriana lost little time getting the infant changed and redressed.

"We're going to church today, because it's Christmas," she told the baby. She had chosen an embroidered white gown that the child's mother had made for her. There were little rosebuds sewn into the bodice.

"Just in case it's a girl," Sally had told Gloriana. "If it's a boy, I can always take them off."

"Your mama made this gown for you," Gloriana whispered. "She's not here to tell you about it, but I am. And I won't let you forget her."

Baby Sally began to fuss again, as if bored with the entire matter. Food was her number one ambition now that she was warm and dry.

"All right. I know what you want, but I

haven't even gotten dressed yet myself." Gloriana decided it would be better to see Sally content than to worry about her own attire for the moment. She took the baby with her to the living room, collecting the bottle from the kitchen on the way.

Sally's eyes widened and her mouth started working before the leather nipple even reached her lips. Gloriana laughed at her. "You little piggy. At least wait until I can put a towel under the bottle." She wanted to protect the gown Sally's mother had worked so hard on.

Gloriana arranged everything just so and sat in the rocking chair by the fire. Finally, they were settled and the baby was content. Just then, however, a knock sounded at the door. A moment of panic washed over Gloriana. It would be Luke. She wasn't dressed, and her hair wasn't pinned up or even brushed out. She hated to let Luke see her this way but felt she had little choice. If she didn't call him in, he'd just keep knocking.

"Come in."

Luke entered as if he owned the place. He had two big bags in his arms. One looked to be full of wrapped gifts and the other held food. "I'm glad you're up. I couldn't wait a minute longer. When I saw the fireplace smoking, I knew I had to bring this stuff over."

"I'm barely up. I haven't even had a chance to dress or arrange my hair."

He smiled at her. "It looks good down. But don't you worry about me. I've got all of this figured out. I want to get the presents under the tree before JT wakes up. He is still asleep, isn't he?" He glanced toward the hall.

"He is. It's just us girls so far this morning."

"Good. That serves my purpose quite well." He set down the bags and immediately began pulling gifts from the larger of the two.

"What in the world did you do, buy out the store?" Gloriana couldn't believe all the packages that Luke was putting under the tree.

"I know it's a lot, but call me sentimental. I got some of it here in town, and some of it I had my secretary pick up in St. Paul. I can't imagine poor Mr. Sedgwick trying to procure some of these things, but it honestly never dawned on me that it might be an embarrassment for him until he was already well on his way."

"An embarrassment? Goodness, Luke, what did you buy that would be embarrassing?"

"Just some clothes and things like that. I want you to have everything you need."

Gloriana had never had a man shop for

her. Not for clothes, anyway. Her father usually left all of that kind of shopping to Mama, and Mama generally made the things they wore. Even their undergarments.

Luke continued putting gifts under the tree while Gloriana fed Sally. Neither chore took long, and when Sally was done, Gloriana set the bottle aside and got to her feet just as Luke grabbed the second bag and headed to the kitchen.

She watched him for a moment while burping Sally. He was completely at ease pulling a variety of cakes and pies from the bag. He held up a slab of bacon and a small basket of eggs. "I didn't know if you had any, so I brought extra."

She nodded but didn't bother to comment, as he was already continuing.

"I have some of those wonderful Swedish doughnuts. I ordered them when we were there after cutting down the tree. I told the woman I needed them for Christmas morning and paid her extra to drop them off to me. I could see she thought I was crazy. But maybe we could make our own pot of chocolate."

"Of course." Gloriana laughed as he filled the table with more food than she'd ever seen for Christmas morning.

"What's going on?" JT asked, yawning

as he padded down the hall in his nightgown and heavy knit socks. It seemed to dawn on him all at once that it was Christmas. He raced to the tree, and Gloriana watched as his mouth dropped open. "There are so many presents!"

"Yes, but it will all wait until after church," she warned, "so you'd best go get dressed."

JT looked at her and nodded. "You gotta get dressed too."

Gloriana smiled. "I do. Come, Sally, you can help me."

It took her longer to comb through her tangled curls than to dress. She was anxious about going to church. She hadn't been there since the memorial. No doubt people were talking. They had probably already formed their judgments about her and Luke living so close to each other and raising Luke's niece together. But the child needed someone to care for her and keep her safe. There was nothing strange about that.

Gloriana did up the buttons on her green wool skirt, then pulled on the matching jacket. It was one of only two outfits she ever wore for church. She'd never had more than one or two dressy things. There simply had never been the money for it. Now she wondered what Luke had purchased for her. How would he even know the right sizes?

They made their way to the church in Luke's new carriage, and all the way, Gloriana couldn't help but feel like they were a proper family. They were comfortable and happy with each other. It reminded her of days so long ago when she had walked to church with Mama and Papa and the others.

Church was crowded, and when Gloriana entered with the baby in her arms, she was immediately set upon by friends who had been worried about her.

"Gloriana, you look so pale. Are you ill?" one woman asked.

Another commented, "You're so thin. You must be working much too hard taking care of that baby."

"How are you getting by without your father? We've heard that Mr. Carson is paying you to care for his niece."

The chatter went on without Gloriana even being able to reply.

"We've missed you so much, my dear," Mrs. Sedgwick declared, coming to save Gloriana from the onslaught. "Sit with me."

Luke and JT trailed up the aisle behind Gloriana as the pastor's wife took charge. Gloriana took her seat with the baby, and Luke and JT joined her. Luke had the good sense to put JT between them. Gloriana couldn't help but feel the entire church was whispering about them.

She raised her chin. Let them think what they would. She'd done nothing wrong. God knew the truth, even if she felt at odds with Him at the moment.

The thought surprised her. God had always been a safe harbor for her, a refuge in times of trouble, but this time she had made Him the enemy.

Everything in her soul rose up against that. He wasn't the enemy. Still, what did she do with a God who seemed so indifferent to her pain?

The service was short. Pastor Sedgwick prayed a blessing on them after sharing his hopes for their new year and the love that he and Mrs. Sedgwick felt for the congregation. To her surprise, it was announced that the ladies' committee had set up a Christmas pounding for them. Each of the congregants had brought pounds of flour, sugar, salt, and coffee to gift the Sedgwicks. There were other things too—jars of jellies and vegetables, as well as fish. Gloriana felt bad that she hadn't known about it.

When the service concluded, it looked as if Gloriana would be set upon by the nosy women of the church again. Luke seemed mindful of this, however, and whisked her and JT from the church. He had them loaded in the carriage and headed home before too many people could react.

"Can we open presents now?" JT asked when they reached the house.

"Of course." Luke laughed. "I won't make you wait anymore."

"I would like it if you would change out of your good clothes," Gloriana told him.

JT moaned, but the second the carriage stopped, he jumped out and raced for the house.

Luke laughed. "I have to go to the livery to leave the horses and carriage. I'll be back as soon as I can."

"It seems like an awful lot of trouble for a short ride to church."

"Not when you care about someone." Luke met her eyes and winked.

Gloriana's breath caught in her throat. She hugged Sally closer, much to the baby's dislike. "Speaking of which, I'd better get the baby down for a nap."

"She has Christmas presents too," he said, smiling. "Maybe you could let her open a few first."

Gloriana nodded. "Maybe a few, although I'm sure she won't care."

When they gathered at the tree a half hour later, Luke had already put food in the oven and started frying bacon on the stove. Gloriana was starved, and as the bacon began to pop and sizzle, she found herself far more focused on food than gifts. Still, she was excited to give Luke his present. She had also managed to get JT a nice present—at least she hoped he'd think so. It wasn't a toy, so it was hard to gauge.

"Here's a present from me to you," Luke said, handing JT a small package.

JT opened the box and found his Christmas ornament with the etching of a dog. He looked at Luke in confusion. "Why did you wrap this?"

"Luke and I discussed it and think it's time for you to have your own dog," Gloriana said. "Papa was already considering getting you one for your next birthday."

"A dog? A real dog?" JT was so excited that he began to dance around the room. "When can we get him?"

"Captain Johnson said their collie had puppies at Thanksgiving. He thought they'd be ready to leave their mother by the end of January. You get first pick of the litter."

"Oh boy!"

Luke grew serious. "But remember, there is a lot of work in training a puppy."

JT nodded. "Will you show me how to take care of him?"

"Of course." Luke smiled. "I've already started building him a doghouse."

JT put the box down and went to embrace him. "It will make me think of you and Papa." He wrapped his little arms around Luke's waist and hugged him tight.

Gloriana smiled at the tender moment.

Luke moved on and drew out a package for the baby. "I hope this will fit."

Between Sally trying to eat the paper and Gloriana doing her best to unwrap it in a neat order, the entire affair was comical. When the gift was revealed, Gloriana gasped. It was a beautiful pink gown with a white lace overlay.

"This is beautiful, Luke. It's too big for now, but it will be perfect soon enough."

He handed her another package. "This is a bonnet to go with it."

Gloriana had an easier time of unwrapping this, as Sally was preoccupied with the paper from the first gift. The bonnet was also a little big but matched the dress perfectly. "Luke, this is so beautiful. I know Sally will look sweet in it."

"And this one is for you."

It was a large box, and Gloriana couldn't manage it and the baby at the same time. "You'll have to take Sally," she told Luke.

He did so, and Gloriana lifted the box

from the floor. It was tied with ribbon, so she quickly unfastened it and opened the lid. Inside was a heavy wool coat trimmed in fur.

"Luke, it's beautiful!" she gasped. She stood and pulled the coat from the box. "I've never had anything so grand."

"Try it on." He was clearly pleased at her joy.

She slipped into the coat and pulled it close around her. "It's perfect and so warm. Thank you."

Luke nudged a similar box toward JT. "I have something in this one for you."

JT tore into the box and pulled out a black wool coat. "Thank you, Luke." He wasn't nearly as enthralled with it as Gloriana was with hers.

"In keeping with the idea of warmth and protection," Gloriana said, reaching for two packages, "I have these for you two." She handed one package to Luke and the other to JT.

They quickly opened them to reveal blue wool sweaters.

"I made them. Originally they were for Papa and JT," she explained. "Fishermen rely on their sweaters, and the women here have their own patterns for each family. This is the Womack pattern."

"I'm honored." Luke held up the sweater

and marveled at the work. "This is so heavy. I'm sure it's very warm."

"They are," JT told him. "Nothing warmer. But they smell because you don't wash them. The wool has special oils on it from the sheep, and that makes them water-proof. So you don't wash them. You wear one of these sweaters and your coat, and you'll never even feel the wind. Except for your face. That gets cold."

Luke chuckled. "I'm sure."

The rounds of gift-giving continued. It was casual and lovely, and Gloriana found herself wishing the morning would never end.

"We have a present for you, Luke," JT said, bringing the wooden box from Glori-ana's room.

"I apologize for a lack of wrapping, but the cost seemed frivolous," she said, look-ing at the waste of boxes and paper in her front room. At least some of the paper could be saved, and the boxes would be useful for storage.

JT handed the gift to Luke. "I hope you like it. It was my idea."

Luke opened the lid. "A compass. How beautiful."

"And useful," JT declared.

Gloriana could see Luke was pleased. "Some people around here say that a man only needs a Bible and a compass to always go the right direction," she said.

Luke smiled. "Sounds quite right."

"We thought the bigger compass could be something to place in your office as a reminder," she continued. She glanced toward Sally, who had fallen asleep without any concern about her gifts. Gloriana turned back to JT. "I have one more thing for you."

She slipped off to her room and reached under the bed for a small wooden box. She hoped JT would be happy with what was inside.

"Here you are," she said, rejoining the men.

JT looked at the box. It was about twelve inches across and maybe six inches deep. He opened the hinged lid and looked inside. "What's this?"

"A memory box," Gloriana said, smiling. "See, here is a letter Mama wrote to Papa once when he had to be far away. And this is a little hair comb Papa carved for Mama long ago. There are other bits and pieces from our family that will always remind you of them. You can add to it over the years whenever something special happens." She held up a small blue stone that had been tied to a leather thong. "Papa could never afford jewels for Mama, but he made this for her the day you were born."

JT took it from her and looked it over. "It's sea glass. See how frosted it is?"

"Papa found it while walking and waiting for you to be born," Gloriana said, pleased that he seemed so in awe of the gift.

He cradled the box close. "I'll always love it."

Pleasure coursed through her heart. She had longed to give him something of their family to hold on to—something tangible. "I'm glad you feel that way, little brother." She kissed his curls. "Now, if you don't mind, I'm starving and intend to eat—even if I need to do so by myself."

"I'm hungry too," JT said, putting the necklace back in the box. "And I want to play with the things Luke got me." He looked at Luke. "Thank you for my soldiers and for the puppy. I wish we could have him today."

Luke smiled. "There's one more gift to give. JT, I believe you have a present for your sister."

JT's mouth dropped open and he nodded with great enthusiasm. "I do!" Luke handed the boy a small box. "This is for you, Glory," JT said with pride. "I earned some money helping Luke and got you this."

"I surely don't need even one more thing. Luke has already been more than generous with the boots, coat, hat, gloves, and gowns.

Goodness, I don't know when I've ever had so many clothes."

"Well, you need clothes," JT declared. "This is just for fun."

She opened the little box and gasped. "It's . . . it's lovely." She pulled out the gold locket cameo and opened it.

"Luke said one day we'll get you some special photograph to put inside," JT assured her.

She hugged JT close. "Thank you, I'll cherish it forever." She looked at Luke. "Thank you for everything. You've blessed us in so many ways. We might not have even had food on the table but for your generosity. Thank God you came along when you did."

He smiled. "Thanking God, are you? That's a good thing to hear."

She stiffened, then let her guard down again. "Be patient with me."

"For as long as I have breath."

Chapter 14

Martin Carson sipped strong coffee and re-considered his son's letter. Luke's message, though sparse with details, made clear the circumstances of his situation.

> *The baby, a little girl who is named for her mother, is healthy and happy. Upon her deathbed, Sally asked that her dear friend, Gloriana Womack, and I take charge of the child and raise her in a manner that would have pleased Scott. We have done this, and I'm pleased to say that Sally Marie Carson is a strong and vital child.*

He set the letter aside and considered the situation, as he had done nearly every minute since receiving the letter two days earlier. It was January, and the baby was nearing four months in age. Martin had started planning what all that would require. Certainly a nurse who had training to care for infants. An entire nursery wing that could house the nurse and babe as well. There was the old nursery upstairs, but it would need to be completely redone.

His plan was to bring the baby to Philadelphia as soon as possible and raise her in ease and luxury. She was his last connection to Scott, and although his son had been rebellious and had married against his will, Martin Carson was not going to allow it all to be for naught. Having a baby in the house would be rather interesting, and with the right people installed, Martin wouldn't even need to know she was there unless he truly wanted to.

Thankfully, most of the house staff had been completely replaced in the last six months, and no one need know much about the child's parentage. Of course, his intimate friends would know she was Scott's daughter, but they needn't dwell on a scullery maid being her mother. Besides, she wasn't the first child of such a relationship, nor would she be the last.

There was the complication of winter in Minnesota. As he understood after checking into it, the harbor was now closed until March or early April. The rail lines had not been completed, and the work there was also ended until spring. Getting in or out of Duluth was not impossible, but it was extremely difficult, and no one with any sense would drag a small infant out across a wintery wilderness.

That meant waiting until at least April to bring the baby to Philadelphia. He supposed it was just as well. He would have someone come in and begin to refashion the nursery. It would give him time to check into qualified nurses.

"More coffee, sir?" the footman asked.

"Yes." Martin waited until the cup was poured, then motioned to the table. "You may clear the rest. I'll take my coffee to the library."

"Very good, sir."

Martin set his napkin aside and rose. He looked at the exquisite furnishings of the dining room. He had everything money could buy, and yet it rang hollow. He was alone. His only remaining son was off in the wilderness, doing the bidding of his boss, and the rest of his family was dead. Baby Sally would be his consolation.

He grimaced. They would have to change her name. Sally was far too common.

He strolled to the library, coffee in hand, and considered his entire lifetime of work.

What had it been for? He was fifty-eight. He had a good reputation in banking and investments. People sought out his advice and wisdom, yet he had never felt so alone and unneeded in his life.

He had pushed Scott aside for his disobedience, and with that action, Martin knew he'd lost some of Luke's respect as well. A part of him had been proud of his sons and their independent streaks, but another part had resented and regretted that they no longer needed him. He had been certain that cutting Scott off from wealth would bring him back around to obedience, but like his mother, Scott wasn't impressed with the things money could buy. He had always had the heart of a poet.

The grand library with two floors of books welcomed him with a roaring fire and draperies pulled back to let in the winter sun. Martin loved this room more than any other in the house and often sought solace here. He had taught Luke about finance in this room. Had tried to teach Scott as well. Scott had always been cut of a different cloth, however. Where Luke thrived on book learning and loved numbers, Scott wanted to use his hands—digging in the dirt, building something with the gardener. He loved the vast outdoors and made more than one trip to wilderness areas to learn about living off the land. Martin had never understood him but supposed it was some influence from his mother's side of the family.

Poor Marie. How he missed her. She had been such a good stepmother to Luke and the perfect mother for Scott. She had been a great wife, with her wisdom and grace and gentle wit. He had truly enjoyed his years with her. How hard it was to be alone again.

He'd considered remarrying. There were any number of widows in the city who vied for his attention, and yet Martin hadn't met any particular one who struck his fancy. He sat down in front of the fire and sighed. A baby in the house would give him something to focus his energy on. He would see that she had everything. The best of furnishings and clothes, the finest tutors and trips. Oh, the trips they could take abroad.

Martin set his coffee on the table beside him and smiled. He would pen a letter immediately to Luke and let him know his decision regarding the baby. He rubbed his hands together. Finally, there was something worthwhile to consider.

Luke went over the house design with the man he'd hired. "I like this very much. I think it's exactly what is needed."

"It will fit the property well," the builder agreed. "There's another parcel of land that can also be purchased behind yours, if you'd like to consider that as well. I wasn't sure how much land you wanted, but the price is reasonable."

"Behind the property, you say?"

The builder nodded. "From that position on the hillside, you'll have a glorious view of the lake. You could build a gazebo for picnics and a stable or servant's house as well. If you purchase that land, all told you'd have five acres."

"I like that idea very much. Get me all the particulars, and let's see if we can't get it for a reasonable price. Otherwise, let's move ahead with these plans. I'd like to see the house built by summer."

He looked once more at the drawing. There would be a grand porch to offer hours of respite shielded from sun and rain. There would be three floors with plenty of bedrooms. Luke thought of Gloriana and JT living there with him and Sally. Of course, they couldn't live under the same roof, but Luke knew his growing feelings for Gloriana meant he was losing his heart.

He often considered telling her how he felt, but he was afraid it might make things awkward between them. He also felt it was too soon after losing her father. He didn't want her to feel that she had to marry to save herself and her brother. Paying her for helping him with Sally, as well as keeping his laundry and preparing his meals, at least gave Gloriana a freedom that many women didn't have. Here in the frontier, when women lost their husbands, their preservation demanded they remarry. It was doubly required when there were small children to consider. But Gloriana would have time to make up her mind about the future, and Luke hoped she would want him in it. There was Sally too. Gloriana was the only mother the baby had known, and it would be difficult for either one to be separated from the other. Still, Luke didn't want to acquire a wife simply as a mother for his niece.

He had to force himself to slow down. He dismissed the builder and stood at the window of his office, watching the man navigate down the icy roadway.

It seemed as though Luke's future had already been decided. He didn't want to be presumptuous, but Gloriana suited him in a way he couldn't explain. She was simple in her desires, content with her sewing and reading or playing with the baby. She had infinite patience for her little brother, who seemed to test her at every turn. JT was a strong-willed young man who needed a man in his life to help shape his course. Luke found the idea of being that caring older brother to JT a welcome one. It filled a void left by Scott. He loved JT—loved his big sister. How had that happened in such a short time?

He supposed tragedy had bonded them more quickly than a mere acquaintance might have, but frankly it seemed as though they had always known each other.

Luke took his seat at the desk again and wondered what Gloriana would think about the house he was building—the future he dreamed of in which they'd be a family. He thought of the long hours he'd spent in prayer regarding his future. No matter what he considered—returning to Philadelphia or staying in Duluth, continuing to work for Cooke or setting up business for himself— Gloriana was always in the middle of his thoughts.

"There is a packet for you from Mr. Cooke," Theodore declared, coming into Luke's office. He paused at the door. "The post office says it's been en route since before Christmas, and here it is nearly February. Such is the way of life in Duluth. News doesn't get here easily or without great difficulty at times."

Luke chuckled. "I am well aware. I tried

to send a telegram only to be told the temporary lines were down and unusable. We need that railroad to St. Paul, to be sure. Life will be so much easier here when that is secured."

"Indeed." Theodore handed him the packet. "If you won't need me for a while, I have those boxes of Northern Pacific correspondence to work through. I believe I can have it in order for you by early afternoon."

"Go right ahead. I have enough to keep me occupied here, it would seem." He had no idea what Jay Cooke had sent him, but it would require Luke's immediate attention, no doubt. Especially since it had been floating around for some time.

Theodore left the room as Luke opened the packet. Inside he found a letter from Mr. Cooke describing the new manager for the Northern Pacific there in Minnesota. A man named Ira Spaulding had been chosen. He had been involved as an engineer in the war, making fortifications, building bridges and railroads, and basically doing whatever was necessary to give the army a clear way to victory. He was exactly what they needed to move the line ahead.

Mr. Cooke sounded pleased with the choice, but less pleased with Congress's demands that building on the Northern Pacific take place from both ends of the system at the same time. The Territory of Washington, with its mountains and such, would be easier to manage than Minnesota with its tens of thousands of lakes and swampland. According to the reports, there was even quicksand to contend with, as well as what was being called "Minnesota black muck." It made conditions such that you could neither swim nor boat it, nor walk atop it. It was simply impassable, and someone desperately needed to figure out what could be done.

The stagnant water also made for mosquito breeding habitats. Workers had learned from the native Indians that the only thing to use to combat the onslaught was bear grease, but the smell was so putrid that many refused it until desperation set in and they could no longer take the constant attack of biting flies and mosquitoes. Luke could understand the dilemma, although he'd come when colder weather had already set in. He had no idea what summer would bring.

Luke continued reading through the packet, learning of Mr. Cooke's frustrations with Congress and their lack of interest in the northern line. The transcontinental railroad had just been completed, and that was surely enough to connect the nation for business and pleasure. They were shortsighted, Mr. Cooke told Luke. And because of their frustrating attitude, Mr. Cooke believed his best bet was to be very public with his railroad venture. With that in mind, he was going to send a large party of newspaper reporters, dignitaries, and other railroad enthusiasts to participate in a groundbreaking ceremony for the Minnesota side of the Northern Pacific. It would take place in February, and Mr. Cooke promised more news to come. He instructed Luke to do what he could to ensure rooms at Clark House Hotel, even though it was still being built. In fact, he pressed the importance of seeing that hotel complete, even if Luke had to personally hire more men for the job.

It would seem the entire world had erupted at once, and Jay Cooke was in charge of putting it back together. Luke would be very busy for the next few weeks.

~

"He's perfect," JT said, hugging the puppy close. The sable-and-brown dog licked JT's face over and over, making the boy giggle. "I think he likes me."

"It certainly looks that way," Luke said, laughing.

Gloriana shook her head. "I hope you get him quickly trained to do his business outside," she said, cleaning up the puppy's latest mistake.

"It won't take all that long, and once he's trained and a bit bigger," Luke declared, "you'll be glad to have him standing guard over you."

"Do you think he'll be a good guard dog?" JT asked.

"The best." Luke rubbed the dog's nose. "See this blaze of white on his nose and forehead?"

JT nodded.

"I had a dog with those very same marks when I was a boy, and he turned out to be the fiercest of guard dogs."

Gloriana gave him a skeptical look. "I have my doubts that that big-nosed ball of fur could ever be fierce. He might love something to death, but I doubt he'll ever be mean."

JT giggled as the dog continued to wiggle and lick his face. "I figured out a name for him." He maneuvered the dog and held him up. "I think we should call him Calico Jack. Papa told me he was a pirate in the Caribbean Sea."

"Calico Jack?" Gloriana tried the name on for size. "Seems kind of long. I suppose we could just call him Jack for short."

The puppy yipped, and JT nodded. "He likes that."

"Then Jack it is." Luke scratched the pup behind the ears. "Now, it might be wise to take him to his doghouse. We don't want him making another mess."

"No, indeed, because you get to clean up all the rest of his messes." Gloriana smiled at JT and Jack. It was good to see her brother so happy.

Chapter 15

With the harbor closed down for the winter, Gloriana missed her father more than ever. Winter layup had always been a time for making repairs and working on the boat, but it also meant Papa was home every evening. When she was a little girl, Papa and his friends would sometimes sit around the house, plotting and planning while Mama supplied hot coffee and baked goods. Often a bottle of something would make the rounds and get added to the coffee, but the men were never drunk nor out of control. Not in the Womack house.

Gloriana had never known a single one of her father's friends or crew to be anything but gracious and polite to her mother and herself. They might tease her on occasion—tease them both about their looks or kindness. One of her father's dearest friends, Sam Jorgenson, used to ask Gloriana to put her little finger in his coffee to make it sweeter. She used to do it too and laugh with delight. Of course, she'd only been a child then, and the world seemed as if it would go on in perfect order forever.

But then Sam had been lost at sea when his ship had been caught in a storm. It was the first time she'd seen her father cry. Over the years, others were lost, and now Papa was among their numbers. The loss bonded the tiny town of Duluth, as it did most fishing or shipping towns. They needed the lake and couldn't walk away from it, even if it cost them their lives.

A thought that had been nagging at her for weeks rose yet again. Maybe most of the people here had no choice in staying, but Gloriana and JT weren't bound by the lake anymore. They could pack up and go anytime. It would mean leaving her mother's and siblings' graves, the house Papa had built them, and all their friends. But it also meant leaving that cursed lake.

The wind began to howl outside as if agreeing with her line of thinking. Storms were a part of life here on the lake. She ought to be used to them. But every new gale brought trepidation. This time of year, at least, the men were off the water, but it was still daunting. Threatening. A reminder to all of them that they had little control over their destiny.

She went to the window and pulled back the heavy curtain. The lake was gray, frozen, and icy. The gunmetal-gray skies were heavy with clouds, and it had begun to snow. No doubt there was a blizzard coming on. She hoped it might wait until JT got home from school. She hated to think of him walking home in such a storm, and yet she remembered her father instructing her not to smother the boy with her worries.

"He's a boy, Gloriana, and as such he will one day be a man. You cannot overprotect him from life. I won't allow for it. Let him explore, let him dare great things. He will get hurt, but he will learn from his mistakes. He's a good boy and he'll practice a certain amount of caution, but not if he feels he needs to prove to you that he's able to go beyond what you believe."

Gloriana always tried to keep that in mind in dealing with JT. That was why she didn't scold when he came in late from school. Still, a boy needed guidance as well as trust. She needed him to understand the dangers, since his mother and father weren't there to do it. He needed to know about blizzards and how easily a person could lose their way. He needed to know when the temperature dropped below freezing how quickly a person could be in danger from the cold.

She let the drapery drop back into place. How could she ever manage to be both mother and father to the boy? She had no understanding or experience of how to make a man out of a child.

The door opened, and the icy wind blew it back so hard that the entire house seemed to shake as it slammed against the wall. JT struggled to take hold of it, balancing Jack in one arm and his books in the other. It took both Gloriana and JT to get the door closed again.

"You're home early," she said, trying not to sound overly concerned.

"Teacher let us go. Said this storm was going to be a bad one. We might not even have school on Monday. Wouldn't that be great?" His expression was filled with pleasure. "I brought Jack inside because it might get too bad to get out to his doghouse later." He managed to put his books on the table despite the wiggly puppy almost squirming out of his arms.

"Well, put some newspapers down for him by the door." Gloriana pointed to the stack she'd started saving. "He seems to understand what they're for, at least."

"He's really smart." JT continued to hold

the puppy while getting a handful of news-papers. He finally set Jack down in order to spread the protection over the floor. He grabbed Jack and put him on the papers. "Remember, you can use these, not the floor."

The puppy yipped and yipped, then shot across the room toward the fireplace.

Melting snowflakes left water droplets on JT's curls, and Gloriana worried about him catching cold. "Why don't you give me your coat and hat? I'll hang them up for you, and you can get warm by the fire with Jack. Would you like some hot milk?"

"No, I want to try coffee. Charley drinks coffee. He said his parents always let him have it in the morning. Can I try it?"

Gloriana thought for a moment. Here was one of those times when she was uncertain what her mother might have done. Frankly, she didn't think JT would like coffee, and maybe that was her answer. Let him try it and decide for himself.

"All right," she said, nodding. "I think there's some left. I'll warm it up and put some sugar in it for you."

JT smiled. "Thanks, Gloriana. You're the best sister ever."

She had baked that morning, so she cut him a piece of cinnamon cake to go with his coffee. When everything was ready, she brought it to him in front of the fire. He was sitting on the floor and used his little stool as a makeshift table while battling to keep Jack from his refreshments.

He sampled the coffee and looked up at Gloriana with a revulsion so severe, she almost laughed out loud.

"This is terrible. This is coffee?" he asked.

She frowned. "Let me taste." She sampled the warm brew. "Yes, this is coffee. A lot of people don't even use sugar."

His nose wrinkled. "It's really bad. Could I have warm milk instead?"

She smiled and kept the mug. "Of course."

And so that battle was dealt with without so much as a single harsh word. JT had tried his first cup of coffee and didn't like it. Would that other situations could be as easily resolved.

"Jacob said his dad is building a house for Luke. Did you know about that?"

Gloriana stopped mid-step and slowly turned back to JT. "A house? No, I didn't know."

"I guess that means maybe he's going to stay a long time. Wouldn't that be great? But I don't know why he has to move away. You didn't tell him he had to go, did you?" Jack rose up on his hind legs and tried to reach JT's cake. JT pushed him down. "No, Jack."

"Of course I didn't." Gloriana looked at her brother and shook her head. "He's welcome to stay in the cottage as long as he likes." She went to prepare his milk. Had she somehow made Luke feel that he needed to go?

"Well, Jacob said it's going to be a big house up by where they're building Robert Munger's mansion."

She stirred the milk in a pan and nodded. Of course. Luke was used to luxury and beauty. A small fishing cottage wasn't going to please him for long.

"It's going to be just as big as Mr. Munger's house too. Jacob said it was huge."

The Munger house was a mansion and was talked about constantly as the pride of the area. Once completed, it was rumored it would have fifteen rooms. Of course, the Mungers could afford such a place. Mr. Munger owned a flour mill, sawmill, and coal dock, just to name a few. He was also the head man pushing for the building of a canal. He had big plans for Duluth.

It seemed only right that a wealthy man like Luke might follow suit. Gloriana had no idea what his future plans were beyond seeing the railroad completed this summer, but maybe he wanted to stay. She knew he was also involved in the Northern Pacific's creation, so perhaps he had agreed to work for

Mr. Cooke in a more permanent capacity that would see him become a long-time resident of Duluth. She could only hope so.

After testing the milk, Gloriana poured it into a mug and then put a tiny bit on a saucer for Jack and brought both to JT. "Here you go. I'm sure this will be more to your liking."

JT put the saucer down for Jack and laughed as the puppy plunged his nose into the milk.

The wind whined against the house. There was a definite leakage of air, but Gloriana wasn't sure where it was coming from nor how to fix it.

"I wonder, brother of mine, would you have time to help me with something?"

"I was going to play with Jack and the soldiers Luke gave me." He put the mug aside and devoted his attention to the cake.

"Well, this was something Papa would have taken care of, but I suppose I can ask Luke when he visits later."

"No, I'll help," JT said, finishing off the cake. "I'm the man of the house now."

She knelt beside him and shook her head. "No, you are the eight-year-old of the house. You don't have to be a man just yet, but I am very grateful for your help and company. I don't ever want you to think you have to take on Papa's duties just yet. You need time to be a boy and have fun, as well as work. I'm only asking that you help here and there."

JT's expression was solemn. "I want to help. Luke said it was important that family take care of each other. I already knew that, 'cause Papa said it too."

Gloriana smiled. "Well, we need to go around the house and find all the places where the wind is getting in. Baby Sally won't be safe if she gets too cold, so we need to figure out how to plug up the leaks."

The wind blew harder still, and JT moved a little closer to the fire. "I can help you do that, Glory. It won't be hard, especially today."

She got back to her feet. "We can start in here and go room to room, if you like. But first, since I feel certain the wind is going to be howling for hours, why don't you go play with your soldiers?"

He popped up, grinning. "I have a battle going on."

"I'll just bet you do." She gathered up his dishes as JT started for his room. Jack followed him. "Try not to be too noisy. Sally's napping. Oh, and don't forget to bring Jack to the papers from time to time."

She took the dishes to the kitchen and set them in the sink. She would wash them along with the supper things later. Thinking of supper, she opened the oven door to check the stew she'd created. Mrs. Sedgwick had given her a crate of canned vegetables she'd put up earlier in the summer. Gloriana had used some of those along with a chunk of roasted beef to make the meal. This would feed them tonight, along with fresh bread and butter, and the aroma was starting to make her mouth water. They had always eaten a lot of fish, and beef was a rare treat. JT would be happy for the change. Papa had always been too.

Gloriana paused and let a memory come to mind. Mama and Papa had once talked about buying a dairy cow, and that had started them thinking about other animals. What if they were to buy a couple of beef calves and raise them to slaughter? The children would be the ones to tend the animals, and Gloriana remembered thinking it a fun idea. The problem came in actually killing and eating the animals she knew would become pets.

She hugged her arms close and smiled as tears came to her eyes. She missed her family so much. Memories were all she had, and those were bittersweet and often too much to bear.

Why, God? Why did You take them all? Did I somehow fail to pray for them correctly? Did I somehow fail You, so You felt I needed punishment?

She had been so hesitant to pray—even to question the Almighty about her situation. After so much loss and pain, she was almost afraid to bring herself to God's attention, and yet she wanted so much to know the answers.

"I'm so alone." She tightened her grip on her arms, trying her best to feel something other than emptiness.

Storms only reminded her of Papa's death—of the fragility of life. She went to the window again and looked out at the lake. Part of the window was iced with frost. Apparently her first leak to plug would be around that window.

The snow made it impossible to see anything. Gloriana thought of her life here in Duluth. She'd never traveled anywhere else or seen any other town, but right now she wished she could be far away.

Tears continued to stream down her cheeks. Why did it have to hurt so much? Why couldn't she just cast aside her pain and be unmoved? There would always be time for tears in the solitude of her bed. Nighttime was the perfect cover for such things. But standing here now, with JT only just down the hall, Gloriana risked showing him her sadness. She had worked so hard not to break down in front of him.

There was a rattle and then a knock at the

door. Gloriana raised her apron to dry her eyes. She knew if anyone looked closely, however, they'd be able to see she'd been crying.

She opened the door to find Luke standing there, covered in snow. "Get inside, quick." She stepped back to give him room.

Luke laughed and came into the house, pulling off his coat at the same time. "Here, let me shake it outside." He turned and gave the coat a snap, then handed it to Gloriana. He grabbed his hat and gave a few swipes with his gloved hand, then slammed the door closed against the wind. "I was worried about JT. I heard they closed school early, and I wanted to make sure he got home."

"He did." Gloriana turned away to hang up the coat. "He and Jack are in his room, playing out some battle, if you'd like to go see him." She drew a deep breath. "I'll put some fresh coffee on in the meantime. There's also some cake if you're hungry. Supper will be a few hours still."

"That sounds inviting, but I can't stay long. I still have a lot of work. Since I was headed over to the Clark House, I thought it would be easy enough to stop here first."

Gloriana pretended to be busy at the stove. She checked the stew again. "What about coffee? Would you like me to make some?"

"No. I'll wait and have it with supper."

He said nothing more, and Gloriana fought to keep her emotions under control. She didn't want to break down in front of him.

"Gloriana, what's wrong?"

She heard the softness of his tone. She hadn't been able to hide her sorrow from him. For a moment she wondered what she could say. He had to know she was still grieving.

"It's just . . ." She paused to choose her words carefully. "It's just a hard day. The storm and all." There. She'd managed to say it without sobbing.

"I'm so sorry. I hadn't even thought about the storm stirring up your sorrow. Forgive me."

She nodded but refused to look at him. "Nothing to forgive. I'll be just fine. JT and I have a plan for scouting out all the drafts in the house. We're going to use newspaper and braided rags to seal off the windows. We can't have Sally getting chilled.

"Oh, speaking of houses, JT tells me you're building one. Does this mean Mr. Cooke wants you to stay on in the area after the train line is complete in the summer?"

"Gloriana, stop." Luke had moved across the room to stand directly behind her. He reached out and turned her to face him. "You don't have to hide your feelings from me."

She glanced up and saw the kindness in his expression. It was her undoing, and tears flooded her eyes. "I'm sorry. I just don't want to upset JT."

Luke pulled her into his arms, and Gloriana allowed herself to stay there for a moment. How wonderful to be held by someone who cared. Just to feel the warmth of another human being—to know she wasn't alone. He held her close while she cried, never attempting to hush her or tell her to be strong. He seemed to understand that she had no strength to give. What a tenderhearted man.

"I should have realized you would be thinking of your father since you lost him during a storm."

"It's not just him," she murmured. "It's everyone. They're all gone, and I am so alone."

"You aren't alone. Not as long as I'm here."

She was grateful he hadn't said anything about JT or Sally. She knew they were still there and dependent upon her, but she was void of people she could count on for counsel and strength. She couldn't even turn to God, and that was the biggest void of all.

As if hearing her thoughts, Luke spoke. "Gloriana, sooner or later you're going to have to reconcile with God. That's what's hurting you the most right now. You may not realize it, but it's the truth. For a young woman who has spent her life honoring God and trusting in Him for her needs, to walk away from Him now at such a difficult time makes everything worse."

She pulled back. "I didn't walk away. He did."

"Did He? Or did He just not keep your life in the order you had become accustomed to?"

"What good is it to be a Christian and serve Him if we cannot trust Him to protect us from evil and bad things?"

"When did He fail you in that area?" Luke asked, his voice barely a whisper.

"By taking my family. My father." Was it really so hard for him to understand?

"There are things that will happen to us over the course of our lifetime. Things that cause us great sorrow and pain, but that hardly equates to God's lack of protection and love. Gloriana, God didn't walk away. You did. You turned your back on Him because He didn't do things your way. It's hard to lose your father, but he was right with God when the end came. I know it's hard without him, and I would give just about anything to give him back to you, but instead I'll give you what I can. Myself."

She looked deep into his eyes and could see the depth of his sincerity. How she wanted to trust in that pledge, but Luke was here today and gone tomorrow. At least that was the way Gloriana saw it.

Before she realized what was happening, she found Luke's mouth upon hers. The kiss was tender and promising. She momentarily lost herself in that single, simple action. It was her first kiss—probably her last. She wrapped her arms around his neck and returned the gesture.

But then reasonable thought returned, and she jumped back, pushing him away at the same time.

"No! I can't. I can't let myself care about you only to lose you when summer ends. Do you realize how hard it is to care for someone you know you will soon be parted from? I take care of Sally every day and grow closer and closer to her, only to know that when your job here is done, you'll take her away from me. I spend time with you and care for you as well, but soon you'll be gone. I can't bear it, Luke. I just can't lose anyone else."

Luke touched her cheek. "I have no intention of leaving you, Gloriana, nor of taking Sally away from you. You are the baby's mother as sure as anything. I wouldn't hurt you that way."

"But by your own admission, you don't know what the future holds. Your father may desire to take Sally, and your own ambitions may take you from here. I just can't do this. Don't ask me to . . . care for you."

She had nearly said the word *love*. She would have begged him not to let her fall in love with him, but she knew it was too late for that. She was already in love with Lucas Carson, and nothing would change that.

As her mother used to say to Papa, *"My heart is destined for you, and nothing will ever change that."* Now Gloriana knew exactly what that meant.

"I'm sorry, Gloriana. I shouldn't have done that." Luke stepped back with a worried look on his face. "Please forgive me. I took what was not mine to take."

She wasn't at all sorry for the kiss, nor for his compassion, but the pain building inside of her was almost too much to bear. "Don't apologize." She shook her head. "Please don't apologize."

She heard Sally's whimpered cry and hurried from the room. The thought of Luke being sorry for having kissed her only made matters worse.

Chapter 16

By Monday they had a foot of snow, and it made moving around town quite perilous. Still, Luke had work that required his attention, and he couldn't forsake it merely because of snow. He trudged up the hill to his office, hardly seeing anyone on the streets. Folks had apparently found ways to do what was needed without having to come outside. They were a smart bunch up here. Gloriana had told him that everyone worked hard all year to ensure survival. Thankfully, wood was plentiful, so keeping warm was no problem. The churches were mindful of the widows and poorer families who had no one to keep on top of their needs. Just last week, the pastor had asked for a team of men to take firewood to a woman with five small children. Her husband was one of the men who had died with Gloriana's father and Luke's brother.

Thinking of Gloriana only brought back memories of their kiss. Luke had kissed other young ladies, but never had it affected him like this kiss. He found himself thinking about Gloriana constantly—about how well they fit together—about how right that kiss had felt. But maybe most startling of all, Luke never wanted to kiss anyone else. The thought of it had no appeal. He was in love with Gloriana and intended to make that kiss the first of many.

She had pushed him away, however. That was something he couldn't ignore. But her feelings for him were clear. She cared for him—the kiss wasn't abhorrent to her, just frightening. It was only fear that caused her to walk away. She was terrified of the future.

Luke opened the door to his office to find the room warm and well lit. Theodore Sedgwick glanced up from his desk, then got up to help Luke with his coat and hat.

"I was told it's minus ten degrees Fahrenheit today," Theodore declared. "Hard on man and beast alike."

"How cold can it get here?" Luke unwound the knitted scarf he wore.

"I believe the record is around minus forty," Theodore answered as he went to hang up Luke's coat on the coat tree.

"Grief, but that's cold. We were never that cold in Philadelphia."

"No, the weather was milder," Theodore replied.

Luke stopped and looked at him. He had a vague recollection that Gloriana had said something about Theodore living in Pennsylvania. "When did you live in Philadelphia?"

"Many years ago. Before the war. I wasn't there long. I was there again just before coming here. It's a lovely town. I very much enjoy the history of our Founding Fathers and how Philadelphia was once the center of our government. It still holds great interest in our country's finances."

Luke nodded and handed his hat and gloves to Theodore as well. "It's a nice town, but while my father desires it for his home, I'm mixed. I have seen a lot of the world and have to admit there are other places that intrigue me more. Duluth being one of them."

"I heard you're building a new house. Does that mean you intend to stay on?"

"Mr. Cooke has asked me to, and I see no reason not to," Luke admitted. "I have quite a few interests here, and investing in this town appeals to me. What do you think? Is it a good place to invest in?"

Theodore seemed taken aback by his question. "I . . . well, I think it is. Obviously, there is reason to believe it might very well be the next Chicago." He smiled. "I would invest heavily had I the means to do so."

Luke chuckled. "That was my thinking too. The lake alone makes it valuable."

Theodore took his seat. "Undoubtedly."

Luke made his way to his office and thought of the various opportunities he'd already heard about. This morning he was set to have a meeting with Roger Munger regarding the canal he wanted to see built. Luke was more than a little interested in hearing all of the details. He had a feeling, given the kind of money being invested in the city by Jay Cooke, it would behoove him to have a working knowledge of other projects that might also benefit his boss. However, he was also looking for personal investments, and the canal sounded like a good one.

"Mr. Rowland is here to see you," Theodore said from the open door to his office.

"Send him in." Luke got to his feet and extended his hand as Archie Rowland entered the room. "Good to see you, Archie. Close the door and have a seat."

The older man did exactly that.

"What can I do for you?"

Archie frowned. "Well, there are some issues with the route that we need to go over. Problems have developed, and even though we've completed work up here for the winter, this must be dealt with before we start up again in the spring."

Luke nodded. "Sounds serious."

"It is. It might very well be that someone within our own people means to see us fail."

Theodore listened at the door, hoping to learn the reason for Archie Rowland's surprise visit. With the line work closed down for the winter, Rowland was supposed to be in St. Paul, working with the others on the final route to connect the Lake Superior and Mississippi Railroad to Duluth.

It was difficult to hear what was being said, however. He heard Rowland say something about failure, but the men were speaking in such hushed whispers that it made hearing impossible. Theodore had to find a way into that office.

He took up his box of notepaper and a pencil. Perhaps Luke would want a record of the matter. He knocked lightly and opened the door. Luke glanced his way.

"I thought perhaps you might like me to record the details of the meeting?" He held up the paper.

"That might be for the best," Luke told Rowland. "If things are as bad as you suggest, we need to make sure we explore every possible angle, and having notes would make that easier."

Rowland nodded. "I agree."

Theodore smiled and took a seat on a wooden chair. "Please feel free to continue." He pulled paper from the box, then closed the lid and wrote the date across the top of the page.

"Well, as I was saying," Rowland said, "some changes to the route created problems for us. We're not sure how the numbers were altered or if it was simply oversight on the part of the engineers and builders. We haven't yet had an opportunity to see the work orders and the final route layout. Once we're able to get a look at that, we'll know if it was an accident or deliberate."

"I suppose we can't ignore the possibility of it being deliberate," Luke replied. "Superior, Wisconsin, has made it more than clear that they believe the railroad should belong to them. If they've managed to get men hired into positions where changes to the route can be made, then we're in some real trouble. What with all the problems we already have trying to lay a route that won't be encumbered by the black muck and quicksand, or swallowed whole by the lakes themselves, this is a grievous situation."

"If someone is working against us, it's best to know it right away," Rowland said. "I've seen tampering of this sort before, and it always ends up costing a pretty penny."

Luke nodded and steepled his fingers as he leaned back in his leather chair. "I'll give this some thought. Meanwhile, we need to find those work orders and original maps. We'll compare the numbers and see if anything has been altered. And if they have . . . then we'll have to figure out who is responsible. Can you leave right away for St. Paul, Archie?"

"I can."

Theodore tried not to react in any way to what Luke said, but he delighted in the trouble he'd already caused. He would see Carson's doom if it was the last thing he did.

After his appointment with Archie, Luke met with Roger Munger. The meeting only furthered Luke's excitement about the town. Munger wanted a canal dug to give ships direct access to the harbors on the Duluth side of the bay. Superior, of course, fought this idea, because keeping the only entry into the bay on their side would guarantee they had the lion's share of business.

Munger felt confident that the canal could

be dug for a minimal cost without damage to the breakwaters. He was convinced there was more than enough shipping for both Duluth and Superior, and with the railroads coming in, Duluth must have this direct approach.

Luke agreed and pledged his intention to invest. He promised also to speak with Jay Cooke on the matter as soon as possible. Munger was pleased and left without any time for socializing. He did, however, invite Luke to come to dinner the following Thursday.

"Be sure to put that on my appointment calendar," Luke told Theodore as he dressed to go back out into the cold.

"I've already taken care of it," Theodore replied. He got up and helped Luke with his coat and hat. "Will you be returning today?"

"I don't think so. I have an appointment with Judge Prescott, and then I believe I'll catch up on correspondence at home." Luke wrapped the scarf around his neck and pulled on his gloves. "Do what you can to find those original work orders. I know we sent the maps to St. Paul, so I may need to send you down there as well. I don't want to if it can be avoided, however. Talk to Archie. If he feels he can handle things from that end, you won't need to go. Otherwise, if he wants your help, then I think we must give it."

"Very good, sir. I will find an opportunity to speak to him."

Luke picked up his satchel and made his way outside and down the street to the judge's office. He had met Judge Prescott at church originally, and while they weren't yet well acquainted, Luke felt he was just the man to help him with Sally's adoption.

"Good day." Luke smiled at the clerk seated in the outer office. "I have an appointment with Judge Prescott. I'm Lucas Carson."

The clerk nodded. "I'll let the judge know you're here. Please have a seat."

Luke did as the man bid and pulled off his gloves. Archie had been right about his needing better gloves than these. Luke had already ordered some with fur lining. An old man down on Third Street was making several pairs for Luke, in fact. Gloriana had promised him new scarves and perhaps even another sweater. The one she'd given him for Christmas was just as JT had promised— warm enough that when he wore it, he never felt the bite of the wind.

"Lucas Carson. It's good to see you again," the judge declared from the open doorway to his office. "Please come in."

"Judge Prescott. Thank you for making time to see me." Luke followed him into the office, closing the door behind him.

"I hope you're doing well. Duluth can be daunting in the winter."

"So everyone says, and I'm starting to learn for myself." Luke glanced around the room and thoroughly approved of the book-lined shelves.

"I see you've spied my library. I have more books than Solomon had wives." The judge laughed and sat down at his desk. "Please have a seat and tell me how it goes with the railroad."

Luke did as he asked, but he wasn't ready yet to speak about the problems Archie had uncovered. "Overall, we're on schedule, no thanks to the difficult landscape. We aren't contending with mountainous terrain or deserts, but what we have is difficult and requires specialized care."

"I can well imagine. There's a lot of water to be mastered."

"Exactly."

"But the railroad didn't bring you here today. Tell me what has."

Luke began his story. "My brother was a crew member on the *Ana Eileen*. He was killed with the others when she went down last September."

"My condolences. We lost a great many good men that day."

"Yes." Luke paused a moment in reverence.

"My sister-in-law was expecting their first child. She had no family save my brother and this unborn child. The night I arrived in town, she was giving birth. Weakness and a broken heart caused her to give up the will to live. On her deathbed, with the midwife as a witness, she asked me and Gloriana Womack to raise her child. Being the baby's uncle, I realized there would be no conflict in this, save the possibility of my father's interference."

"Your father? Tell me about him."

"He's a banker and financier in Philadelphia. He was a harsh taskmaster to my brother and me. When my brother decided to marry, our father did not approve and irrevocably cut him off from the family fortune."

"Rather severe," the judge commented.

"Yes. Very. He ordered Scott and his wife to leave the family house and never be in his presence again. When he learned of the baby, our father showed some interest. He called my brother back with promises of accepting him into the fold should he divorce his wife after the child's birth and take the child from her."

"Cruel, indeed."

"My brother was livid. There was much arguing and many hateful things said, and my brother took his wife and came here to Duluth, where he took a job as a fisherman.

This happened last spring. He kept in touch with me, and I even helped financially until they were able to get on their feet again."

"And now?"

"Now I fear my father will have his regrets and desire to take the baby to raise as his own. I would like to prevent that from happening, not only for my sake and that of the child, but for Gloriana Womack, who has become a mother to the baby. I would like to adopt my niece so that I might offer her stability and love. It is even my hope to marry Gloriana so that we might become a regular family."

The judge smiled. "I know that young woman well. She has always impressed me with her demeanor and loyalty. When her mother died, she pledged herself to care for her father and brother without even a hint of regret or disdain. Mrs. Sedgwick told me she has always been a generous soul."

"I can believe that. Her first priority since losing her father has been to her brother. And let me tell you . . . he's a handful." Luke grinned. "But I want him too. I want us to be a family. Right now isn't the proper time to propose that to Gloriana. She's in deep mourning for her father, and I wouldn't dream of trying to interfere with that process. However, I fear I don't have time to delay where the baby is concerned. My father knows about her, and his intentions, unless I'm mistaken, will be to come here and take her."

"Then we will push through this adoption and get matters settled. I don't want to see Gloriana hurt any more than she has already been. Give my man the information about the midwife in attendance at the birth. We'll take her statement and use that as a foundation for the adoption. I believe we can have all of this resolved very shortly."

Luke got to his feet and extended his hand. "Thank you, Judge Prescott. I appreciate your compassion. Baby Sally will appreciate it too, as well as Gloriana and JT."

"We definitely want to do what is best for all."

Luke bid the judge good day and made his way outside. The wind was making the air feel even colder than it had before. Pulling the scarf tighter around his face and neck, Luke pushed on toward the post office. He would see if anything had come for him, despite the winter service being more sporadic, and then head home. The thought of ending his day with Gloriana and JT and the baby was more than enough to quicken his steps.

He thought of Gloriana and her frustration with God. Would he be any different if he'd suffered so much loss? Of course, he had lost his mother and stepmother and now his brother. They had quite a bit in common, if one looked at it that way. However, where Gloriana had adored her father, Luke felt as if he barely knew his. Martin Carson was all about business and making money. The time he had spent with his sons had also been about business and finance. Luke couldn't remember a time when he and his father had just talked about life, about their desires or ambitions, unless it related back to work.

That was a void Luke had struggled to fill by inviting the friendship of other older men and advisors. He always gravitated toward mentoring relationships. His brother was the only person who was different. Luke was Scott's mentor, and now Scott was gone, and Luke felt that void as well.

Perhaps that was what kept him wanting to be there for JT. The boy reminded him of Scott in many ways. Scott had always been more physical—more interested in things that went on outdoors rather than inside. College had bored Scott nearly to walking away. He'd been too young for the war but hung on Luke's every word about battles and strategies. Their father had been appalled. His boys had been raised to follow in his footsteps, and nothing else would suffice. Scott had always felt he could never measure up to his father's desires.

Luke thought again of Gloriana and her anger at God. God hadn't lived up to her expectations. It seemed there were disappointments enough to go around. Luke only wanted to help her find her way back. Only that close bond with God would see her through this depth of pain.

"Father," Luke whispered, lifting his gaze heavenward, "help her. I care for her so. I don't want bitterness and anger to harden her heart. Help her to see You for the loving Father You are. Amen."

He felt a calm come over him. No matter what, he knew that seeking God first was how peace would be found, and for now, he could rest in that.

Chapter 17

Luke's peace was short-lived. A letter was waiting for him at the post office from his father. Father had paid a high price to see it delivered, and the postmaster spoke of how a man had been hired in St. Paul to see it through personally.

Several days had passed, but the words of the letter still bothered Luke a great deal. His father wanted Luke to bring Sally to Philadelphia, just as Luke had feared. Father had declared himself the logical choice to raise his son's child and demanded that upon the first possible chance to bring her out of that "godforsaken frozen wilderness," Luke would comply.

Now he would have to write to his father and break the news that, thanks to the judge's fast work, he had already adopted Sally and that she would remain in Duluth with him and with Gloriana. His father would be livid—possibly to the point of fighting Luke for possession of the child.

He glanced over to see the baby asleep in Gloriana's arms as Pastor Sedgwick spoke of Moses leading the Hebrew children through the desert. JT squirmed uncomfortably in one of the outfits Luke had bought him for Christmas. The boy hated dressing up, and Luke couldn't say he blamed him.

They were, for all intents and purposes, a family. Luke had fallen into the role of protector-provider without even needing to be asked. Gloriana was a natural nurturer and mother figure. They suited each other, worked well together, and respected each other. Why shouldn't it follow that they remain a family? Luke had given that strong thought—especially with his father's threat to Sally. It wasn't that his father was evil or would necessarily do the child harm, but Luke knew Father wouldn't raise Sally in a way that pleased Scott, and so it brought out the fight in him to keep the child away from such influences.

Scott would never want his daughter judging people by their appearance and social standing. Scott would never want Sally to decide on a husband or friends based on what they could do for the family, but Father would. Luke knew from the pressures Father had put on him to marry women who could advance the family fortunes or had social connections. Love played no role in marriage as far as Father was concerned. That would follow, and if it didn't, then at least there would be enough money to keep everyone happy with something else.

"In conclusion," Pastor Sedgwick said, "we often cannot see the place where God is taking us, but obedience on the journey will save us much sorrow. Trusting God for the outcome—for His faithfulness—is not easy, by any means. Especially when you are stuck in the middle of the desert and nothing seems possible."

He stepped away from the pulpit with the Bible in his hand. "But with God, all things are possible, and we must remember that. Deserts and death are but a momentary obstacle to us, and certainly no obstacle to God. We may wander for a time in the desert, but God will never leave nor forsake us there. He asks us to trust Him, even when He seems aloof, distant, or unreachable. The Hebrew children had to learn this, and we must learn it as well. Let us pray."

Luke bowed his head, wondering if Gloriana had found any comfort at all in the words.

She hadn't wanted to come to church, pointing out that the bitter cold was hard on the baby, but Luke reminded her that the carriage would be warm and protect them all. He had arranged extra blankets and even some warmers with hot coals to keep their feet toasty. It was hard to argue against such things.

When the service concluded, Luke talked to several of the men and finally to the pastor. He thanked Sedgwick for the thoughtful and well-delivered sermon, then once again made his way to Gloriana.

"I'll bring the carriage around," he said.

"Can I help?" JT asked. He was fascinated by the team and wanted to learn to handle the carriage. Such things were oddities to fishermen's sons.

"Of course. If it's all right with Gloriana."

She nodded as she wrapped the sleeping baby for the journey home. "Just be sure to do everything Luke tells you to. Horses are dangerous beasts."

Luke smiled and ruffled JT's hair. "So are little boys, if they aren't properly handled."

JT grinned and looped his arm through Luke's. "I'm not dangerous, just busy. That's what Papa used to say. He told me that he'd never known anyone who was busier than me, but Papa never met Jack."

Gloriana laughed, and Luke thought it was the nicest sound he could hear. "He's right. Papa did say that."

"Then come along, you busy bee. Let me show you the right way to bring the carriage around."

Gloriana watched Luke and JT disappear through the congregation and out the door. She didn't relish being left alone to deal with the women of the church, but she squared her shoulders and continued her preparations for going outside.

"Oh, Gloriana," Mrs. Sedgwick said, coming to her side. "Let me see that precious babe."

Gloriana handed Sally over, grateful for the opportunity. She pulled her fine wool coat on as the pastor's wife fussed over the sleeping child.

"She's grown so much. I can scarcely believe it. She's doubled in size since Christmas."

"She has, and she's such a happy baby. She's a delight. She keeps me from ever being too sad. JT has his puppy, and I have Sally. They have gotten us through our deepest sorrows."

Mrs. Sedgwick met Gloriana's eyes. "I'm so glad you came today, my dear. I've missed our chats. Do you suppose you might come for tea sometime this week?"

Gloriana hadn't wanted to participate in any of the winter social events and had made herself scarce. There had been invitations, but usually she refused. This time, however, she thought she might as well accept.

"Will it just be us?"

"Of course. And bring Sally. Why don't you come Tuesday at two? That will give us plenty of time to visit before you have to worry about JT getting home from school."

Gloriana nodded. "I think I'd like that."

"So, are you excited about Luke adopting Sally legally?"

Gloriana tried not to betray her surprise. Adoption? Luke had said nothing about adopting Sally. She supposed it made sense that some sort of legal arrangement needed to be made, but why hadn't he told her?

She kept her gaze on the infant. "It will give her stability and protection."

"True. I'm sure that's uppermost on his mind." Mrs. Sedgwick handed Sally back to Gloriana. "I think perhaps there is more on his mind than that, however. I've seen the way he looks at you, Gloriana." She grinned. "I think the young man is in love."

Gloriana felt her cheeks grow hot. "I . . . don't think . . . I . . . ."

"My dear, you needn't explain. God has put the two of you together for a reason, and I think you make a handsome couple. I wouldn't worry about the rumors or other nonsensical talk going around. You have conducted yourself quite honorably, as I see it. Just don't let love slip away from you because of your sadness. Love might very well be God's answer for seeing you through these difficult times."

"Love? Should I love someone else only to lose them as well?" Gloriana asked, temporarily losing her anger that people were gossiping about her and Luke.

"Oh, my dear, it is so hard to lose someone we love." Mrs. Sedgwick patted her hand. "But we can hardly stop loving because of it. What is life without love?"

Gloriana wasn't sure, but it seemed it might very well be less complicated and painful. "I'm sorry, I must go. Luke probably has the carriage brought around. I'll come and see you Tuesday." She gave Mrs. Sedgwick a quick peck on the cheek. "Until then."

She hurried down the aisle, making sure the baby was completely wrapped up before heading out the church doors. Several women commented and bid her greetings, but Gloriana barely had time to give them a nod. No doubt it would send their tongues wagging once again.

Oh, who cares what they say? People were always going to say something about something. Gloriana couldn't allow it to bother her.

Luke stood waiting beside the carriage when she reached it. He took the baby and waited while Gloriana settled herself in the carriage, then handed Sally to her. He climbed up and squeezed in beside her, then took up the lines.

"I think it's colder now than it was this morning. Is that even possible?"

"Of course, silly," Gloriana said, putting aside her disgruntled feelings. "It often happens that way. Didn't you see the skies? It's going to snow again."

"Then I'd best get you home and the horses to the livery."

JT squirmed. "Gloriana said we're having meat pies for lunch with gravy poured all over them. She got some pork from Mr. Griggs. He butchered one of his pigs."

"That was very generous of him," Luke declared.

"It was. I promised him an apple pie in return," Gloriana said. "Folks do a lot of trading around here in the winter when supplies are harder to get."

"Luke, what's a doption?" JT asked out of the blue.

"What?" He sounded almost startled by the boy's question.

"A *doption*. I heard the judge say that Sally is getting one. Is it a toy?"

Luke chuckled. "No." He glanced at Gloriana. She wasn't quick enough to hide her frown, but Luke didn't seem to notice, or perhaps he didn't care. "Adoption is a process that makes Sally legally mine. No one can take her away from me, and she will have my name and protection."

"But she's already a Carson. Why does she need adoption?"

Luke turned to Gloriana. "I'm sorry I've had no time to talk to you about this. I had a letter from my father. He intends for Sally to go to Philadelphia to live with him. I couldn't let that happen. I couldn't let him take her from you—hurt you that way."

She hadn't imagined that she had been a factor in his decision. It touched her deeply to think that Luke was worried about her being hurt in the matter.

"Look, we can discuss this over lunch," he said as they reached the house. "I'll get the horse settled and be right back."

She nodded, still uncertain of what to say. She had always known that despite Sally Carson asking her to raise the baby, the child had no relationship to Gloriana. She was Luke's niece, and that made her blood kin. Gloriana was just a friend who happened to be the only mother the child had known.

Luke helped her and the baby from the carriage, while JT leapt out—jumping into a pile of snow as if he could fly. He laughed with glee as he crashed into the mound. "Can we go sledding this afternoon?"

Luke raised a brow. "It sounds like fun. What do you think, Gloriana?"

"I think the baby and I would prefer the warmth of the house, but you boys do as you see fit."

"Very well. After lunch, then, Master JT. We'll go and conquer a few hills. Do you have a sled?"

JT nodded. "A really fast one. Papa helped me make the runners really smooth. I'll show you."

"Excellent. I'll be back shortly, and you can do exactly that."

"After you change your clothes," Gloriana instructed.

Inside, she built up the fire and then unwrapped the baby. Sally kicked and squealed. She was becoming such a force to be reckoned with, and her personality was more apparent every day. Gloriana often tried to decide who she looked more like, Sally or Scott. Always she came to the same conclusion. The baby had Scott's mouth and chin, but Sally's eyes and nose. She was the perfect combination of both.

Gloriana checked on their lunch and then warmed the baby a bottle. She thought about the adoption and what it would mean for the future. She had always known that she had no legal rights to the child, but Luke could have at least discussed his plans. It was hard to learn it from Mrs. Sedgwick. No doubt the rest of the congregation already knew as well. News traveled very fast in Duluth.

JT bounded back into the front room, doing up the buttons on his play shirt. "I put on long underwear and will wear the sweater you made me."

"Wear double socks too. You know how cold your feet get, even with those good boots."

It wasn't long before Luke returned. His cheeks were red from the cold, but he seemed no worse for wear. "You were right. It's starting to snow again."

"I've lived here all of my life. It seems only right that I should understand the weather. Now, as soon as I finish giving Sally her bottle, we can eat our lunch."

The baby didn't appear even the slightest bit tired, so once she was fed, Gloriana spread a blanket on the floor near the table and gave

Sally a cloth doll to play with while the boys took their seats.

"She'll be sitting up and crawling before we know it."

"Babies change fast," Gloriana admitted. "The first year is a whirlwind of mile markers, Mama used to say."

Luke said grace, and then he and JT began to pass the food. Gloriana took a meat pie and drenched it in gravy.

Luke took two of the pies. "They look wonderful. I haven't had meat pies like this since I was a boy."

"Gloriana puts vegetables inside with the gravy," JT explained. "I don't like those as much as the meat, but I eat them anyway. Papa always said vegetables were good for my const . . . consti . . ." He looked at Gloriana.

"Constitution," she relayed.

"Constitution," JT repeated. "I don't know what that is, but Papa thought it was important, so I do too."

Luke chuckled. "A good constitution will see you through many a bad time."

They ate in silence while the baby cooed and babbled. Finally, after his second pie was gone, Luke spoke up.

"Regarding the adoption, I apologize for not talking it over with you. I knew I needed to act fast."

"You hardly need my permission. She is your niece."

"But I feel it is important to discuss everything with you that is related to Sally. She is yours as much as mine. I want you to know that I mean that."

"Maybe you could adopt all of us," JT said, grinning. "Then we'd be one big family."

"I'd like that," Luke said, surprising Gloriana. "I really would."

She didn't know what to say. She looked down at her plate. It wasn't exactly a proposal, but she couldn't help but feel that was his intention. The thought made her tremble. Everything would be wrapped up in perfect order if they married. She knew there were strong feelings between them, but they never talked about it.

She met his gaze, knowing he was expecting her to say something. *Be brave*, she told herself. *Speak up and let him know how you feel. Don't hide from love.*

Gloriana swallowed the lump in her throat. "I'd like it too."

Chapter 18

"I'm so glad you could come to tea, Gloriana. I miss having time with you and your mother." Greta Sedgwick handed Gloriana a cup and saucer while Sally slept soundly on the little settee.

Gloriana lifted the steaming liquid to her mouth and paused to breathe in the rich aroma. "I'm glad I could come. I've missed our times together." She didn't add that it was still hard to leave the house—to talk to old friends and, worst of all, pretend life was normal.

Mrs. Sedgwick took her seat and nodded. "Life without your mother must be quite difficult. Every girl wants to be able to consult their mother, especially on matters of the heart. In her absence, might I be a substitute, albeit a poor one?"

"You aren't a poor substitute, Mrs. Sedgwick." Gloriana offered her a smile before sampling the tea. It was quite good. She lowered the cup. "You were my mother's dearest friend, and as such you are the natural substitute. Mama would be honored to know you were here, sharing such love with me."

If only I can bear it without tears.

Mama had been close with Greta Sedgwick, and the friendship shared by the two women was admired by many. Gloriana had never really considered how much the older woman must miss Mama. Gloriana had been so concerned with her own misery that she hadn't given anyone else consideration.

"I miss her so much. Some days when I'm at the house and the baby is asleep, I think I hear her call my name." Gloriana shook her head. "I close my eyes and imagine she's there, and I answer."

Mrs. Sedgwick nodded. "It's to be expected. You were very close."

"Sometimes I still can't believe how quickly she passed. It seemed that one day she was in good health and the next day, dead. How these things can possibly happen baffles me." Gloriana licked her bottom lip. "I'm sorry that I haven't given your feelings much consideration. I know it must be terribly hard on you to have lost her. I know how much you relied on each other."

"I never got to say good-bye," Greta murmured. "I was going to bring a pie for you and your father that day. I had planned to visit with her and see how I might help, but before the pie was done, my husband returned to say your mother was gone. The children too."

"They did go very fast. The doctor said it wasn't at all the usual way of the disease. He thought perhaps there was an infection in the heart and lungs." Gloriana shook her head, not wishing to dwell on the memory. "And now Papa is gone as well." She sighed. "And the house seems so empty sometimes."

"Perhaps it would be good to move away from the memories. I understand Luke is building a new house."

"Yes, he is. But that's his house—not mine."

Mrs. Sedgwick smiled. "Gloriana, I believe that young man is in love with you. With the way you two have borne each other's sorrows, helped each other care for the baby and JT . . . well, I believe it's just a matter of time until he proposes."

Gloriana felt her cheeks warm. "It's happened without my even noticing it. At least at first. Luke was just like an old friend or family member who showed up to help in a time of need. I feel like I've known him all my life." She marveled at her feelings. "It just happened so naturally—as if it was always meant to be."

"Perhaps it was. You both suffered loss, and that brought you together to share the pain," Mrs. Sedgwick said, her voice tender. "God knew your need."

"Ah, yes. God." Gloriana sampled the tea again. "I've been thinking long and hard about my anger toward Him."

"And what conclusions have you come to?"

"God is all-knowing. He knows how I feel—knew how I would react to losing Papa. I've not surprised Him, although I fear I have greatly distanced myself from Him." She glanced toward the windows to find it was snowing again. "When I sit back in the calm of the day, I am shocked at myself for reacting as I have. I would never have thought myself capable. But nevertheless, I put that distance between us."

"Distance can be overcome, but it takes a willingness to return. Do you have that?"

Gloriana's shoulders slumped. "I feel so alone, and I know it's my own fault. Mama once said she didn't worry about leaving JT in my care. This was hours before she died.

She knew she didn't have long. She told me she knew I would love and care for JT, but most of all, she knew I would share Jesus with him every day because God was so important to me and to who I was that I wouldn't be able to help myself. Now I know that I've failed her."

"It's not too late, Gloriana." Mrs. Sedgwick's consoling voice soothed Gloriana's heart. She wasn't at all condemning, just encouraging. "Your mother was a wise woman. She knew there might come times of frustration and disappointment, but she also knew you would never waver and leave the truth behind. Your heart hurts for the loss, and you want someone to take the blame. Give it to God—His shoulders are big enough. Leave it at the cross. Jesus has already died for your anger and disbelief."

Gloriana began to weep. She put the cup and saucer aside as her hands began to tremble. "Can He forgive me—even now— knowing the way I've been? My heart has been so hardened by all of this."

"I doubt that. If it were truly hardened, you wouldn't care. Your heart is aching, and that's why there are tears. Gloriana, God can and already has forgiven you. He won't force you to come to Him, but He will willingly wait for you to return."

Her hands trembled all the more as Gloriana thought of the last few months. "I've been so unkind—said regretful things. I said . . . I told Him that I couldn't believe He really loved me. But I know He does. I know, too, that love sometimes takes on different looks to different people. Please tell me it's not too late." She buried her face in her hands.

Nothing had prepared her for this moment. She hadn't come to see Mrs. Sedgwick thinking they would talk about God and her hard heart. Why now? Why was all of this crashing down around her now? She'd worked so hard to keep her sorrow contained in a neat little box. Why must it spill out now?

"Oh, my sweet girl," Mrs. Sedgwick said, coming to sit beside her. She put her arms around Gloriana and pulled her into a warm embrace. For several minutes she said nothing and Gloriana simply cried. She cried for her sinful heart. Cried for her mother's and father's passing—for her brother and sister. Cried for the future without them.

And in the middle of all of it, Gloriana felt the most amazing comfort. The love of Mrs. Sedgwick was a huge part of it. She cared deeply—loved completely. There was no pretense in her manner. She was sharing her heart and love with Gloriana, knowing that it was the only thing that could help in true healing. She didn't condemn or leave Gloriana to feel hopeless for the way she'd behaved. She just loved her.

"I don't know how to go on without them," Gloriana finally murmured. "They were everything to me."

"I know, but they would want you to be relieved of the pain. It would break their hearts to think you couldn't live life, fall in love, and have a family of your own because their shadow fell too heavy on your heart." Mrs. Sedgwick straightened and drew Gloriana's face up to meet her eyes. "Your dear mother would want you to return the love of that good man—to marry him and mother this babe—to raise your brother as a godly man. If you cannot do it for yourself, then honor those who've gone before you and do it for them. Do it to perpetuate the love they taught you."

Gloriana nodded. "And God . . . will He forgive me?"

Mrs. Sedgwick nodded. "He will. Just ask Him and see."

Luke glanced over the day's schedule once again. February fifteenth had been set for the Northern Pacific groundbreaking, although it seemed silly to call it that. Very little real construction would take place. The cold was bitter and the ongoing problems too numerous to resolve. Still, Jay Cooke had arranged for three to four hundred of his wealthy friends and dignitaries to be there for the celebration. He had all but paid the newspapers to be there in force and made sure that every man, woman, and child from Superior and Duluth who could attend did so. He even somehow managed to have additional sleighs brought in to take everyone to the site. Luke thought it all ridiculous but made sure there were multiple bonfires to keep the people from freezing to death. One of the local pastors prayed for the new line, and then J. B. Culver of Duluth shoveled out a scoop of dirt to officially break the ground. This was followed by several other men taking a turn with the shovel, and then an orator came to the dais and spoke of the grand and glorious line they had just begun.

"This is such a farce," one man told another next to Luke. "They've scarcely got ten miles of solid ground on this route. Wait until spring when they have to deal with those floating islands. We'll see just how great a railroad Mr. Cooke has then."

Luke said nothing, but he knew the men were right. There had been nothing but conflict lately. It was going to be hard enough to finish the Lake Superior line. That should have been Mr. Cooke's focus, since he was financing the drive north. What would it have hurt to delay until August, when that line was finished, before making a fuss over the Northern Pacific? Who could even tell if the plans would move ahead? Congress had no particular love for the northern line, as they'd expressed on more than one occasion.

Theodore caught Luke's attention. His secretary stood huddled with several other men from Superior, Wisconsin. Luke knew this because they'd been introduced earlier, and Theodore had made it clear he didn't know any of them. Now, however, they conversed and laughed as if they were all old friends. There was something about the way they interacted that suggested a closeness that Theodore had claimed didn't exist.

"I hope you aren't disappointed in the celebration," Archie said, joining Luke. "It would seem everyone's having a great time. Folks are always happy when there's plenty of food and warmth and something exciting to celebrate."

"Yes, but I'm not convinced we have

something exciting to celebrate. There's more problems with this line than I anticipated. Who knew we were going to have so much trouble with the ground?"

"Well, I did, for one, but no one was listening to me. I watched as the company bought four of those new Otis steam shovel scoops and only one pile driver. I told them over and over that we were going to be sinking a great many pilings if we wanted to create a solid roadbed, but that's how they treated my recommendation."

"Only one pile driver?" Luke shook his head. "How do they intend to strengthen the roadbed?"

"It's probably not as much a problem that they've only got one. After all, I don't think they're going to be able to find solid ground in any case. We may need to bury a ton of trees before we can even begin to create a road. And even that may not work."

"What are we going to do, Archie?"

Archie smiled. "I suppose we will raise a glass with the other fools and pretend that this railroad has every chance of success. Even if it will take a miracle to secure it in Minnesota."

"And what about the Lake Superior line? Are we any closer to getting information on the changed route?"

"I've compared a couple of older section maps to the new map. The route has been altered on some and kept to the original on others. I've been unable to locate the detailed line map we had, but it would seem the bulk of the changes are between Fond du Lac and Moose Lake. We had enough trouble with that section to begin with. Hardly any decent solid ground to build on. We should have stuck to aligning the tracks with the old wagon road. I guess it's too late now."

"But why would someone change the route? Do you suppose they actually know a better way?" Luke asked.

"I'd like to think this was done for our benefit, but I'm more inclined to think it was to harm us. Those men from Superior have fought Duluth having this line every step of the way. And when we avoided them altogether by steering far off the wagon road, which would have put the railroad in their backyard, they've been looking for ways to make us fail. No," he said, shaking his head, "I don't think this was done for our benefit at all."

Luke thought about the issues and problems with the line the entire journey back to Duluth. He was discouraged by the reality of what others had tried to hide. There were plenty of rumors that employees were sending back sunny reports and ignoring the major issues that came up on a daily, if not hourly, basis. People liked spending money and giving at least a pretense of progress. Luke wondered how he could possibly help Mr. Cooke see the truth.

The only thing that kept him from losing all hope was the thought of Gloriana. She always seemed to understand his frustrations, but even more important, she helped him forget about his work for a few precious hours. She would give him a sense of family and home, and they would talk about the days when his brother and her family had been alive. But what Luke really wanted to talk to her about was the future.

"She's not ready for the future," he murmured.

"Did you say something, sir?" Theodore Sedgwick asked.

Luke looked at him for a moment. He had a strange feeling about his secretary. There was just something that didn't sit right. It never had. He couldn't for the life of him figure out what it was, and no one who knew Sedgwick seemed to say anything negative about him. And why should they? Sedgwick had done nothing wrong. He was performing his duties well. He was never absent or sick, and he always had a working knowledge of what Luke needed.

So why did Luke feel so suspicious of him? Gloriana had mentioned that Sedgwick had lived in Pennsylvania, and Sedgwick himself had admitted to living in Philadelphia before the war and just before coming here. Maybe Sedgwick had done something illegal during that time and it had been written up in the newspaper. Maybe Sedgwick had wronged someone. He tried to remember any mention of Sedgwick's name, but nothing came to mind.

He shook off the feeling. It probably had nothing to do with Theodore at all. It was this cursed railroad line and all the problems of the black muck and floating islands. Only recently had Luke learned that one of the smaller townships near Duluth was built entirely on this floating debris. There was no sense of security or promise that it would even be there the next day, and yet people had built a small village on it and called it Freemont.

He shook his head. He wanted permanency and a solid foundation. He wanted a future that would bear fruit and leave a legacy of truth behind. A legacy that would last for the ages. Why did everything suddenly feel so temporary?

He breathed a sigh of relief when the boat returned to Duluth. There had been a lot of ice, making the journey difficult, but the ship's captain knew how to navigate the water and managed to get them back without issue.

Luke walked home without saying much to anyone. The officials and dignitaries were headed to the Clark House to celebrate, but Luke had no heart for it. He felt tired—weary from the entire façade. He couldn't figure out what was wrong, but there was such a sense of disappointment that he was actually considering giving up his job with Jay Cooke.

He headed to his little cottage and then thought better of it and headed to the main house. He needed his family. He needed at least to pretend they were his. No. Pretense was not what he needed nor wanted. He wanted Gloriana and JT to be his family. He wanted Gloriana to marry him.

He knocked on the door and smiled when JT opened it with great gusto.

"Luke! You've come home early." Jack started yipping. "See, even Jack is happy you're home."

Home. That word sounded so perfect. He was home. This was home.

"Did you have the celebration for the railroad? We talked about it at school today," JT declared, helping pull Luke's coat sleeve down.

Luke shed his coat and let JT hang it up.

JT scooped up the puppy. "Jack has learned to use the newspapers if I don't get him outside in time. Isn't that great?"

"It is," Luke said, rubbing JT's head and then Jack's.

He glanced toward where Gloriana was heating a bottle for Sally. She looked so beautiful. Her blond curls were done up in that haphazard way that suggested she'd been working hard and hadn't had time to worry over her looks. Luke found her lack of concern endearing. She was a beautiful woman, but she didn't feel the need to flaunt it.

Their eyes met, and he smiled. "I hope I'm welcome this early."

She laughed. "Of course you are. However, you should know that I have plans for our evening. We're going to have a very serious conversation."

Luke was torn. She looked happy and even sounded as though she were teasing, and yet there was something very significant in her eyes.

"All right. I'm all yours," he said.

"We shall see." She turned back to the stove and tested the bottle.

"How was school today?" Luke asked JT.

"Well, we talked about the railroad a lot.

Mr. Nelson said that the railroad was critical to the civil-zation—"

"Civilization," Luke corrected.

"Yes. Civil-la-zation of our country. He said that countries don't get settled until people civilize them. So with the railroad, we can have an easier time moving to those parts of the country where there aren't very many towns yet."

"And would you like to move away from the lake?"

JT shrugged. "I don't know. The lake is hard to live by. It's hard on the families because people get killed. I don't know if I want us to stay here."

Gloriana said nothing, but Luke could tell she'd heard his comments. "Well, I believe God has a place for everyone. If He calls someone to move somewhere special, He'll make sure they know. Like when He told Abraham to get out of his country. Abraham got his family together and moved far away."

"Or like when the angel told Joseph to take Mary and baby Jesus and go to Egypt," JT said, nodding.

"Exactly. Sometimes God calls us to leave a place and go."

"And sometimes He calls us to stay," Gloriana finally said. She held up the bottle. "I'm going to feed Sally. She's been extra crabby today, and I'm hoping to get her to bed early. If you're too hungry to wait for supper, there are cookies and buttermilk."

Luke watched her go, wondering what she wanted to speak to him about. JT was already heading for the cookie jar, bouncing Jack in his arms.

"I don't want any buttermilk, but I always want cookies." JT put the puppy on the floor, then reached into the cookie jar.

"Just get one for you and one for me," Luke instructed. "We don't want to ruin our appetites. Your sister has worked much too hard on our supper, and we don't want to disappoint her."

"What about Jack?"

"No, I don't think cookies are good for Jack. Let's stick with giving Jack leftover meat and bread."

JT frowned but didn't argue. He brought Luke a sugar cookie. "So was the celebration a good one?" Jack danced at his feet.

"A lot of people came to see us start the new railroad," Luke admitted. "But I don't know if it was a good celebration. There are a lot of problems that we have to find answers for, and I don't know where those answers are going to come from."

"Did you pray?"

Luke smiled. "I should have, huh?"

"Yup." JT shoved most of the cookie in his mouth and spoke around it. "That's the only way to be sure you get the right answer." He let a piece of cookie drop to the floor, and Jack quickly scooped it up. Luke pretended not to notice as JT continued. "Mama always said prayer should be our first resort, not our last."

Out of the mouth of babes. Luke ruffled JT's hair and handed him half of his uneaten cookie. "Here. You deserve this for pointing me back in the right direction."

JT smiled. "Thanks, Luke." He gave Luke a hug before dashing off down the hall. The puppy followed him like a shadow.

Luke sat thinking about the simplicity of JT's suggestion.

He's right, Lord. I've been way too caught up in trying to do things in my own power. My fears and concerns over the railroad and the baby and this family have caused me to lose focus on You. I am sorry for that. I know You will provide my answers. You will give me direction—if I let You—if I listen. Forgive me for trying to wrestle with this in my own strength.

Gloriana thought about what she intended to say. She needed Luke to understand that she had worked through her anger at God and that, while she still felt overwhelmed by the loss in her life, she was ready to move forward. She was in love with him, and she knew he cared for her as well. She felt he had made certain implied suggestions for their future, and she wanted them both to be frank with each other about what that future should be.

After supper she asked JT to play in his room so she could have time alone to talk to Luke. She put Sally to bed for the night and stopped a moment to pray.

"Father, I am sorry for the way I've acted, just as I told You earlier," she whispered as she stood watching over Sally. "I want to change. I want my heart to be yielded to You in every way, but I need Your help. I know I'm willful and easily given to my own emotions. Help me, please. Help me tonight to say the right things. Let Luke understand. Amen."

She drew a deep breath. It was now or never.

Luke was waiting for her by the fire. To her surprise, he'd already washed up the dishes and cleaned the kitchen.

"What a pleasant surprise."

"You work much too hard," he said, smiling. "I just wanted to offer what I could."

She took a seat in her mother's chair and relished the fire's warmth. "I hope I haven't made you uncomfortable with my request to talk."

He pulled up the rocker and sat down. "Not at all. I enjoy our talks, so please begin."

"First I want to thank you for your patience with me. You've never quite had my best. When you arrived, I was already steeped in sorrow and anger over Papa and Scott. I felt God had forsaken us, and it made me so bitter. Upon reflection and with the passing of time, my heart has come to an understanding that my grief does not equate to God's absence. Mrs. Sedgwick and I had a long discussion about that today, and I feel I am ready to release my bitterness and rage at the Almighty. Better still, I know that I have His forgiveness."

"I'm so glad, Gloriana. I've been praying for you. I know your pain has been acute."

"It has." She met his gaze. "And I knew you were praying. You've been so kind. So caring, so patient. I honestly do not know what I would have done without you, and I want you to know that I've come to care for you more deeply than I thought possible."

"What exactly are you saying?"

She struggled for the right words. "I . . . I have . . ." She sighed. "I have never felt like you were a stranger. From the moment I found you in the cottage, it seemed I knew you. We have so easily become friends—family, of a sort—and I cannot imagine the future without you in it." She drew in a deep breath. "Nor do I want to."

"Nor do I." He moved from the chair to kneel in front of her. "So, will you marry me?"

Gloriana smiled. She didn't feel surprised by his words—just pleased. "Of course I will."

Chapter 19

When the harbor opened again in April and welcomed the first ships of spring, the cities of Superior and Duluth celebrated. They put aside their differences and instead focused on the joy of having the harbor once again open to commerce and badly needed supplies. Railroad work had already started up again, and there were some new ideas about how to build up the roadway for the railroad. A combination of gravel and woodchips was being experimented with, as well as drainage systems suggested by some Dutch experts. Perhaps they would get this railroad built on time after all.

The two major railroads that would tie Duluth to the rest of the United States required more workers than ever, and with this in mind, Jay Cooke had sent word to hire immigrants. They were grateful for work, wouldn't argue about the wages, and many had special skills related to the railroad. He told Luke in a very detailed letter to start plans for immigrant railroad housing. He wanted the housing in place by the next year and suggested using some of the excess land near the depot and railyards.

Every day, Luke could see the progress being made and wondered at the future of this growing city. When he'd first heard of Duluth, there couldn't have been more than a few hundred people living there—if that. Now there were nearly three thousand. Housing was difficult to find, and because of that, Luke had purchased additional tracts of land for himself and hired builders to put together simple one-story houses. He knew he'd have no trouble renting out the places once they were complete in the summer. He felt that Duluth was rapidly advancing and proving itself to be worth the investment, and now he had his future with Gloriana and the children to consider.

"That's the last of it," Archie said as he checked through a stack of papers. "Everything we expected with this first order is here. I'll get the men to move it out onto the line."

Luke nodded. "Thanks, Archie. I know

this isn't your job, but given Ray is so sick, I appreciate you stepping in to help me." Ray Willis, the supply manager, had taken on a bad pneumonia and was even now abed, fighting for recovery.

Believing his duties complete at the docks, Luke made the trek back to his office. The day had turned out sunny and brilliant but still quite chilly, and he was grateful for the warmth of the offices when he returned.

"You have a visitor waiting," Theodore announced. He got to his feet to help Luke with his hat and coat as he did every time Luke came or went. "If you don't need me, I have some paperwork to deliver to Mr. Rowland."

"That's fine. Who is my visitor?"

"I am."

Luke knew the voice immediately. He turned and met his father's stern expression. He finished handing his gloves to Theodore before forcing a smile. "Father. It's good to see you."

"More like a surprise, I would warrant."

"That too." Luke looked at Theodore. "Feel free to get those papers to Archie. He plans to oversee the supply delivery."

"Very good, sir." Theodore took up his own hat and coat. "I shouldn't be gone long."

Luke waited until his secretary had

departed to question his father. "Why didn't you let me know you were coming?"

"I was afraid you wouldn't approve."

"And why would I not approve a visit from my father?" Luke motioned to the office. "Please, let's sit, and I'll stoke up the fire."

"Your man already did that."

Luke nodded and brushed past his father to claim the seat behind his desk. "I take it you arrived this morning on the *Athena*. I hope your journey was smooth."

"It was." His father moved slowly to the chair opposite the desk.

"I wish you had let me know you were coming. It's going to be hard to find you accommodations. The Clark House is finished, but we already have quite a few visiting dignitaries occupying it at the moment. Duluth is growing at an astonishing pace."

"Why can't I simply reside with you?"

Luke smiled. "Because I live in a fisherman's cottage at the moment. I am building a house, but it won't be complete before summer. But never fear. I shall find you accommodations."

His father folded his hands. "I suppose you know why I've come."

Luke shook his head. "No, not exactly. My guess is you've come to see how I'm doing and perhaps to meet your granddaughter."

"I've come to take my granddaughter back to Philadelphia." He fixed Luke with one of his no-nonsense expressions. When Luke was a boy, it was this look that always let him know there was no room for negotiation.

"Well, I'm sorry to disappoint you, but my daughter is staying with me . . . and her mother. You see, I've adopted Sally and will soon be married to Gloriana—the woman your daughter-in-law asked to raise her baby."

His father's eyes narrowed. "You had no right to adopt the baby. Not without consulting me first."

"I had every right, Father. I was appointed guardianship by the baby's dying mother. In front of witnesses, I might add. I'm the only father the child has known, and Gloriana has been her only mother. It just so happens that through our ordeal and sorrows, Gloriana and I have fallen in love. We intend to be married very soon."

"I will disinherit you!" his father growled.

"Do as you will, Father, but remember what happened the last time you acted out of haste and anger. You can't undo the past. Would you make the same mistake again?"

"I have a right to that baby. She is my flesh and blood."

"And mine. And her mother chose me to raise her." Luke leaned back in his chair.

"You are an old man, and I am young and will hopefully have other children who can be siblings to Sally. She can grow up with the love of a mother and father, as well as brothers and sisters. Surely even you can see the blessing of that. What life would it be for a child to be raised in a museum-like house with an old man who has nothing to do with her but to show her off on Sundays?"

"She would have everything. You cannot give her the life I can."

"Nor can you give her the life I can," Luke countered. "My life is better, because she will have family and love. Your money and possessions cannot fill the emptiness that will be hers should she be ripped away from those who love her."

"I won't allow for this. I'll take you to court."

"You may do as you feel necessary, but the adoption is complete and quite legal. The witnesses gave testimony, and Sally is thriving and happy. I do not wish to be threatening, but I will guard and protect that baby as if she were my own. Scott would never want her raised by you in Philadelphia."

His father's face grew red. "She is my granddaughter. Her father and mother are dead. I have a right to raise her and will not allow you to rob me of that opportunity."

Luke drew a deep breath. "I have no wish to keep you from knowing Sally. In fact, I will take you to meet her—if I have your word that you'll do nothing to interfere with her staying here, with us."

"I will not give you my word on that. I am her grandfather!" He pounded the arms of the chair. "She is mine by right of survivorship."

"You'll have to take that up with Judge Prescott. He finalized the adoption, and I believe the matter has satisfied all the laws of this state." Luke paused and then leaned forward, arms on his desk. "Father, I don't want to argue with you. I know this news is not what you expected, but it will be what it is. It would be far better for everyone involved if you would admit defeat and accept the role we offer you."

"Which is what? An occasional visit? I want an active role in my granddaughter's life. She should have the privilege to which she's been born."

"She wasn't born to privilege. She was born by the lake to a fisherman and a kitchen maid. Did you forget that you cut her father off from privilege?"

"It didn't have to be that way. I made offers."

"You told my brother that if he would

divorce his wife and steal their child, you would reinstate him in the family. You were heartless and cruel. Scott loved Sally with everything he had, and they were happy, yet you couldn't allow that. You cared about status and keeping up appearances so much that you denied your own child. What would happen if Sally chose a different life? Would you cast her off as easily as you did Scott?"

"Scott was a grown man acting like a child. He knew the price of his ridiculous choice."

"And now you do as well." Luke shook his head. "If you want any role at all in the life of my daughter, you will reexamine your heart and repent of your harsh ways."

"I will fight you on this. You will not win. I have far more money and lawyers who will know what is to be done."

Luke got to his feet. "If you attempt to steal my child, you will regret it." He fought to control his anger. "I do not wish to fight you, but I will not have Sally be caught in the middle of your struggle for power. Now, I think it best that we head over to the hotel and I see about getting you a room."

Gloriana stood back to survey her handiwork. She had been cleaning since early that morning. Spring cleaning, her mother had always called it. They did a thorough clean of the house each spring and fall as a sort of ritual. Mother likened the springtime to renewal of life and thought the house should have its own refreshing as well.

That morning Gloriana had started with cleaning the fireplace and doing what she could to clear the chimney. Next, she had moved on to dust and sweep the house from top to bottom. After that, she took rags and hot soapy water to wipe down everything from the ceiling to the floors. Sally had watched her from the beautiful walnut baby chair Luke had found in one of the little shops in town. Gloriana had padded the chair with blankets so Sally couldn't escape. At nearly seven months old, the baby seemed quite content as Gloriana moved her from room to room and kept her entertained with her cleaning.

At noon they had stopped for lunch, followed by Sally taking a long nap while Gloriana battled cleaning out all of the cupboards. She had just gotten everything back into place when JT walked through the door with muddy boots.

"Stop!" Gloriana jumped down from the chair she had been standing on and pointed to his boots. "You should have taken those off outside. Where did you get into all that mud?"

"We were playing, and it's been raining," he said. Squatting down, he worked to get them off. "I'm sorry. I didn't mean to track it in."

"It's all right, but try to remember next time. I've been cleaning all day long."

"And it really smells good in here too. What are we having for supper?"

"Fish and rice, and berry tarts."

JT grinned. "Can I have one now? I'm really hungry."

Gloriana shook her head. "No, but you can have two cookies and go get your homework done."

"Luke said he'd help me with it. It's grammar." JT frowned. "I don't like it."

"I never did either, but I know it's very useful." Gloriana helped him discard his coat and hat. "Clean up your boots and then go get started. When Luke gets here, I'll have him come see you straightaway. Since he trained as a lawyer, he probably knows lots about English."

But Luke didn't arrive at the usual time. Where could he be? It was just a half hour until supper. She added wood to the fireplace and waited to make sure it caught. Sally was cooing and playing in her bed as if the world were a perfectly ordered place.

"Well, just look at you," Gloriana said, checking to see if Sally needed a fresh diaper. She did. Gloriana went to work, talking and smiling as Sally reached for her. "You are such a pretty baby."

And she really was. Her golden blond hair and chubby cheeks were just part of her charm. Her big blue eyes had the longest lashes, and her nose was a little button.

"Just wait until you can move about on your own. What fun we'll have then."

Gloriana finished with the diaper and lifted Sally. "When you're walking and running and climbing, I'll probably wish you were back to the sitting and scooting stage, but honestly I find myself eager for your first steps." She kissed the baby's cheek. "Oh, my darling girl, how I love you."

"They want me to mark all of the nouns," JT said from the doorway. "Where's Luke?"

"I don't know." Gloriana turned with the baby in her arms. "Maybe Sally can help. Sally, what are nouns?" She looked at the baby, who began to babble. Gloriana laughed. "Sally says they are people, places, or things."

JT came to see her. "She's gotten so much bigger. When is she going to really talk?"

"Oh, probably not for a long time. Babies just like to make their own words for a while."

"Do you think other babies know what

they're saying?" JT ran his finger along Sally's cheek. She reached for him and drew his finger toward her mouth.

"Oh, no you don't," Gloriana said, pulling JT's finger away. "You'll have a bottle in a moment." She looked at JT's forlorn expression. "Why don't you wait on the homework? I'm sure Luke just had extra work to oversee."

A knock sounded on the door, and Gloriana smiled. "See there? I'll bet that's him. Why don't you go see?"

JT scurried off, and Gloriana followed with Sally on her hip. She reached the kitchen just as JT was explaining to Luke all his frustrations and reminding him to take off his shoes.

"I'm sure we can figure it out together, so don't fret," Luke replied. He glanced past JT to where Gloriana stood with Sally. His expression changed to one of adoration. "There are my two beautiful girls."

Gloriana smiled. "I was just about to get her bottle ready. She had a nice long nap and now, with her dry diaper, I believe she is more than ready to visit and play."

"But Luke is going to help me with nouns," JT protested. "He can't play with the baby and help me at the same time."

"No, he's quite right. Why don't I wash up and go help JT? You can feed Sally, and then I'll entertain her while you finish up with supper." He glanced around. "Is something different? It seems, I don't know, brighter or something."

"Gloriana's been spring cleaning today," JT informed him. "It always smells extra good when she does that."

Luke looked at her and shook his head. "You are amazing, you know."

She laughed. "I'm tired, not amazing. Now, go help JT. Sally and I will be just fine."

There was something in Luke's expression that changed. "I do have something to tell you."

She had known him long enough to know it was serious. Whatever it was, she knew it might not be pleasant. "I'll be here."

She warmed Sally's bottle and tried not to fret. Whatever Luke needed to tell her, they would just face it together and do whatever needed to be done. Perhaps something had gone wrong with the house or with his job. Maybe Jay Cooke wanted him to return to Philadelphia. Oh, what if it were that? What would she say or do? Would he leave Duluth to do his work? He did have a responsibility. How could she fault him for honoring that?

When the bottle was ready, Gloriana sat in the rocker by the fire and fed Sally. The baby took hold of the glass bottle herself and half chewed, half sucked on the leather nipple. They would have to replace it soon. Mrs. Sedgwick had even suggested feeding the baby by using a little mug and teaching her to drink from it. To Gloriana it sounded like a lot of work and cleanup.

Luke came back just as Gloriana was burping Sally. "Here, that's a job I can do." He reached down and drew the baby up to his shoulder. "Hello, little one. Aren't you looking pretty today?"

"You'd better have this towel. You don't want your suit ruined." Gloriana handed him up a towel, which he promptly used to cover his shoulder.

He patted Sally firmly on the back until she let out a loud burp. "I think that should suffice," he said, laughing. "I've heard grown men belch more delicately."

Gloriana grinned. "She's just very enthusiastic. By the way, how's JT doing with his nouns?"

"He's fine now. He was just confused by pronouns. When I left, he was racing through the problems. I'll check all of his answers after dinner."

She had no desire to avoid the obvious. "What is it we need to discuss? Has something happened?"

"It has." Luke sat down and bounced Sally on his knee. "My father has come to town."

"Your father?" Gloriana felt a chill go up her spine. "Why is he here?"

Luke met her gaze. "To take Sally."

Chapter 20

"Take Sally?" JT asked from the other side of the room. "You aren't going to let him, are you?"

"Indeed, I will not. That's why I was late getting here. I had to stop off to see Judge Prescott. I told him about my father and what he had said and what I feared he might do."

"Which is what, exactly?" Gloriana asked. She wanted to snatch Sally out of Luke's arms but held back.

"Father believes he can give Sally a better life in Philadelphia. With his money and social standing, he thinks that Sally will have every advantage life can afford. I pointed out she would be lacking the most important thing: love."

"Love is the most important," JT declared, coming to stand beside Gloriana.

"Sally has us to love her, and she wouldn't be happy if we weren't there."

"No, I don't believe she would be," Luke said, smiling at the baby. "Judge Prescott said we have nothing to fear." He handed Sally to Gloriana. "And although I wish my father were not in such ill spirits about the matter, I do not intend to let him spoil our happiness."

"Did the judge offer any other advice?"

Luke nodded. "He did. He suggested you and I be married immediately. He said even if we want to have a bigger wedding later, he believed it would further solidify our case to be married and show a strong family unit. I assured him I would speak to you on the matter."

"I don't need a big wedding. Let's get married right away—even tonight."

Luke chuckled. "I don't think we have to run out right now and get the judge to marry us, Gloriana."

"I just don't want anything to happen to cause us to lose Sally. I have agreed to be your wife, so why delay any further?"

JT looked at her and then Luke. "I can go get Pastor Sedgwick."

"Just hold on," Luke declared, taking a seat on the sofa. "You are both getting way too excited. My father isn't going to do anything just yet. All of his lawyers and money are back in Philadelphia. My desire is to convince him that he should put aside his plans, but I believe the first order of business is for us to pray. As a family."

Gloriana had to admit that her first thought was to question God again. Why was He letting this happen? Why couldn't He just intercede and keep Luke's father from causing trouble? She drew a deep breath.

I'm sorry, Lord. I'm just so weary of trouble.

"My father can be difficult, but I intend to show him how happy we all are together. I want him to see us as a family. That's why I think we should invite him to come for dinner one night."

"Here?" Gloriana barely managed to squeak the word out. "You want to entertain your father here? With my cooking?"

"You're a wonderful cook, and the house is lovely. This is our home."

"Can I be there when you get married?" JT asked.

Gloriana looked at him with a smile. "Of course. You can give me away."

"Give you away?" JT frowned. "I don't want to give you away."

"You'd just be giving her to me," Luke said, rubbing JT's curls.

"Why couldn't we just take you to be with us instead of me giving Gloriana away?

I don't want to lose anything—I want to gain having you in our family."

"He makes an excellent point." Gloriana laughed as the baby did her best to clap her hands. "I believe Sally agrees. We won't give anything away. Instead we will increase our fold. We will add Luke to the family."

"I like the sound of that."

They shared supper, continuing to talk about Luke's father and when they might entertain him. Luke wanted them to marry the following day, and because of that, he suggested they keep JT home from school.

"We can walk over to see the judge first thing in the morning. Better still, I'll get my carriage, and we'll drive. The streets are muddy but passable."

"I'd rather we get Pastor Sedgwick and his wife," Gloriana replied. Over the last few years she'd never figured to wed, but prior to that, whenever she thought of marriage, she imagined having the ceremony in the church.

"That's fine by me. I can go speak to him tonight, if you wish."

Gloriana nodded. "That would be good."

"I got a headache," JT said, rubbing his eyes. "I think I did too much English."

Gloriana laughed. "Then why don't you get washed up and ready for bed? It sounds like we're going to have a very busy day to-morrow."

JT nodded and came to lay his head against her shoulder. "I love you, Glory. I'm real happy that we're getting married to Luke."

She frowned and felt his head. "You're awfully warm."

"He was sitting by the stove," Luke offered.

"True." She smoothed back her brother's curls. "Go get ready for bed, and I'll come tuck you in."

"Can Luke do it? He's been telling me this story about a man and his friend who went on an adventure across America. He and his friend made maps and everything."

Gloriana looked at Luke, who shrugged. "I thought the story of Lewis and Clark was fascinating. Amazing, actually, when you consider they made their trek nearly seventy years ago when there was nothing settled at all."

"It is fascinating. I wouldn't mind hearing it myself, but I understand it's something you boys have going on, and I won't interfere." She pulled Sally out of the baby chair. "Besides, I must ready this little miss for her own bedtime."

They went their separate ways, and Gloriana put Sally to bed and then went back to clean the kitchen. But she couldn't stop dwelling on the fact that someone out there wanted to divide her family. They wanted to take her happiness from her once again.

Why should it matter so much to Luke's father that Sally be his? He wouldn't be the one caring for her. No doubt there would be a nurse and the baby would be hidden away in an opulent room in the old man's grand house. He would bring her out and show her off from time to time like a beautiful painting or thoroughbred horse. Then he would send her back to live with her caregivers and grow up all alone, devoid of love and a normal family.

"I won't let that happen," Gloriana murmured as she finished washing the last of the dishes. No matter what she had to do, she wouldn't let Mr. Carson do such a horrible thing to Sally.

She picked up a dish towel and suddenly remembered that on the morrow she was to become a bride. It was almost an afterthought, and it amused her that it wasn't the grand event or monumental moment that she'd always thought it might be. She remembered friends planning their wedding days. They talked and planned constantly until the event was upon them.

Gloriana went to the window and looked out into the dark night. The lake was nothing but blackness in the silence. Nevertheless, she knew it was there. The threats posed in the day seemed doubly so at night. She'd never liked to gaze upon the lake at night, be it at peace or churned up. It was always a dark omen—a silent warning.

She let the curtain fall back into place. She wasn't going to let Mr. Carson nor Lake Superior ruin her mood. She needed to focus on the good things that were about to happen. She needed to dwell on her love for Luke and the life they would have together.

I love him so much.

The words were still foreign on her lips. The love had developed in such a subtle way. There hadn't been any fanfare or time for romantic strolls or courtship. It was a relationship that was matter-of-fact yet extraordinary.

How could she not have seen its development? With each kindness, each gentle encouragement, love grew between them. Mama had once said that she knew she was in love with Gloriana's father when he had stopped to calm a young boy who sat by the road crying.

"He knelt beside the child and asked what the trouble was, and when the boy told him that he couldn't find his favorite marble, your father didn't chide him or laugh at him. Instead, he took the boy's hand, and together they searched until the lost marble was found. I could not have loved him more for that act of kindness."

Luke was kind like that. He had such a gentle spirit and tenderness that amazed Gloriana. When he was dealing with JT and the boy was in a particularly bad mood, Luke seemed to have endless patience. Yet when speaking of his father's threats, Luke was all strength and deliberate refuge. He would not see his family harmed. He would protect them.

It was how her father had been—how her heavenly Father was. Fierce and powerful on one hand, but loving and gentle on the other. If she'd ever had any doubts about Luke being the right person for her, this thought completely dissolved them. Luke was a godly man—a man her father would have respected and loved.

"You look deep in thought," Luke said from the hallway.

"I am." She smiled. "I was just thinking of how tomorrow we'll be married."

"I still want to give you a big church wedding if you want one."

She shook her head. "No. That's never

really been my desire. I always thought of a small intimate ceremony with my family and friends. Now my family is gone, and so are many of my friends. Sally was my best friend of all."

"I know we've had so little time to talk and consider what this means." He came to stand directly in front of her and put his palm against her cheek. "I never thought it would be like this either."

Gloriana smiled. "Papa would have said it was just what he expected from me. I was always doing things different from everyone else."

"Some people will probably talk. Their curiosity will be stirred by us marrying quickly and quietly."

"Let them talk. My friends know my beliefs and trust me to make wise decisions, and those who believe otherwise are of no consequence. They aren't real friends if they're setting out to believe the worst about me."

"True." He ran his fingers through her errant blond curls. "You've given up so much to care for others. You are the type of woman a man can always count on for support and honesty. I know that my heart will be safe with you. I hope you know that yours will be safe with mine."

"I do, and yet there is no reason either

of us should feel so confident." His fingers traced her jawline, and her heart quickened its pace. She loved his touch.

"Sometimes," he began, "God does things in such a way that all the pieces fit neatly together. There's no striving. No conflict. Some would call it miraculous, and perhaps it is, for how could two people otherwise come together for the first time, yet feel as though they'd already lived a lifetime in each other's presence?"

"God is the only answer." She was as sure of that as she was of anything else. Only God could have seen the need JT and Sally would have—the need that Gloriana and Luke would have—and then make such utter and complete resolution and restoration.

"I love you, Gloriana. Never doubt that, I beg you. Ours might be a different kind of courtship, but my love for you is no less filled with passion and wonder. I know we will be happy together."

"I love you too, Luke. The wonder of it leaves me amazed and overwhelmed." She searched the depth of his blue-gray eyes. "I never thought I'd fall in love—yet here we are."

"I never thought I'd live here and meet someone I love. For a long time, I was expected to live a certain way. I used to be so prideful. I was always considered a prime catch." He chuckled. "And I almost believed it for a time. But God straightened me out on that. He made it clear that He had plans for my future—that love would come in time. I've always known I would be a husband and father one day. I just didn't know God would send me someone like you."

"Luke, I don't fit into that world of yours. You must see that and remember it." She frowned. "I will never be good enough for Philadelphia society. You're forsaking your upbringing and the privilege that goes with it by marrying me."

"It's a price I happily pay. It was never a world that made me happy. Not like you make me happy." He took her face in his hands. "And, Gloriana, I've never been so happy."

He kissed her tenderly, and she melted against him. Tomorrow she would be a bride and a wife. She could scarcely draw breath. After tomorrow, they would never have to part again. Never leave to go to their separate houses. Never be alone.

"They aren't going to change their minds," the man declared as Theodore Sedgwick sipped his whiskey. "Are they?"

"Not at this late date," Theo admitted.

"However, we can still make it costly to them. Perhaps if we plan it right, it will even be financially disastrous." He had always seen this as the prized goal anyway. He didn't care whether Duluth or Superior got the railroad. Not really. It would have pleased him to see Duluth fail because that would hurt his father, but he honestly didn't care.

What he wanted was for Luke Carson's name and reputation to be destroyed. Now that Luke's father was in town, Theo had even tried to figure out a way to harm the old man as well. After all, it had been his bank Rafael had embezzled from and the elder Carson who had pressed the charges to the utter limit of the law. If there was a way to destroy father *and* son, that would be perfectly satisfying.

"We can do nothing about the railroad. Cooke has that sewn up, and despite our having swayed a good number of congressmen to see things our way, money is what will always move railroads. However, we've another matter to consider. The canal."

Theodore knew the man who was speaking only by reputation. They'd never been formally introduced, nor did he imagine they would be. The man had no interest in someone of Theo's lowly status, unless of course that someone could actually accomplish something. Theodore had failed in his eyes, and that made him less than useful to the likes of this politician.

If Theodore could figure out a way to put an end to the canal plans, then perhaps the politician might have other uses for him. After all, Theodore's quest for revenge against Luke and his father wouldn't last forever. He'd ruin those two or kill them. Maybe both. Either way, he would still need powerful friends in the future.

Chapter 21

At breakfast the next morning, Luke was more than a little excited. "Pastor Sedgwick said to come to the church at seven tonight. He will marry us then. Mrs. Sedgwick said she'd even invite a few of your closest friends to witness the occasion, and there will be a little reception afterward."

"It sounds like a simple affair is growing more elaborate," Gloriana said, glancing at her brother. "JT, are you feeling all right?"

He shrugged. "I'm tired." He cut into his pancake and said nothing more.

Luke put several pancakes on his own plate. "I'm sure the excitement of it all gave him restless sleep. I know it did me. I kept thinking about how everything would come together tonight. I'm not sure how to manage it all. The new house won't be complete until

July, maybe August. I'm content to live here with you until then, if that meets with your approval."

Gloriana poured him a cup of coffee. "What else would we do?" She put the pot back on the stove and took her seat at the table beside Sally's high chair. The baby was enjoying playing with a couple of wooden spoons.

"Do you need me to pick up anything in town?" Luke asked.

She considered his question a moment, then shook her head. "I can't think of a thing. I figure I'll have supper ready for us, and after we eat, we can go to the church."

Luke nodded. "That sounds perfect, although I wonder if either of us will be able to eat a bite. I don't know about you, but I already have butterflies in my stomach."

"Butterflies?" JT asked. "How did you get butterflies in your stomach?"

"It's just a saying, JT." Gloriana reached for the syrup. "Would you like some more?" She held up the crock and offered to spoon it onto JT's uneaten pancake.

"No. I think I got butterflies too."

Luke laughed. "It is a momentous occasion. Still, I would be grateful for syrup."

He was still thinking about butterflies later when he joined a meeting Roger Munger had arranged regarding the canal.

"As most of you know, the canal is something we've wanted for years. There have been numerous difficulties in getting it established, however. We all know that the Panic of '57 put a stop to everything, and then, of course, the war was a difficulty for all, even though we had no battles in Duluth.

"Still, there have been attempts to further the cause of a canal. After the war, the Army Corps of Engineers built us a breakwater to protect the outer harbor. But as you gentlemen also remember, they advised against a canal due to an unreasonable fear that the flow of the St. Louis River might be altered and become more hazardous."

Munger looked at his notes. "Others have said there would be no damage and that digging a deeper channel would resolve any issues with the river. The fact of the matter is that no one knows for sure what will happen once a canal is in place, except that our commerce will be greatly benefitted."

There were murmurs of approval from around the room. Luke could see that the majority of these men were avid supporters of the canal. And for him, it sounded like the best idea for the city. Not only that, but he was certain Jay Cooke would agree and want to be in on the earliest plans.

"My personal engineers assure me that

a canal will not harm the harbor. If anything, it will benefit it greatly. I've already made arrangements to purchase or hire a steam dredger, and I believe by summer we should be able to begin digging," Munger announced.

There was something of a free-for-all of questions after that. The powerful men of Duluth wanted to know all of the details, and Luke found his mind again on his father and the wedding. Part of him wanted to invite his father to witness the nuptials, but he wanted the occasion to be without conflict, so that was out of the question.

When the meeting broke up, Luke went back to his office. He was surprised to find correspondence awaiting him from Mr. Cooke, but not so shocked to see that it was all about the railroad. Scanning through the pages, Luke read Mr. Cooke's concerns for reaching the August deadline to complete the Lake Superior and Mississippi line. They must, he wrote, focus on completing that railroad, even if the Northern Pacific was delayed. Yes, Congress had demanded progress from both ends of the northern line, but Mr. Cooke was certain Luke could at least make it appear that the work was progressing.

Luke knew land was being cleared now

that a warm spring was upon them. At last count, over thirty miles had been graded and looked ready for the laying of rails. The problem was, they needed more workers. Perhaps if he could hire on more people to finish up the Lake Superior line, they could then transfer all of those people to the Northern Pacific once the job was completed. Thankfully, Mr. Cooke had advertised abroad to encourage immigrant laborers to consider coming to work for the Northern Pacific. If enough of them signed on soon, Luke could use them with the Lake Superior line as well.

The real frustration was the tampering with the route. Luke and Archie had been unable to find the original maps that had been drawn. They had been lost somewhere between offices. There were numerous section copies, but that didn't help. They needed to find the original reports and maps to see exactly what had been compromised. Until then, there was no telling what trouble might come.

Theodore came into his office, barely stopping to give a light rap. "Your father is here to see you, sir."

"I need no introduction," Luke's father declared, pushing past the secretary. "Now leave us so that I might talk to my son in private."

Theodore looked as if he might say something, but then he gave a curt nod and looked to Luke. "Will there be anything else, sir?"

Luke felt sorry for Sedgwick. His father could be such an imposing figure to handle. "No. I believe it would be a good time for you to take your lunch. Father and I will likely do the same."

Theodore nodded and left with only the slightest glance at the senior Mr. Carson. Luke waited until he heard the outside door close before meeting his father's disgruntled expression.

"I thought I would see you at breakfast," his father declared.

"I had other plans and then a meeting." Luke put away the correspondence from Mr. Cooke and got to his feet. "Luncheon will have to suffice, as today my schedule is quite busy."

"This is preposterous. I came all of this way and haven't yet seen my granddaughter. You hide her away from me as if you think me some sort of villain. I am here to give her everything, not hurt her. You have made me out to be some sort of thief."

"You want to steal my daughter. That makes you a thief in my eyes."

"She's my granddaughter by blood and your daughter only by paper."

Luke's eyes narrowed. "I will not argue

with you about the validity of my claim. Nor of the love I hold for that child. I also will not allow you to see her until you agree to put this ridiculous notion aside."

"What ridiculous notion?"

"That you believe yourself capable of taking her from me. That will not happen." Luke drew a deep breath. "Now, let us go to lunch and speak of more pleasant topics. Perhaps you can tell me how your investments played out last fall. You were quite excited about a couple of them, as I recall."

Gloriana made certain her dress was ready. At Christmas Luke had given her several store-bought gowns, and this was one she had thought much too fine to wear for everyday use. She hadn't even managed to wear it for church because the silk material was too lightweight for winter. Now, however, with this unseasonably warm spring, Gloriana thought it would be perfect for her wedding dress.

She lightly fingered the fabric and smiled. The pale coral color was trimmed in a slightly darker coral cord. The neckline was modest and edged with lace, and the sleeves were long and fitted. In keeping with the current fashion, the front of the gown was layered and drawn up to the back in a sweeping fashion that connected to form part of the bustle. There was a small matching hat for the gown that Gloriana thought quite charming. It had been designed to sit to one side, with tulle and feathers decorating its simplicity. She couldn't imagine it being any more perfect. It would accent her blond hair and pale complexion.

As she finished making sure every detail was perfect, she heard the front door open. "Is that you, JT?"

"It's me," she heard him reply. He didn't sound right.

She left the dress hanging and went to see what might be wrong. She found JT slumped in a chair at the table.

"Looks like you had a rough day."

"I don't feel good, Glory," he murmured.

Gloriana raised his face to meet hers. His cheeks were red and his skin hot to the touch. He had a fever. There was no doubting it this time.

"Come on. Let me get you to bed, and we'll see what the problem might be."

"I can't. We're getting married tonight."

"I know, but maybe it isn't something that will keep you from being there. Let me look you over and give you some medicine. You can rest until supper, and if you feel well enough to eat, then fine. If not, we'll see what else needs to be done."

She helped him to his feet and led him to his room. "You get your clothes off, and I'll grab your nightshirt and pull down the covers."

Just the fact that he wasn't protesting left Gloriana gravely concerned. It wasn't like JT to be so sluggish, even when he was sick.

She pulled down the covers and turned to see him standing in front of the window. The light streamed in, touching his small chest and face. There, Gloriana could see the source of his illness. A fine rash had developed all over his torso.

"Oh, JT." She went to him and touched his arm. "You have the measles."

"It's the measles, all right," Abigail Lindquist declared. "Nothing to be done but keep the fever down and put him in a dark room. He'll need lots of fluids. Measles dries a body out something fierce." She got up and gathered her things. "I'll let folks know you're in quarantine. You need to post a sign."

Gloriana nodded. "Are there other cases?"

"JT is the third child I've seen this week. I hope we won't have a full epidemic, but you can never tell. Someone probably brought it in on one of the ships. You know these things spread fast."

Gloriana nodded and then remembered Sally. "What about the baby?"

Abigail shook her head. "There's no way of telling. She is definitely susceptible. Keep her away from his sickroom, but it's probably too late to keep her from getting sick if she's going to take it. You've already had the measles, so you won't get them again."

The entire situation was terrifying. Her mother and other siblings had died from scarlet fever, and now JT was sick with the measles. She tried not to race to the obvious conclusion that JT could die, but it was all she could think about.

"It's most important to get JT's fever down. Children usually fight off these things better than adults, but the fever can still burn his brain and leave him blind or deaf. You must be vigilant to bring it down. Use the willow bark tea; that will help. I'll show you how much to use for someone his size. Come with me to the kitchen."

Gloriana followed Abigail, hesitant to leave her little brother. He was already sleeping, but she didn't want him to be alone. It was terrifying to be sick and not know what might happen. She didn't want him to be afraid.

Abigail showed her the exact amount to

use in JT's tea and told her how often to use it, but Gloriana wanted only to return to his side. She was so thankful that Sally was content to play in her crib. The baby's brand-new trick was sitting up. It wouldn't be long until she was pulling up and then walking. Gloriana decided to put Sally's crib in her father's old room so Sally would be closed off from the rest of the house.

Once Abigail was gone, Gloriana found a piece of brown paper and some burnt wood. The charred pieces would make nice black lettering. She wrote the word *quarantine*, then set the paper aside to make a flour-and-water paste. Once this was complete, she plastered the sign to the front door.

Poor Luke. She hoped he'd already had the measles.

Then it dawned on her that they were to have been married that evening. "Oh, grief!" She sighed. What if this caused problems for them with the baby? What if Luke's father was somehow able to get the edge because they hadn't yet wed?

She tried not to think of her disappointment in having to forgo the wedding she'd been anticipating with great joy. Such thinking was selfish. Her little brother was sick— possibly on death's door. How could she worry about something such as getting married?

Taking the willow bark tea and a pan of tepid water, Gloriana made her way back to the bedroom. JT was sound asleep, but she had to do what she could to bring down his temperature.

"JT, I need you to wake up and take some medicine," she said, trying to sound as cheerful as possible. She shook him gently and waited as he opened his eyes. She smiled down at him. "I have some tea you need to drink. It'll help with the fever. After you do that, I have to wipe you down with vinegar water. It smells terrible, but it will help with the fever too."

"Do I have scarlet fever again?"

"No, this time it's the measles."

"Oh, I remember you saying that. Billy and Matt have been sick too, and Teacher said it was measles."

Gloriana nodded and helped him with the mug. "Mrs. Lindquist said there are several children sick with it. It'll be all right, though. You just need to rest and drink a lot of fluids. We'll have you well in no time."

"But tonight . . . we were supposed to go to the church."

She was surprised he remembered. "It's all right, JT. We'll still have the wedding sometime, but right now it's more important that we get you well."

"Is measles really bad?" He looked at her with glassy, fevered eyes.

"It can be, but we're going to make sure it isn't. Now, you rest while I bathe your body. It won't take long. I don't want you to take a chill."

Sally began fussing in the other room, and JT shook his head. "Does the baby have measles too?"

"No. At least I don't think so. I hope not."

"We gotta pray so she won't get sick. Will you pray with me, Glory?" he whispered.

Rather than rage in anger at God, Gloriana was too afraid to do anything but cling to Him. He had the power to heal her brother and to keep the baby from getting sick. But God had also had the power to heal her family of scarlet fever. Doubt crept in, and Gloriana fought to push it back.

"I will pray." She squeezed JT's hand. "Dear God, we need Your help. We need healing for JT and the others, and we need Sally to stay well."

What if He didn't hear her now any more than He'd heard her prayers for Mama, Tabby, and Aaron? But He had heard. He had. He had heard and He had been there. He was here now. Prayers might not always be answered the way Gloriana thought they should, but God was here.

Tears flooded her closed eyes. *Please don't take him from me, Lord. Please. I know Your will is all we should seek, and I do want to be mindful of that, but please . . . please . . . I need JT. I need him to live.*

When she opened her eyes, JT was once again asleep.

~

Luke saw the quarantine sign and frowned. He knocked on the door as he always did, but this time he didn't open it. When Gloriana finally showed up, he could see she'd been crying.

"What's going on?" he asked.

"JT has the measles. He's very sick."

"And Sally?"

She shook her head. "So far she's fine, but she has been exposed, and there's no telling how it will go with her."

"Is there anything I can do? I've had the measles, so I won't catch them again."

"No. I'm sorry, but it means we can't go to the church tonight. JT was upset about that." She twisted her apron in her hands. "He was worried about us not getting married."

Luke gave her a smile. "Tell him not to fear. We will be married as soon as possible, and he will be there to share in the celebration."

"I'm so worried about him, Luke. I'm so afraid."

He pressed open the door and pulled her into his arms. "I promise it's going to be all right."

"You can't make that kind of promise. Diseases don't care about promises."

He lifted her face to his. "Don't let this fear take ahold of you, Gloriana. The devil wins then. He wants you to be so afraid that you'll again put up walls between you and God. Probably between you and me as well. We're going to see this through with God's help. Neither of us is going to leave you, Gloriana. And that's a promise you can count on."

Chapter 22

For two days and nights, Gloriana fought to get JT's fever to break. Instead it seemed only to climb and the boy to grow ever sicker. She tried her best not to fear what might or might not happen.

On the second night, Abigail Lindquist stopped by to resupply Gloriana's willow bark tea and to check on them.

"You're doing everything right," she assured Gloriana.

"Then why won't the fever come down?"

Abigail shook her head. "It's just often the way of it. Don't despair. Keep getting fluids into him. That's the most important thing right now."

"Luke wants to help. He's had the measles. Do you suppose it will be all right to let him see JT?"

"Of course. The quarantine is for those who haven't had the disease. We keep it contained here, and hopefully those who haven't had it will refrain from taking it. Luke should be fine to come and go."

Gloriana breathed a sigh of relief. She was so worn out. Despite Sally being such a good baby and remaining well, she was in constant need of attention. Having Luke around to help with the baby might allow Gloriana a few minutes to herself.

After Abigail left, Gloriana went to check on her brother before starting a bottle for Sally. JT slept peacefully, although he now had some congestion. She could hear it rattle in his chest as he breathed. Abigail said it was important to keep moving him and even make him sleep propped up so his lungs would drain properly. Gloriana touched his forehead. He seemed a little cooler. Or was that just her own wishful thinking?

Sally began to fuss, and Gloriana knew it was only a matter of time until she was crying in earnest. Still, it was hard to leave JT. What if he needed her and Gloriana didn't hear him? She desperately needed Luke to come by so she could tell him it was all right for him to stay. No matter what anyone thought.

She went to the basin in the kitchen and poured hot water into it. Next, she washed her hands with soap. She didn't know if it really helped or not, but keeping clean seemed a good way to avoid spreading the disease. She started the bottle warming, then went to change Sally and get her up from her nap.

"Hello, beautiful girl." Gloriana smiled, and the baby immediately calmed and looked up.

Gloriana undressed Sally to rid her of the wet diaper. Each time she'd performed this task over the last two days, Gloriana had held her breath, looking for the telltale signs of measles. So far there was no rash and no sign of fever. She let out a sigh and put the diaper to soak with several others. Laundry would have to be done soon.

"Oh, I hope you stay well, little one. I cannot imagine the misery you and I would both suffer should you fall ill."

Sally kicked and cooed as if she understood.

Once she had a dry diaper and new gown in place, Gloriana lifted the baby and snuggled her against her neck. How she loved this child. She had never really thought of the fact that she had become Sally's mother, only that she loved this child enough to sacrifice anything for her. Even life itself. It was clear that Gloriana needn't have carried Sally in order to love her.

"And I do love you, little one. With all my heart." She kissed the baby's face, and Sally pressed her fingers against Gloriana's mouth. Gloriana pretended to nibble on the baby's fingers, and Sally giggled.

For just a moment, Gloriana could forget about the miseries of the day—the week. She longed to rest in the moment and enjoy the sweetness of Sally's amusement. Closing her eyes, she pretended that the world was in right order and all was well. But, as if to keep her from even that momentary pleasure, a knock sounded on the door.

She opened her eyes and looked at the baby. "Well, so much for a quiet moment."

Crossing the room, Gloriana could see through the window that the visitor was a man. Perhaps Pastor Sedgwick had come to check on them. She opened the door.

A stranger looked at her with a stern scrutiny. "Quarantine? For what, if I might ask?"

"Do I know you?" Gloriana returned the man's studying gaze.

"I'm Martin Carson, Lucas Carson's father." He looked at the baby on her hip. "Sally Carson's grandfather."

Gloriana was determined to show no fear. "I'm Gloriana Womack, soon to be your son's wife, and yes, we're under quarantine for measles."

He was still as sober as a Puritan minister. "Does my granddaughter have the measles?"

She hugged the baby close. "No, at least not yet. We've seen no signs, but the disease varies as to when you might see symptoms. So far Sally is quite healthy."

"And this . . . is Sally?" he asked, nodding toward the baby.

"It is."

He gave the first signs of softening. "She reminds me of her father."

"Yes, but she also bears characteristics of her mother, as you can probably see for yourself. Luke tells me you knew her. She was my dear friend."

"She scarcely lived here long enough to form much of a friendship with anyone, I daresay."

Gloriana held her temper. "Some friendships are formed more easily and quickly. When Scott and Sally arrived, they had no one, and our family quickly took them under our wing. Scott was like a son to my father. They worked well together."

"And died together."

"Yes, tragically so. The lake is unforgiving when storms come up without warning. My father sailed her for over fifty years and knew her well, but there is no accounting for rogue storms."

"Still, a man with such experience should know better than to risk the lives of everyone on board. No doubt he felt he could take that chance, but it has robbed me of a son."

Gloria stiffened. "Your son went willingly, as did the other members of the crew. They were loyal to the ship and one another. They entrusted their lives to one another." Gloriana found it harder and harder to hold her tongue. "I would wager a guess that you know nothing of such a bond. You strike me as a man who has trusted solely in himself."

She saw the edge of anger in his eyes and regretted her words. She let out a sigh. "I apologize. That was uncalled for, but I am quite busy, and your appearance has called me away from my duties. Luke isn't here, so you should check at his office or even the cottage next door if you're looking for him."

"I came to see my granddaughter."

She nodded. "And so you have." Sally played with one of Gloriana's loose curls. "But now you must excuse me, because she's hungry and I have a bottle warming."

She backed up and began to close the door, but Martin Carson put his hand out to stop it. "I won't be dismissed. This is my granddaughter, and I've come to take her back with me to Philadelphia. I'm sure Luke has probably made you aware of that." He stepped forward as if to cross the threshold, then seemed to reconsider.

"You really should take this matter up with your son, Mr. Carson." Gloriana didn't want to say any of the harsh things she was thinking. She could easily remind him of how much he'd hurt Scott by disowning him. She could remind him of the terrible way he put Scott and Sally from the house without money or much more than the clothes on their backs. But she held her tongue, knowing that speaking of such things would only make matters worse.

"Father, what are you doing here?"

Thank the Lord, Luke had come. Relief poured over her.

Martin Carson turned. "I wanted to meet my granddaughter, and I arrive here to find her in a house of disease."

"Yes, Gloriana's brother has the measles. And as I recall, you have not."

The older man frowned. "No, I have not."

"How does a man go through life without having contracted measles?" Gloriana murmured, immediately wishing she'd kept the question to herself.

"My upbringing shielded me from most of the diseases this world has to offer. My determination to live in a healthy manner has helped me elude the rest," Luke's father said in a haughty manner.

"In other words, Gloriana, when there were sick people to deal with, my father let someone else see to their needs."

"And why not? I'm neither a doctor nor a nurse. My care has kept me from harm. How can you fault me for such a thing? No man willingly walks into a den of vipers."

"No, I suppose not, Father. But if Sally accidentally walked into that den, I would risk my life to save hers. Would you?"

Sally began to fuss, and Gloriana took it as the perfect opportunity. "I'm sorry, but I must feed the baby. Luke, Abigail said that because you've had the measles, you are safe to enter the quarantine." She looked at Luke's father. "I'm glad to have met you, Mr. Carson."

"I hardly believe that," he replied with a sneer.

That was all she could take. "Then you misjudge me. I'm glad to have met you, because now I know who to avoid in the future."

"How long was he here?" Luke could see how upset Gloriana was by the way she paced back and forth while feeding Sally.

"Not all that long, but long enough. How did he find out where we live?"

"It's not that big of a town, Gloriana." He

gave her a reassuring smile. "But stop worrying. He cares far too much about himself to come back here until we're out of quarantine."

"He scares me. Like you said before, he is a man used to having his own way."

Luke went to take Sally from Gloriana. "You're exhausted. I want you to go rest. Have a nap. It won't hurt for you to take some time away from all this. I'll stay here and take care of JT and Sally."

"But you don't know what to do for JT."

"So tell me." He grinned and put Sally to his shoulder to see if she needed to burp. She did.

"It's too complicated. JT has to get the willow bark tea every six hours to help with his fever, and he has to drink plenty of fluids otherwise. He's just now starting to feel a little cooler, so I dare not relax my concern now."

"You aren't. You're letting me take it on for you. Now go to bed. I'll be here to oversee it all. I know how to warm a bottle and change a diaper. I can even wash out dirty clothes if I need to." He adjusted his hold on Sally. "We'll be just fine."

"Well, maybe for just an hour or so, but it wouldn't be appropriate for me to sleep with you here."

"Then sleep next door. It won't hurt a

thing. We're going to be married as soon as you feel it safe enough to slip away and do so. No one has any right to fuss over you taking a nap next door while I mind the sick and very young." He kissed Sally's face, and she squealed in delight and reached for his nose.

Gloriana watched them for a moment, then nodded. "All right. I'll go next door and take a nap. If I'm not back in an hour or two, however, come wake me."

"Go on. We'll be just fine, and you'll be much better once you've slept."

He watched Gloriana hesitate as she wrestled with the decision one more time before finally leaving the house. She was barely functioning. He could see the exhaustion in her eyes. Her drive to care for JT—to see him through this sickness and save his life—had taken such a toll. No doubt her worry that Sally might catch the disease had also kept her from being able to relax for even a moment.

"Well, here we are, pretty miss," he told Sally. "I suggest we go check on JT, but since I don't want to give you any extra exposure, I'm going to put you in your crib to play."

Luke set Sally up with her toys, then lit a lamp, since they were starting to lose the light. He took another lamp and went to check on JT. He placed the light on the dresser and then went to the window and looked out across the yard toward the lake. It had been a lovely day, and there were quite a few fishing boats still on the water. He couldn't help but think about Scott. He had written to tell Luke how much he loved being on the water.

"It's a mix of raw emotions that wells up in me," Scott had written. *"I feel upon seeing Lake Superior that my spirit has only just come alive. It calls to me, and I find I must go."*

Luke didn't feel that way about the lake, but maybe that was because the lake had cost him the life of a beloved brother. He found the setting lovely enough, but it hardly stirred him the way it had Scott.

"What's out there?" JT asked, his voice barely audible.

Luke turned and smiled. "A lot of water. About the same amount that you need to be drinking." He came to the bed. "How are you feeling?"

"Itchy." JT looked around. "Where's Glory?"

"I made her go next door to take a nap. I'm in charge now. Are you hungry? Want me to make you something to eat?"

JT shook his head. "You could read to me or tell me more about Lewis and Clark, though."

Luke pulled up the chair. "I would love

to. We were just about to get to a very exciting part where some hostile Indians happen upon their camp."

The boy's eyes widened. "Hostile Indians? What happened?"

Gloriana opened her eyes to find that it was still light. Thankfully, she'd only slept a short time, but she felt amazingly rested. She got up and smoothed the covers back into place. She hadn't even bothered to get under the quilt, but had instead used the extra one hanging over the end of the bed. She hadn't wanted to feel obligated to change the bedding before returning home.

She got to her feet, marveling that the rest had given her new strength and resolve. They were going to get through this and be stronger for it. Luke's father would be dealt with, and JT would recover. She was sure of it.

Gloriana folded the quilt and replaced it at the end of the bed, then went to the mirror and did what she could to repair her hair. Thankfully, with her natural curls, it was easy to pin her hair up and make it look somewhat orderly. Other women would need a curling iron, but not Gloriana.

As she finished that task, she thought about what they might eat for supper. Luke had been bringing bread from the bakery and other things to make her daily tasks much easier, but it was still necessary to cook, and now that she knew for sure it was all right for Luke to be at the house, he'd expect supper.

Entering her house, Gloriana was immediately assaulted by the aroma of something delightful. She made her way to the oven and found a casserole of some type.

"Too many cooks spoil the broth," Luke announced as he came into the room.

"This smells wonderful. Did you make it?" She closed the oven door and straightened.

"I can't take credit for it. Mrs. Sedgwick brought it by. I'm just the man who put it in the oven to warm. How did you sleep?"

"Wonderfully. I never knew a short nap could help so much."

He laughed. "Short, eh? You've been asleep for twenty-three hours."

Gloriana's mouth dropped open. "What? No. I couldn't have."

"I'm afraid so. I actually had Mrs. Sedgwick check on you last night. She and Pastor Sedgwick stopped by to visit. I told them what was going on, and she promised to bring us supper for tonight. I could hardly say no, since I had no idea when you might wake back up."

"JT?"

She started for the hall, but Luke caught her waist and swept her into his arms. "Is doing much better. He's awake and starting to eat a little gruel. Mrs. Sedgwick told me to start him on that and graduate to soup. So, you see, we're quite under control here." He kissed her nose.

Gloriana shook her head. "I want to see him for myself."

He nodded and released her. "I knew you would."

She went to JT's room and found her little brother sitting up in bed with all his toy soldiers lined up around him.

"Glory! You're awake. Luke told me you were so tired that you slept all day and all night."

"You did a lot of that too." She felt his forehead. The fever was gone. "How do you feel?"

"Itchy, but Mrs. Sedgwick told me not to scratch. She said when it got really bad to just put my hand on top of where it itched and pray." He shook his head. "It doesn't help much."

"A baking soda bath might do the trick. Not that prayer is a bad idea." She smiled, feeling such relief that she had to sit down. "I've been so worried about you."

"I'm strong, Glory. You said so yourself. I'm going to get better and better, and then I'll never get the measles again. Luke told me that."

She nodded. "Thankfully, it's true. Although I did hear of a man who caught the measles more than once. The doctor said he was just prone to it. He never got as sick as you did, though."

"Well, I'm better now." He beamed her a smile. "And pretty soon I'll be well enough that we can have the wedding. Pastor Sedgwick said we could even have it right here."

Gloriana smiled. "We just might have to."

Chapter 23

Once JT had completely recovered from the measles, Luke and Gloriana decided it was in their best interests to invite Luke's father to supper. She made some of her best dishes, hoping to impress him. Before he arrived, she donned one of the gowns Luke had purchased for her at Christmastime. The navy-and-red plaid skirt had threads of gold running through the pattern. The bodice was gold to match those threads and trimmed with navy-blue cording and buttons. Gloriana thought it a very tasteful and modest design.

"You look really pretty, Glory," JT said, his eyes wide in wonder. "Like an angel."

"She does, doesn't she?" Luke had just finished changing the baby's diaper and carried her to the high chair. Sally squealed at the sight of Gloriana. "I think the baby agrees."

"You both look smart in your suits, as well. I don't know what your father will think of any of this, but I think we all clean up quite nice."

Luke laughed as he secured Sally in her chair. "Father won't care unless it somehow benefits him." A knock sounded, and Luke turned to answer the door. "That will be him now."

Gloriana stiffened and tried to draw in a deep breath. She wanted to relax and put her mind at ease. Luke had assured her that his father could do nothing legally to take Sally, but he had been so angry the last time they'd met that Gloriana feared he might try.

"Father, I'm glad you could make it for supper," Luke said, greeting the older man.

JT tucked himself against Gloriana. He clearly felt much as she did, and she put her arm around him. "It'll be all right," she whispered. It was as much for herself as for JT.

Mr. Carson glanced toward Gloriana and JT. He gave a curt nod. "I must say, the invitation was a surprise. You've hardly seen me while I've been in town."

"I'm afraid we've been quite busy. JT is just a couple of days out of quarantine," Luke replied. "Not only that, but my work with the railroad requires much of my time. We have an August deadline to see the line complete, and there have been a myriad of problems." Luke gestured to Gloriana and JT. "I know that you've met Gloriana and Sally, but this is JT—Jeremiah Thomas Womack. He has become a younger brother to me and has helped me better understand life along the lake."

JT smiled, but Gloriana could feel his rigid stance. He was still unsure of the elder Mr. Carson.

"Young Master Womack," Luke's father said, giving the boy a nod.

Gloriana excused herself and turned back to the stove while Luke encouraged his father to take a seat. She tried not to feel anger toward their visitor, but this man wanted to tear Sally from their family. He didn't value the love they had for her or the way they had bonded with her over these last months. He obviously didn't care and was used to buying whatever he wanted.

"I think you'd find some of the railroad work quite fascinating, Father. You should accompany me on one of my line inspections."

"Railroads have only ever interested me as they related to increasing my profits," his father said without emotion.

Gloriana brought a platter to the table. There was baked fish—a fresh catch brought to her by Captain Johnson—as well as creamed peas and potatoes. She had baked bread and rolls that morning and hoped that Mr. Carson could appreciate the effort.

"We're having fruitcake for dessert," JT declared as he took his seat at the table. "With fresh cream."

Gloriana grabbed the coffeepot and poured Luke and his father a cup. "Would you care for sugar or cream, Mr. Carson?"

"No. Thank you." He looked at the china cup as if surprised.

"The china was my mother's. A wedding gift. I've always loved the delicate flower pattern."

Gloriana recalled the first time she had seen her mother use the set. It was at an anniversary party for one of the old sea captains and his wife. They were celebrating fifty years of marriage. Quite a feat, considering the dangers of earning your living on the lake. Gloriana had declared them the prettiest dishes she'd ever seen. Her mother told her that one day they would be hers, and she hoped Gloriana would think of her whenever she used them.

Mr. Carson said nothing.

Gloriana brought a glass of milk for JT and tea for herself. Luke helped her into her chair and then claimed his own. "Let's pray."

They bowed their heads, and Luke offered grace. Gloriana couldn't keep her mind on the prayer, however. She was almost afraid that Mr. Carson would grab the baby and run while their eyes were closed. She was grateful that Luke kept the prayer short.

The food was served, and as they began to eat, JT shared about school. "A lot of children caught the measles. I was just one of the very first. Half of the people are gone from class. Mr. Nelson sends their schoolwork home to them just like he did with me. I think that's mean, 'cause when you're sick, you can't think about English and history."

"Perhaps he only wants them to have it for when they do feel better." Gloriana handed him the butter. "Would you pass this around, please?"

JT did so but wasn't yet ready to let the topic drop. "I think when you're sick, you shouldn't have to do any of that work. If you miss it, you miss it."

"Yes, but English is especially important to take in steps, JT," Luke replied. "History might be acceptable to move from era to era, but often you'll find that, too, has great emphasis placed on the foundation of what passed before." He took the butter and applied a generous amount to his fish and dinner roll.

"We raised our children to be silent if they joined the adults at the dinner table,"

Mr. Carson stated without bothering to meet anyone's gaze.

"We believe in letting JT speak his mind so long as he's polite and gives others a chance to talk as well. We enjoy his conversation," Luke replied. "And we believe it's a good time to catch up on his interests and activities."

"Those are topics to share with a nurse or nanny." This time the older man did meet Luke's gaze. "There are appropriate and inappropriate ways to raise a child."

"And you are suggesting our way is inappropriate. Perhaps for the house of a man focused on his own interests, that might well be the case." Luke turned to JT. "My brother and I all but lived in the nursery. We went for occasional outings with the nanny, but we were carefully kept hidden away, lest we embarrass our parents in front of others. We seldom saw our father."

"My papa used to do all sorts of things with me," JT said, smiling. "He taught me how to build and fix things. We were going to paint the house and cottage this year, and he showed me how we were going to do it and how to use a ladder."

"Perhaps you and I can do the painting together. The house definitely needs our care."

JT gave an enthusiastic nod. "We can

paint the shutters too. Papa wanted to paint them green."

"Sounds good."

Mr. Carson snorted. "Manual labor. My son, who was raised to rule over industry, has been relegated to the position of a common laborer." He dabbed his napkin to his lips. He'd hardly eaten anything.

"Father, hard work has never hurt anyone. It has expanded my skills and helped me better understand those who work for me. Surely that is knowledge worth obtaining."

His father leaned back in his chair. Gloriana thought he looked very tired, but she said nothing. She wasn't feeling overly kind toward this man who had already suggested her brother was unwelcome.

"I can't help but feel that when you understand the tasks required to work a job," Luke continued, "it betters your ability to deal with the workforce required to accomplish that job. After all, how can you properly manage men if you don't understand what you've asked of them?"

"That is precisely why I stay out of it and hire others to oversee. Honestly, Lucas, you have been raised and educated to stand far above others. You were never intended to be an overseer to anyone. I plan to speak to Jay Cooke upon my return. It's ridiculous for you to be here in the middle of nowhere. Come back to Philadelphia and work for me. Better still, I will turn over part of the Carson industry to you. You'll see for yourself that instructing others to do your bidding is the better way."

Luke's eyes narrowed, and Gloriana could see his father's words had piqued his anger. "Do not think to interfere in my vocation, Father. I have chosen the path I desire. I have no desire for you to speak with Mr. Cooke, and should you do so, it will most assuredly alter my respect for you."

Mr. Carson looked just as frustrated by his son's response as Luke had been at his suggestions. Furthermore, JT had grown silent as he watched his elders speak out against each other. Gloriana reached over and gave his hand a pat. JT looked at her for a moment, then refocused his attention on the food.

They all ate in silence for several minutes until Sally decided enough was enough. She had eaten the bits and pieces of food Gloriana had placed on her tray and now wanted more of a role in the evening's entertainment. She slapped her hands on the wooden tray of her chair and babbled loudly.

Mr. Carson seemed taken aback. He stopped his coffee midway to his lips and stared at the baby. Gloriana wondered if he'd ever before sat at a table with a baby.

"She seems to have liked the fish and bread," Luke declared with a grin.

"I'm certain she'll enjoy the creamed peas and potatoes even better." Gloriana finished mashing a portion, then scooped up a small amount on her spoon. "Here you are, little miss. Try these."

Sally opened her mouth for the offering. Her tongue worked over the food as she seemed to be considering whether it was acceptable or not. Soon enough she opened her mouth for more. Gloriana fed her another spoonful and laughed at the way part of it spilled back out. She quickly caught it with the spoon.

Mr. Carson turned to his son. "And you want this kind of spectacle at your dinner table?"

"Babies have no table manners, Father, but they will learn in time."

"And are best taught in the nursery."

"Not everyone has that luxury, Mr. Carson," Gloriana declared, immediately regretting her comment.

"But I do, and I can have Sally trained up in a proper fashion that befits her status."

"And what status would that be?" Luke looked him square in the eye. "She's the daughter of a kitchen maid and a fisherman who was disinherited by his father. I think we're doing just fine by her."

"I won't stand for this. I will not allow you to keep her here and make her some sort of commoner—a hoi polloi of lower-class refuse."

Luke set aside his napkin and got to his feet. "Perhaps this was a mistake. Gloriana, I am sorry for my father's rudeness."

Gloriana didn't know what to say. She was shocked by the older man's malice toward her and others like her.

Mr. Carson stood as well. "I speak only the truth. The sooner you recognize how blind you've become to the matter, the better for all of us. But especially . . . especially . . ." He swayed a bit and pulled at his collar.

"Mr. Carson, are you all right?" Gloriana jumped to her feet.

"Father?" Luke moved closer. "Father?"

Instead of a reply, however, Luke's father collapsed in a faint. Luke managed to keep him from falling to the ground.

Gloriana headed for the hall. "I'll turn down my father's bed. You can put him there."

Luke lifted his father and carried him to the bedroom. Gloriana helped settle him by arranging the blankets and pillows. She reached to loosen his necktie.

"What do you suppose is wrong with him?" she asked.

Luke shook his head and began unfastening the buttons on his father's waistcoat.

"I have no idea. I've never known him to be given to fits of fainting or anything else that would show weakness."

Gloriana unbuttoned the top of his shirt and gasped. The unmistakable rash seemed almost to glow against his hot skin. She looked at Luke. "He's sick. He's contracted measles, poor man."

"I'll send for the carriage and get him to the hospital."

"No, just send for the doctor. Let's find out how bad it is first and then decide what must be done."

"I'll go now." Luke headed for the door while Gloriana continued to undress the older man. "I won't be long."

She dug through one of her father's old trunks and pulled out a nightshirt. Carson was shorter than her father and smaller in the shoulders, but it wouldn't matter. She wrestled the older man out of his remaining clothes and into the nightshirt before pulling the covers around him. He gave a soft moan as she felt his forehead. He was burning up.

Luke was glad to find the doctor finishing his dinner when he arrived. He explained the situation, and the doctor willingly accompanied him back to Gloriana's house.

"We've returned," Luke said, pushing open the door without knocking first. "The doctor is here."

JT and the baby were still sitting at the table. JT was eating fruitcake and slipping an occasional piece to Sally.

"The baby probably shouldn't have fruitcake," Luke whispered to JT as they passed by on the way to the bedroom.

They found Gloriana sitting at his father's side, wiping his brow with a wet cloth. He marveled that she should even bother, given the way his father had treated her.

"Dr. Moore, this is my father, Martin Carson."

Luke's father opened his eyes. "I'm not sick. Just . . . tired. You needn't fuss." He closed his eyes. "Needn't fuss."

"I'll be the judge of that," Dr. Moore said, motioning Gloriana aside.

"I'll step outside so you can examine him," she said, heading for the door."

Luke followed her. "I'm touched you were willing to care for him. He's done nothing but stand against us. I wouldn't have blamed you if you'd thrown him out."

"He's sick. Perhaps that colored his reactions and responses to us."

Luke shook his head and heaved a sigh. "I'd like to be able to give him that excuse, but

I can't. My father is something of a pompous bully."

She put her hand on his arm. "I want to take care of him." This time she shook her head. "Not because I hold any love for him . . . but because I don't."

"I don't understand."

"I've been afraid of your father. I've been angry at your father. I've prayed he would leave and do so quickly. I've never had a kind thought for him. What kind of Christian am I, to feel so unkind toward another of God's creatures? What gives me the right? I'm ashamed of my thoughts."

Luke kissed the top of her head. "You are something else, Gloriana. I'm humbled by your words and I, too, am ashamed. I haven't honored my father as I should. I haven't even treated him as well as I might a complete stranger."

The doctor emerged from the bedroom. "It is measles, just as you thought. He's already congested, and I fear in his weakened state he will have a difficult time of it. Would you prefer I move him to the hospital?"

Gloriana looked to Luke. He smiled. "No. We'll take care of him here." He took out his wallet and handed over several large bills. "Would you please stop by daily to check on him?"

"I will." The doctor looked at Gloriana. "Since I presume most of his care will fall on you, are you familiar with what is needed to care for him?"

"My little brother just recovered from measles. I will simply extend the care to Mr. Carson."

The doctor nodded. "Let me know if you have any trouble."

Luke showed him out, then returned to find Gloriana once again mopping his father's brow. "I'll sit with him for the first watch. You go ahead and get some sleep."

"I'll get JT and the baby to bed first. JT won't like an early bedtime, but I'll explain it. Oh, Luke, we'll need another quarantine sign."

"I'll take care of it."

When she rose, he pulled her into his arms. "I suppose this means our wedding is once again delayed."

"Let's just get the pastor to stop by with his wife and be done with it," she replied, placing her head on his chest. "We're already managing through sickness and health."

Chapter 24

Gloriana bathed Mr. Carson in a vinegar solution and prayed for him as she did. She wasn't sure what to think of the situation. She wanted nothing to do with this angry, selfish man, but it was clear that God had called her to nurse him. Every time Luke suggested they send him to the hospital, Gloriana knew it wasn't what she was supposed to do.

Lord, I don't understand why You are directing me to take care of this man. He wants to ruin my family and already hates us.

She continued the gentle ministrations. He was very sick. Sicker than JT had been. The doctor said it was very hard on adults to endure the measles.

The old man began to cough, bringing Gloriana's attention back to what she needed to do. She covered him up so he wouldn't take a chill. He already had pneumonia, which was common with measles, but in his situation might very well be fatal.

Gloriana helped him sit up and pounded on his back with the flat of her hand as he coughed and moaned.

He waved her off, and Gloriana allowed him to ease back onto the propped-up pillows. "Why?" He gasped for air. "Why are . . . you . . . doing this?"

She looked at his swollen and reddened eyes. "I've asked myself that a few times." She wasn't sure, but it seemed there was a hint of a smile on the older man's lips.

"You . . . hate me."

She shook her head and helped Mr. Carson take a spoonful of honeyed tea. "I wanted to, but I don't hate you."

Another moan escaped as he closed his eyes. "I hate myself . . . sometimes." His voice was low and raspy.

She had no idea what to say and so said nothing. Instead, she focused on making sure she had plenty of willow bark tea and vinegar solution. She thought Mr. Carson had gone back to sleep, but when she glanced over, she found him watching her.

"You need to rest and keep your eyes closed as much as possible. The irritation can cause a great amount of pain. We want to avoid further damage."

He gave a weak cough. "Not sure it will matter."

"But it does. Luke just lost his brother, and it would be terrible to lose his father as well. I know that pain, and there is nothing like it."

"You were . . . very fond of your father . . . weren't you?"

Her mind flooded with memories. "I was. He was a very good father to us." She picked up the wet cloth and wrung it out. Once again, she began to wipe Mr. Carson's face and neck.

"I'm sorry. That he . . . died. Sorry too . . . for things I said."

She didn't know whether these were just the words of someone who thought himself about to die, or if the old man actually felt remorse. Either way, she would forgive him. She was determined she would forgive him.

"Tell me about him. About . . . your . . . life here."

"It was a good life."

"Seems it was . . . a hard one," Carson murmured.

"Sometimes. But we worked together, and that made everything better. When my mother and brother and sister were alive, we shared the workload. JT was too little to be of much help, but even he was taught early on to lend a hand. My father always provided financially, and Mama said it was our job to make a happy home for him." Gloriana smiled, remembering those days. "But that wasn't hard. We were just happy by nature of who we were."

"And your . . . father. Was he . . . happy?"

"Oh yes. Maybe even more than we were. He loved to be on the lake fishing. Scott did too. I don't know if he told you that. For both of them, the lake was in their blood. Some men have described it as a bond they just can't break. Papa used to say he could no more live without the lake than live without air."

"Yet . . . it killed him."

She nodded. "It did, as it has many a man and even a few women. Still, Papa knew the dangers, as did Mama. I don't think she ever rested easy until he was home from fishing. Each day when he left, she would pray for him, and she continued to pray throughout the day until he returned home, and then she'd pray again and thank God for his safe return."

"Sounds like . . . she prayed . . . a great deal."

"She did. She was very close to God and taught us to be close as well. Are you close to God, Mr. Carson?"

He shook his head. "I never . . . saw it as
. . . important. Didn't believe . . . in God."

"And now?" She put the cloth aside.

"I don't . . . don't know. Seems wrong."

She frowned. "What?"

"Seems wrong to . . . ignore God . . . only
to cry out . . . to Him at the end."

"Nonsense. It's never wrong to seek God.
He wants us to seek Him, and it doesn't matter
that you've waited a lifetime. The important
part is that you acknowledge Him—confess
Him as Lord. When you do it isn't nearly as
important as doing it.

"Now, you need to rest, and I need to see
to the baby. It's a wonder she hasn't caught
the measles. We've done what we could to
keep her away from the sick, but still it's a
miracle." Gloriana headed for the door. "In
a little bit I'll bring you some broth. You have
to keep up your strength, so just determine
here and now that you will eat what I bring."
She smiled. "I don't want to argue with you."

Leaving the older man to rest, Gloria
went to the stove and poured hot water into
the basin. Abigail had told her to wash thoroughly after she dealt with the sick person.
Gloriana had taken this to heart. If it kept
Sally from exposure to the disease, Gloriana
knew there wasn't much she wouldn't do.

Checking in on the baby, she found that

Sally had fallen asleep playing. She was surrounded by her little toys and hugged her blanket close. Sweet child. Gloriana moved most of the toys to the end of the bed except the cloth doll that had become Sally's favorite. This she left beside the baby and spread the blanket out to cover them both.

There was a stack of dirty diapers and bedding that needed Gloriana's attention, so she started the process. It would take all afternoon, but she would accomplish what she could. With the weather chilly but nice, she built a fire under the outdoor caldron and then began the process of filling it with water. Before long, she had the water hot enough and put in the soft soap she purchased from one of the local women. Next she put in the wash and began to stir it around and around. The action was second nature, and Gloriana found herself gazing down over the lake and thinking back to other times when she and her mother and Tabby had shared the chore together. How she missed those days. Mama had often told them stories about her parents, people Gloriana had never known.

Now JT and Sally were her only family. Well, there was Luke too. He had made it clear that they would always be a family. She shook her head and left the clothes to soak. They had decided they would marry as soon as possible, but it seemed every time they arranged it, something kept it from happening.

Now Luke's father was very sick. The doctor was afraid he might die. Mr. Carson was older and not in the best of physical condition. A sedentary life of luxury and rich food had done him no favors. Gloriana hated thinking that if he did die, they wouldn't have any more trouble from the old man. She hated feeling anger toward him and found it had abated somewhat with her responsibility to nurse him. But in the back of her mind, she couldn't help but remember that he wanted to take Sally away from her.

"Lord, please help me put my trust in You and not fear for the future. I know that You already know what will happen in that future, and I don't want to hate this man."

She filled the rinse tub with water and made certain the clotheslines were clean. She went back inside to check on Sally and Mr. Carson a couple of times, retrieving her clothespins on the last trip.

After seeing that all of the clothes were properly scrubbed, Gloriana rinsed them out and began to hang them on the line. She knew the day was getting away from her. She should have started the laundry that morning, but there just hadn't been time. Now, glancing to the west and south, it looked like it might rain. She shrugged it off and decided to hang the clothes anyway. If it rained, they'd just get an extra rinse.

She actually enjoyed hanging the clothes. She usually spent that time in deep prayer. Before Sally came, laundry day was always on Monday. Mama had done it that way, and Gloriana just naturally kept the schedule. However, she remembered when JT had been young that there were often extra washes of baby clothes, bedding, and diapers throughout the week. Babies just weren't all that much for laundry schedules.

Once all of the laundry was finally hanging in neat rows, Gloriana made sure the fire was out and headed back inside. Sally was beginning to fuss. No doubt she was hungry. Before she went to see about the baby, however, Gloriana checked on Mr. Carson.

She went to his bedside and felt his head. It seemed a little cooler, but she couldn't be sure. Her action, however, woke him. He opened his eyes, then frowned. He drew his hand up and began to rub at his right eye.

"I told you that you mustn't rub your eyes," Gloriana said. "You can damage them."

He shook his head. "I think . . . it's too late." He raised his head and turned it from side to side. "I can't see."

When JT arrived home from school, Gloriana immediately sent him for the doctor. Within the hour, Dr. Moore was examining Mr. Carson while Gloriana nervously paced the living room with baby Sally in her arms. She didn't know whether to send for Luke or just wait until the doctor rendered his verdict. She knew measles often caused blindness but also that it might only be temporary. She prayed fervently that this might be the case.

When the doctor came from the bedroom, Gloriana motioned JT to go sit with the old man. She wasn't sure what the doctor might say, and she didn't want the boy upset any more than he had to be.

"Just go and tell him about your day at school," she told JT.

He nodded and hurried down the hall.

Gloriana went to the doctor. "Well?"

"The blindness is caused by the measles, as you probably already surmised," the doctor replied.

"Is it permanent?"

He put something in his black bag and closed it. "There's no way of telling. I've seen people recover from it, but others don't. Only time will tell. You can wash the eyes in a boric acid solution. You can get the boric acid powder at the apothecary. Mix a quarter teaspoon to one pint of hot water, then put it in a sterile canning jar and store it in a dark place. After it cools, you can use it. Shake it well and then pour a small amount to flush the eyes. Be very gentle so as not to cause more harm. Just pat the eyes dry. Do not rub—that will only cause pain and possibly damage the eyes."

"But there's no way to tell if he'll regain his vision?"

"Not at this point. We'll watch him over the next week or two and see what happens."

Baby Sally reached for Gloriana's hair, babbling as if she had something important to add to the conversation. The doctor smiled.

"I'm glad she seems to be immune to the measles. Of course, when she's older, that may well change. But when they're this little, it's so hard on them. Hard on the elderly and the very young." He took up his bag. "Just send for me if anything else happens. Oh, and I wanted to tell you that his lungs sound better."

"Well, at least that's something good." Gloriana pulled Sally's hand from her hair. "Thank you for coming so quickly."

"If you like, I could stop by Luke's office and tell him what's happened. I could also ask him to pick up the boric acid."

"That would be wonderful. Thank you. I know you've been busy, and it's kind of you to take the time to do that."

He smiled. "It's no trouble."

She saw the doctor out and then tied Sally in her high chair. She gave her a couple of wooden spoons to play with then laid out some milk and cookies for JT. After this, she headed to her father's room. JT was talking and Luke's father was sitting up—a captive audience. She paused at the door to hear what they were discussing.

"So you see why you have to get well. I know I'm not your blood relative, but I would like you to be my grandfather. I don't have any other."

Gloriana was stunned by this request. She wondered what Mr. Carson would make of all this. She didn't have to wait long.

"You have all . . . been very kind to me when I didn't deserve it." He stopped to cough. "I have always . . . wanted a grandson." He paused to catch his breath. "I think I should like very much . . . to be your grandfather."

JT clapped his hands. "We'll have a lot of fun. I know you live far away, but you could move here. That way you could see me and Sally all the time. I could show you how to fish. My papa taught me."

"I've never fished before."

He looked away from JT, but Gloriana knew he couldn't see anything. She wondered if the doctor had told him the same thing he'd just shared with her. Maybe he felt Mr. Carson was in too fragile a state and had said very little.

"Is it scary that you can't see?" Gloriana heard her brother ask.

The older man paused for a few moments before answering. "It is." He coughed and coughed, and JT patted his hand.

When the spasm subsided, JT spoke again. "You don't have to worry about anything. We'll take good care of you. That's how it goes when you're family."

Gloriana wasn't sure if it was due to the coughing or JT's words, but there were tears in the older man's eyes.

"JT, thank you for staying with Mr. Carson."

"Sure, Glory. I asked him to be my grandfather and he said yes. Isn't that great?" He came to stand in front of her. "I've got a real grandfather now."

Gloriana smiled. "I think he will be a very good one." It amazed her that only days earlier she had hated this man. Now she just felt sympathy for him . . . and perhaps a little compassion. "You go get your homework done. I left you milk and cookies on the table. Please keep an eye on Sally for a little while as I need to tend to Mr. Carson."

"Grandfather Carson."

Gloriana smiled. "Grandfather Carson."

JT left and she approached the bed, wondering what Luke's father truly thought of all this. "The doctor said we will need to rinse your eyes in boric acid. He's going to stop and let Luke know about your condition, and Luke will bring boric acid home from the apothecary."

Carson nodded. "Your brother is a good boy."

"Yes, he is. I hope he didn't bother you."

"No. I enjoyed our talk."

"I need to wipe you down. You're still feverish. That may well be why you can't see." She opened his shirt and helped him out of it. Carson offered her no resistance.

"I'm sure you both miss your father," he said.

His remark surprised her. He had been quite ugly in his comments about her father prior to this. She held her tongue and asked God for a merciful heart.

"We do," she finally said. "We miss him very much."

"I apologize . . . for any of my comments that suggested . . . he was to blame for the death of my son." He coughed again and seemed a little less raspy.

"Apology accepted." She said nothing more, not knowing what else to say.

She finished wiping his chest and arms, then helped him sit up straight and wiped his back. This brought on spasms of coughing, so Gloriana gave him some honeyed tea.

"The doctor said your lungs are clearer. This coughing is good for getting the mucus out, but I know it also wears you out. Sitting up will also help. When you feel well enough, I'll bring in a chair where you can sit and rest while I make your bed."

A rumble of thunder sounded. The storm was moving in, just as Gloriana had predicted.

"Why are you doing all of this?" Carson asked.

Gloriana hadn't expected this question. "You're sick and you need to be tended."

"But there was money aplenty to have someone else play nursemaid. You could have sent me to the hospital."

"Hospitals are places where people go to die." She shook her head and helped him back into his shirt. "I have some willow bark tea that you need to drink. It will also help bring down the fever."

Carson reached out, fumbling for her. Gloriana frowned and took his hand.

"What is it?"

"I gave you no reason to help me, and yet you do."

"God laid it on my heart. I can hardly marry Luke and then stand by and let his father die."

"I don't deserve . . . your mercy."

Gloriana frowned again. "I have to admit I didn't understand why anyone would want to tear a family apart. When I heard you had come, I was afraid. I love Sally and couldn't bear it if anything happened to her."

"I can see that now." He chuckled and started to cough again. When it passed, he shook his head. "Maybe I had to be blind to see."

"You said you never believed in God, Mr. Carson."

"Not much, anyway. Why do you ask?"

"God has gotten me through all of this. JT's sickness, my father's and Scott's deaths, Sally's death and the baby's birth, and now you being here. When the boat went down and Papa and Scott died, I was so angry at God. I felt He was cruel. Then Sally went into labor and had the baby but could summon no will to live. That convinced me all the more that God didn't care. But He did. Sometimes His way of doing things seems so foreign to me. It makes no sense, and I have to remind myself that I'm not God. I don't have to understand. I have only to trust. That's where you are right now. We neither one understand why you have gotten sick, much less become blind. Nor why it had to involve me. But as I have cared for you in your sickness, my heart has softened. I no longer feel hatred or anger toward you. I'm no longer afraid. I feel God's presence as I act in mercy. I know that I am doing His will."

"I've never met anyone like you. I'm glad my son has found such a woman to wed."

"Even though I'm not rich? Or a part of society? I'm just a fisherman's daughter."

"No, you're so much more."

"So was Sally." Gloriana hadn't meant to speak the words aloud, but now that she had, there was no taking them back.

"Yes. She was a much better woman than I gave her credit for. I am deeply ashamed of how I acted. Deeply ashamed."

Gloriana adjusted his pillows, then helped him lie back. "Scott still loved you. He told me once that when you had time to sort through everything, he knew you would take him back. He never cared about the money— just about you."

Tears came again to his eyes. "My son. My dear son."

Gloriana squeezed his shoulder. "He always loved you, and he always knew that in your own way, you loved him. The loss is tremendous, but Scott loved Jesus, and Sally did too. You will see them in heaven one day if you love Him as well."

The routes were off by as much as twenty to thirty yards in places. Luke had finally managed to locate an original map and could now see exactly where the route should have been laid. He wasn't sure what could be done now except for tearing up the track and re-routing it to the tune of millions of dollars.

Worse still, the evidence kept pointing back to one person. Theodore Sedgwick—his secretary. Luke was sick at heart. How could this be? Why would Sedgwick do such a thing? He was even now returning from St. Paul. He always seemed so helpful—so willing to go the extra mile. Why would he seek to destroy the much-needed and anticipated railroad?

Luke glanced at the clock. Sedgwick should be back by six. He was taking the boat from Fond du Lac, and they were generally on time. Luke wondered if he should be at the dock to meet him or just wait until morning to confront him. A night's sleep might do them both a lot of good.

He heard the front door open and went

to see who had come. The doctor stood just inside, rain dripping from his hat and coat. Luke extended his hand. "I didn't expect to see you today. Is everything all right?"

The doctor was rather grim-faced. "I'm afraid not. Your fiancée sent for me. Your father is blind."

"Blind?" Luke was sure he'd heard wrong. "Did you say he's blind?"

"Yes. Measles often causes blindness. Sometimes it's permanent, and sometimes it's temporary."

"Which is it this time?"

"I don't know. That's the trouble. It might last a few days or even weeks, and then the vision returns, or it could be permanent. I'm sorry. I told Miss Womack that I would instruct you to bring home boric acid powder. You can get it at the apothecary. She knows how to mix it and use it."

"Of course. I'll go right now." It definitely answered the question of confronting Theodore tonight. "Is there anything else I should know?"

The doctor nodded. "His lungs are clearer and his temperature is lower. I believe he's come through the worst of it."

"I would say being blind is the worst of it." Luke couldn't imagine his father bearing blindness with any good grace.

"Well, as I said, it could be just a few days, or it might be permanent. We can only leave it in the hands of God. Soon enough we'll know the truth."

Luke sat by his father's bedside and watched him sleep. Gloriana had told him about JT seeking to form a bond with Luke's father and of his acceptance of the role of grandfather. She had also told him of their discussion and his father's regret for how he'd acted.

"Who's there?" his father asked.

"It's me, Luke. The doctor told me about your eyes, and I came right home. I'm sorry you're having to go through this, Father."

His father's eyes were open, but Luke knew he saw nothing. How awful it must be. How terrible to be confined inside the darkness when he had once known light and sight. Luke felt overwhelmed with grief.

"Sometimes God has to do . . . something drastic . . . to get a man's attention. Especially a man as stubborn as I am," his father replied. His voice was much stronger than it had been yesterday.

"And does God have your attention now?"

Father chuckled and began to cough. Once he regained control, he shook his head.

"Sorry about that. Gloriana tells me it's good because . . . I'm clearing my lungs." He began to cough again, and this time it was less severe. "But to answer your question, yes. God has my attention now. There's little else for me to do but contemplate Him and my life."

"The doctor said this isn't necessarily permanent."

"I know." His father shifted his weight in the bed. "But there's also the possibility that it is. I have to accept that I might never see again. That isn't easy to grasp."

"No. I can't imagine it is, but know that you will be cared for."

"By you?"

"Me, Gloriana, JT, and one day, Sally." Luke took his father's hand. "We won't give you over to strangers."

Father smiled at this. "Even though I deserve it?"

Luke couldn't help but smile in return. "That's what grace is all about—not getting what we deserve. Gloriana told me when I came home that if you needed to remain with us for the rest of your life, she was all right with that."

"She's a remarkable woman. You really should marry her."

Luke laughed. "You wouldn't believe how many times I've tried to do just that."

His father smiled. "I've never known you to be stopped from doing what you set your mind to."

"No. That's true enough."

"You sound tired, wearier than I've ever heard you sound. Then again, maybe I just wasn't listening. Maybe my hearing will improve now that I have no vision."

Luke saw no reason to worry his father with his concerns about the railroad. "I guess I'm extra tired and worried for you. I want to make sure you know that despite the way things started out between us when you arrived, that is all past us. I hold no grudge against you. You will have the best of care. We will see you through this."

His father nodded. "I know. JT told me that's what families do."

Luke smiled. "He's a very clever boy."

"Indeed, he is. I'm going to look forward to being his grandfather."

Chapter 25

Theodore felt more than a little anxious about reporting for work after his trip to St. Paul. He knew the word had already been telegraphed to Luke that the route was off in more places than they'd originally figured. It was all one section of the route, but Theo had made certain that the variance was significant. Well, to be honest, it was the engineer's new route that changed things, but no one would ever know that. Everything had been signed in Lucas Carson's name, even if it had been forged.

He fumbled for his key. He was already celebrating Lucas Carson's demise. When Jay Cooke learned it was his fault that the rail route was off, surely Luke would be fired and his good name ruined. The idea had excited

Theodore so much that he'd hardly been able to sleep.

As he moved to unlock the door, he found it was already unlocked. When he came inside, he could hear voices from Luke's office. He crept closer.

"Who could have known what this would do? I'd like to think the numbers were changed for the purpose of improving the line, but my gut tells me otherwise."

Theo wasn't sure who was talking, but then Luke responded. "It's actually a miracle. Definitely God's blessing. The engineer said the new route was far more stable. We might have had only a few runs before the rails broke had we put the track in the original area. Who could have known about that bedrock? It's made for the best of foundations and will keep the line solid for years to come."

Theodore frowned. What were they talking about? Surely not the new route his engineer had helped figure out. He continued to listen.

"Well, whoever was responsible has saved Jay Cooke millions," the other man replied. "You're sure to be rewarded."

Theodore went to his desk and sat down without even bothering to remove his hat and coat. He had a sinking feeling. From what he could surmise, the new route had not caused the railroad the harm he'd intended, but rather made the line better. This couldn't be. He got up again and headed for the door. He needed to speak to the engineer. He needed to understand what was going on.

~∞~

Luke reread the telegram from Jay Cooke. His employer was more than a little pleased at the changes to the route and all the money it had saved them in the long run. He praised Luke for taking the initiative to get another engineer's opinion. But Luke couldn't take the credit and began to pen a personal letter to Cooke.

> *I cannot take credit for this. In truth, I believe it was meant to harm us, but God took what was meant for evil and used it for good. I have my suspicions as to who was responsible but haven't yet collected the proof. I assure you that I am seeking the truth and will share this news with you as soon as I have it.*

He paused and put the pen aside. If Theodore was to blame as he suspected, Luke was clueless as to why. He had been a good secretary—attentive to every detail. Obviously, now Luke could surmise that that attention was for his own benefit.

"Luke, are you in?"

It was Archie. "Sure, come on back."

Archie came into Luke's office with another man on his heels. "This is Homer Sanders. He's a retired railroad route engineer from back east."

Luke stood and extended his hand. "Mr. Sanders."

"Pleasure to meet you, Mr. Carson. Archie tells me you've been looking for me."

Looking back at Archie, Luke shrugged. "Have I?"

Archie nodded. "You have. This is the man who planned out the second route. He lives around Fond du Lac and knows it and the area to the south quite well. That's how he knew where the solid bedrock lay and which areas were more prone to flooding."

"Well, then it is indeed a pleasure to meet you, Mr. Sanders, but I am curious as to how we came to be in your debt. I know I didn't hire you."

"Oh, but you did. The man told me that Lucas Carson was extending me employment to reassess the route. He made sure I knew your name."

"I think you'd both better sit down and explain everything." Luke took his seat, and

Archie pulled up a chair. Sanders did like-wise.

"We met at one of the local taverns. I was several beers ahead of him, but we enjoyed some conversation as the beer put us at ease." Sanders grinned. "I don't think the poor man was used to alcohol, because when he began to mention what was needed, he had his words and goals pretty mixed up. At one point he said you wanted a route that would fail. I'm pretty sure he meant *wouldn't* fail."

"And this man, did he have a name?"

"Sedgwick. Said he was your secretary, but that we were to keep this mission a secret. Said it would be a problem if the railroad men found out, because they thought their route was better. But I could see it wasn't. They didn't check with folks who'd lived in that area for a long time. I grew up there as a boy. Besides that, I know just by looking at land where you can get some bedrock and stability. It's a gift I have, and it's allowed me to lay some of the best railroads around."

"And Mr. Sedgwick told you that I had ordered this new route?"

"Yes, sir."

After listening to Sanders for the next twenty minutes, Luke finally had a clearer picture in his mind. Theodore Sedgwick had approached the older man and hired him on

Luke's behalf. He told Sanders that there was grave concern about the line, and Sanders agreed to look over the route. Sedgwick wasn't as drunk as the man thought, however, because Luke was certain Theodore had meant for the line to fail. Thank God Sanders believed otherwise.

"You've saved the railroad millions of dollars, and I will see that you receive an ample reward." Luke got to his feet. "I've also got a job proposition for you, Sanders. I'm overseeing the Northern Pacific start-up. We're having a devil of a time finding decent ground for this railroad as well. Maybe you could help us out?"

"Well, I am retired. I don't know that my wife would appreciate me taking on another job. She was happy with the money from the last job, but I don't know about another."

"I promise to make it more than worth your while. Name your price."

"Let me talk to the missus, and I'll get back to you." Sanders grinned. "I like the idea of naming my price."

Luke turned to Archie. "I appreciate you bringing Mr. Sanders to meet with me, Archie. You deserve a bonus as well."

"Just happy to see that we've got a solid line, Boss. I'm delighted not to have to dig up all that track again and start fresh."

"You and me both."

Luke heard the front door open. Hopefully that would be Sedgwick and he could confront him with what he'd done. Maybe he hadn't done it for a bad reason. Maybe he remembered the areas that often flooded from his childhood and had worried the line was in jeopardy.

They made their way into the outer office as Sedgwick was hanging up his coat and hat. When he turned and saw Sanders, however, his face paled, and a look of guilt washed over him. When his gaze met Luke's, Luke knew for certain that Sedgwick had meant the deed only for harm.

"Mr. Sedgwick, I believe you know Mr. Sanders and, of course, Archie."

"Ah . . . yes. Good day, gentlemen."

"Thank you again, gentlemen." Luke walked Archie and Sanders to the door. "I'll be in touch, Mr. Sanders."

"I'll speak to my wife and let you know what she says."

Luke laughed. "Maybe I should be offering her something as well."

Sanders chuckled. "She has her eye on a new icebox."

"Well, tell her it's hers if she'll let you go back to work," Luke promised, laughing.

The men left, and Luke sobered and

turned to face Sedgwick. "I think we should talk."

He walked to his office and sat at his desk. For a moment he wondered if Theodore would join him, but finally the secretary appeared. He was still quite pale.

"Please have a seat."

Sedgwick did as instructed. He gripped his knees and kept his head slightly bowed.

"Do you know why I've asked you to come for this talk?"

"I believe I do." Theodore still refused to look up. Instead he began twisting at his pant legs and rocking ever so slightly back and forth.

"Do I understand correctly that you are the one responsible for changing the numbers on the engineer's plans for the route from Forest Lake to Fond du Lac?"

Sedgwick's breathing quickened. "It did no harm."

Luke nodded, though his secretary still would not look him in the eye. "Perhaps not, but that wasn't your original plan. Was it? You wanted to do harm."

When Sedgwick raised his face, Luke was shocked at his contorted expression. "You killed my dearest friend, and you talk to me of harm?"

Luke's eyes narrowed. "I killed your

dearest friend? Who was this person? Was it someone in the war?"

Theodore jumped up, knocking the chair over backward. "You never even cared about what you did." He paced back and forth. "He hadn't hurt anyone, and yet you saw to it that he was imprisoned."

"Who are you talking about?"

"Rafael Clarington."

Luke shook his head as he scrambled to remember the name. Who was this man?

"You don't even remember him! That's how much it meant to you. He was noth-ing—no one. You didn't care that he wasn't able to endure the hardship of prison. He was an old man, and you killed him as surely as if you had put a gun to his head." Sedgwick's voice raised to a screeching cry. "And I will make you pay. I will. You and your father. I will see you both pay."

He pulled a gun from his pocket.

Luke had never expected such action from this seemingly mild-mannered man. He held up his hands. "Please, Theodore. Tell me more. I want to understand."

"He wants to understand. He doesn't know who you are, Rafael. He doesn't re-member." Sedgwick continued to pace and wave the revolver around. "How can he not remember?" He stopped and turned to glare at Luke. "The bank. Your father's bank in Philadelphia. Rafael and I had found the perfect way to take money from you, and for the longest time no one knew. But you figured it out when no one else could even see it. You, a mere boy."

The memories came rushing back. Luke had been working at his father's bank before going to college. He had busied himself by doing an audit of the books and found a discrepancy. It had been so innocuous that no one else had noticed it. Luke had pointed it out, and after detailing his search, they realized that thousands upon thousands of dollars were involved.

"Rafael Clarington." Luke remembered the old man. He'd worked for his father's bank for years in the audit department. The perfect place to hide his plan. But Luke hadn't realized Theodore had worked at the bank as well, much less been involved. Clarington had always sworn he acted alone.

"Yes." Sedgwick raised the gun. "You put him in jail."

"I'm sorry. He broke the law."

"He was a good man," Sedgwick retorted. "He was good to me. No one was ever good to me but him."

"Theodore, put down that gun," a new voice boomed.

Luke's gaze darted to the door.

Pastor Sedgwick stood in the entryway, looking aghast. He moved into the office. "You heard me. Put down that gun."

Theodore shook his head. "You don't understand. You never understood. You never cared."

"Of course I cared." Pastor Sedgwick kept moving steadily toward the desk. "If I hadn't cared so much, I would never have let you get away with the money you stole when you were younger." He looked at Luke. "One of the local merchants hired Theodore just out of school. He was to be a clerk and keep the books. Unfortunately, he took some of the money for himself."

"The man was rich," Theodore said, seeming happy to change topics. "He had more than he needed."

"Which was probably the only reason he was willing not to press charges so long as you paid him back."

Theodore laughed. "So long as *you* paid him back."

"Yes, that's true. I paid him from my meager savings and salary." Theodore's father lowered his head. "I thought I was helping, but instead you learned nothing."

"I learned to be more careful," Theodore replied in a snide tone. "So careful, in fact, that no one knew I was helping Rafael." His expression grew sad, and he looked down at the gun. "Rafael was good to me. He knew my pain. He knew, and he helped me. He was a much better father to me than you!" The anger was back. He glared at his father. "You should die with Carson. You both are the reason for my suffering."

By now Pastor Sedgwick had backed against the desk, positioning himself between Luke and Theodore. "I won't let you hurt Luke. He's been good to you."

"I tried to get rid of him, but it didn't work. Nothing works. He seems to have all the luck. All of it. He's stolen it. He's robbed me."

Pastor Sedgwick shook his head. "That's not true and you know it. Now put down the gun."

Theodore began to laugh. He shook the gun at his father. "I will kill you too. You deserve to die. You always had your rules. You were never happy with me. God is not happy with me." He pulled back the hammer. "I hate you both."

"Theo, your father isn't to blame for any of this," Luke said, no longer able to remain silent. "He's your father. If you kill him, it will hurt your mother."

"Mother?" Theodore shook his head

and lowered the gun a bit. "Mother is good. Mother wasn't cruel."

"Then you don't want to hurt her."

The words seemed to make him hesitate. Theodore shook his head over and over and began to pace again.

"Why don't you go ask your mother what you should do?" Luke suggested. "She's always loved you. She'll give you good counsel."

"That's right, Theo," Pastor Sedgwick declared. "She will give you wise counsel."

Theodore moved toward the door, then stopped. "No. I know what to do. I know. Rafael told me. I know."

He turned from the door and stood transfixed. Pastor Sedgwick moved toward him, doing his best to keep between Luke and Theo.

Without warning, the door to the outer office opened. Archie called out, "Luke, I'm back."

Pastor Sedgwick flew across the few short feet and tackled his son. The revolver went flying, causing a shot to fire. Luke hurried to help the pastor as Theodore began screaming. Archie was soon there to lend a hand as well.

"Is everyone all right?" Luke took Theodore in hand while the pastor got to his feet.

"I'm fine," Pastor Sedgwick said. He

looked to where Archie was nodding. "Would you go get the police?"

⁓

"Are you certain you're both all right?" Gloriana asked after Luke and the pastor had related their story.

"We're just fine. Fine enough to finally have a wedding," Pastor Sedgwick answered, putting his arm around his wife. The sorrow in their eyes was clear, however.

"We could get someone else to perform the ceremony. I don't want this to put an extra burden on you."

"Nonsense," Mrs. Sedgwick said, lifting her chin a bit. "Theodore has long been a thorn in our side. We will go on loving him, but we cannot take on his sins or bear his consequences for him. Believe me when I say that we have spent a good many years mourning for our child. It's not changed a thing. We will let him face his consequences and press forward with our own lives."

"Yes." Pastor Sedgwick nodded. "Just as we should have done when the trouble first started. I suppose we were slow to learn."

"You wanted to have hope." Gloriana glanced up at Luke. "Everyone needs hope."

"Well, we plan to do what we can to get him the help he needs," Pastor Sedgwick assured them, "but for now, we have a wedding to perform."

Gloriana smiled and looked to Luke for confirmation. He nodded. "Let's not put it off a moment longer."

JT started clapping, which caused Sally to do likewise. Jack danced around him, knowing that something big was about to happen. He gave several yips of approval.

"Grandfather!" JT yelled, scurrying down the hall with Jack at his heels. "Grandfather, we're getting married."

"We'd probably best conduct the ceremony in the sickroom. Since my father is here, he might as well be a part of this quaint affair." Luke smiled and put his arm around Gloriana and the baby.

"We'll need to put Sally in her room. I can't risk her getting sick now." Gloriana smiled and shifted Sally to her left hip. "Although I would love for her to be a part of the wedding."

Mrs. Sedgwick reached for the baby. "Why don't I hold her just outside the room? That way I can bear witness, and Sally can be a part of everything without getting too close."

Gloriana handed the baby over. "I think that's the perfect solution."

"Maybe we can have another ceremony

once everyone is healthy and everyone can be there," Luke said. "You could invite the entire town."

"No. This ceremony is more than enough. I've never needed a big wedding." Gloriana looked up into Luke's eyes. "I just needed the right man."

Epilogue

August 1, 1870

"There's a lot of people here, given that it's nearly eleven thirty at night." Gloriana suppressed a yawn.

Earlier that evening, at eleven minutes past eight, the final stake had been driven into the track and the Lake Superior and Mississippi Railroad was finished. Luke, his father, and JT had attended the event, but Gloriana, knowing she'd be up late for the celebration, had decided to stay home with Sally.

Now, standing in the night with a great many other people, Gloriana admired her husband. He'd worked hard to see this route completed despite the problems they'd had with weather, the town across the bay, and, of course, Theodore Sedgwick's interference.

"Are you excited, Glory?" JT asked, dancing circles around her and the baby.

The first train to travel the completed line had left St. Paul at seven that morning and was due in momentarily, and the atmosphere was festive.

"Everyone's excited about the train." Gloriana laughed, and Sally did likewise, seeming quite content to be out in the middle of the night. "This is definitely a grand celebration. It seems like they could have timed it for daytime, though."

"People were too excited to wait," Luke replied.

"I agree with your beautiful wife," Martin Carson declared. "I would have waited for the next day."

"I didn't get a say in that part. Besides, this is history in the making." Luke shook his head, marveling at the moment. "And we're a part of it."

A blast from the train sounded, and those who'd gathered to celebrate cheered in response. The engineer sent another blast and then a third.

The evening was pleasant, but the breeze and dampness of the air made it chilly. Gloriana wrapped the blanket a little tighter around Sally, who wasn't sure what to think of the distant train whistle.

"This is the best thing we've gotten to do all summer," JT said, grabbing his grandfather's hand. "Aren't you excited, even if it is late?"

"I am. Especially now that I can actually see what's happening."

Gloriana was so glad and grateful to God that Luke's father could be here to witness the event. He was blind for over three months, and then little by little his vision returned. The doctor had feared he might remain blind forever and counted it a miracle. One thing that the blindness had necessitated, however, was that Martin Carson needed round-the-clock care, so he had remained in Duluth with Gloriana and Luke. Luke had worried at first that it would be a bad idea, but it turned out just fine. They moved to the new house up on the hill, and his father slowly adjusted. Gloriana had come up with an idea for helping her father-in-law move around the house by using a knotted rope strung from room to room. She had designed a series of knots in each line of rope so that he could find his way around and know by the number of knots which room he was in. After all, he was not one to lie about. He had picked up the system in quick order and before long was moving about the house with the rest of the family.

"I wish Jack could be here," JT said, still dancing circles around the family. "He would love trains."

"He would probably get run over or hurt. The trains are very dangerous," Luke warned. "Many a man has challenged them only to die."

Gloriana hoped her brother would heed the warning and not let his curiosity lead him into danger. "Luke knows what he's talking about, JT. Please heed his words."

"There it is!" someone in the crowd yelled.

As the train came into town, a railroad worker stood on either side of the engine, waving a lantern. The crowd began cheering so loudly that it startled Sally, and she tightened her grip on Gloriana.

Locomotive engine number eight pulled into the LS&M Railroad depot and came to a halt, lining up its baggage and two passenger cars with the platform. The engineer gave three short blasts in welcome. Sally didn't care for the noise and tucked her face against Gloriana's neck.

"It's all right, Sally," JT said, reaching up to pat her back. "It's just a train. You'll have to get used to it, 'cause there's going to be a whole lot more. Luke is going to build more and more railroads."

Gloriana laughed. "Well, not all by himself. He's going to be too busy taking care of our family. After all, we're going to have another member come February."

Luke looked at her and smiled. "I'm so delighted about the baby, I can hardly wait all those months."

Martin Carson nodded. "Time does seem to drag when you're waiting for something good to happen."

"Well, you'll be busy finishing your move here." Gloriana patted Sally's back to calm her. "I'm glad you decided to relocate, Father Carson. It's such a blessing for the children to have their grandfather nearby."

"And I'm glad to have my father here."

Gloriana knew Luke couldn't have said those words four months ago, but his father had changed after enduring the measles and blindness. Her father-in-law had told her how their kindness to him had been humbling. The fact that they took tender care of him throughout his sickness had shown him the ugliness in his heart, and one day when he was still blind and uncertain about the future, Luke had led him in prayer to confess Jesus as his Lord. Gloriana couldn't have been happier. Well, not unless her own family could be with them again.

Someday she would see them again in heaven, of this she was certain.

Passengers began to disembark the train. Gloriana knew there were several important railroad dignitaries on board and it would be her husband's job to greet them. Luke and his father made their way to the first group of men while she and the children held back.

Gloriana heard his introduction. "I'm Lucas Carson, Mr. Cooke's associate. I'm here to welcome you to Duluth."

One man extended his hand. "So you're the brilliant man who changed my original route. William Wallace Hungerford, chief engineer and superintendent."

They shook hands, and Luke smiled. "Good to have you here. This is my father, Martin Carson."

"I'm pleased to meet you both, but especially you," Hungerford said, turning back to Luke. "You saved this railroad millions, and we aren't likely to forget that."

"Yes, well, we can discuss that at a later time. For now, welcome to Duluth. Is President Banning with you?"

"No, he'll arrive tomorrow. In the meantime, let me introduce you around."

Gloriana watched as Luke met each of the important dignitaries and exchanged pleasantries before the men were surrounded by the mayor and Duluth's key officials. Luke waved her over, and she and JT joined the group.

"I'd like to introduce my wife and her little brother. Gloriana, this is Mr. Hungerford, the chief engineer and superintendent of the line."

"Mrs. Carson, it is a pleasure," he said, giving her a bow. "And what a beautiful little girl. She looks a lot like her mother."

Gloriana didn't correct him. Others had commented on Sally looking like her, even though they knew the two weren't related.

Sally burrowed her face into the neck of Gloriana's jacket. "I'm afraid she's shy."

"I was also shy when I was a boy." Hungerford smiled and shook hands with JT. "It's nice to meet you as well. Perhaps you'll one day work for our railroad."

JT shrugged. "I don't know. Maybe." They all laughed at this.

Luke finished introducing the men and then stepped aside. Gloriana could see that Mr. Munger had already commanded Hungerford's attention.

"Isn't that something?" Pastor Johnson declared as he joined them. Johnson had taken over the church when Pastor Sedgwick and his wife decided to move east with Theodore. There was a great hospital in Boston that might help their son, and they wanted to see that he had what he needed. Everyone missed them, but Pastor Johnson and his wife had ably led the congregation through the transition.

"It certainly is," Luke agreed. "This is going to change everything."

Gloriana had heard Luke mention this before. He had filled her head with stories of towns that tripled in size within a year of getting a railroad. She wondered if that would be the case for Duluth. Already there were a great many more people living here. She'd had no trouble renting the larger house to a family and the cottage to a father and son who fished. The money was making a nice nest egg for JT, should he desire to go to college.

There were two short speeches, with the promise of more on the morrow. It wasn't long before the crowd dispersed, much to Gloriana's relief. The railroad officials were taken to the Clark House. By the time Luke had the family loaded and headed home, JT was asleep with his head on Martin Carson's lap, and baby Sally slept in Gloriana's arms.

At home, Luke bid his father good night

and then carried JT upstairs to bed while Gloriana followed with Sally. Once the baby was tucked into bed, Gloriana made her way through the adjoining door to their grand bedroom. Never in her life had she had such finery, but Luke had insisted she was worthy of such a house and room.

"Finally, the day is done," Luke said, coming into their room.

"Seems like everyone was pleased." Gloriana began to pull the pins from her hair. "I'm sure tomorrow will be more of the same. I know your father is certainly proud of you, and I am too."

Luke just leaned against the closed bedroom door and watched her. She could feel his gaze follow her as she readied herself for bed. She had scarcely known Luke even a year, and yet she couldn't imagine her life without him.

She finished with the pins and carefully began to braid her curls into order. "I never figured so many people would turn out that late at night."

"Well, it's not every day you get your first train."

"I suppose now they'll focus on the canal, while you busy yourself with the Northern Pacific."

"About that . . ." Luke came over to her.

"Would you mind terribly if I didn't work with the Northern Pacific?"

She tied a ribbon on her braid, then turned to face her husband. "Jay Cooke would mind terribly, but I'm content with whatever you choose to do."

He smiled and ran his hand along her cheek. "Good. Mr. Cooke will not be put out at all. I'm still going to work for him, but I'm going to remain here in Duluth. I'm going to focus on getting the immigrant housing done, seeing rail operations run smoothly here, and maybe even help with the canal. This way, however, I won't be traveling back and forth and having to be away from Duluth so much."

"I do like the sound of that." Gloriana wrapped her arms around his waist and placed her head on his shoulder. "I love you dearly, and the hours you are gone seem to last forever."

He held her close. "I love you, Glory. My existence would mean nothing without you and JT and Sally. Even having my father here with us and seeing his transformation has made changes in me that I never expected. I'm so very blessed." He kissed her and pulled away just enough to look into her eyes. "It would seem I was destined for you."

"And I for you. God knew we would need each other to get through the hard times of life." She smiled. "And even though I couldn't understand what He was doing, I'm so glad He didn't give up on me. I'm glad you didn't give up on me either."

Luke lowered his mouth to hers, and after that Gloriana thought of nothing else.

Tracie Peterson is the award-winning author of over one hundred novels, both historical and contemporary. She is often referred to as the "Queen of Historical Christian Fiction," and her avid research resonates in her stories, as seen in her best-selling HEIRS OF MONTANA and ALASKAN QUEST series. Tracie considers her writing a ministry for God to share the Gospel and biblical application. She and her family make their home in Montana. Visit her website at www.traciepeterson.com or on Facebook at www.facebook.com/AuthorTraciePeterson.

Sign Up for Tracie's Newsletter

Keep up to date with Tracie's news on book releases and events by signing up for her email list at traciepeterson.com.

More from Tracie Peterson

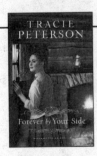

Accompanied by her best friend, Thomas Lowell, Constance Browning returns from studying in the East to catalog the native peoples of Oregon—and to prove that her missionary parents aren't involved in a secret conspiracy to goad the oppressed tribes to war. As tensions rise amid shocking revelations, Constance may also have a revelation of the heart.

Forever by Your Side, WILLAMETTE BRIDES #3

BETHANYHOUSE

Stay up to date on your favorite books and authors with our free e-newsletters. Sign up today at bethanyhouse.com.

 facebook.com/bethanyhousepublishers @bethanyhousefiction

 Free exclusive resources for your book group at bethanyhouseopenbook.com

You May Also Like . . .

When Madysen Powell's supposedly dead father shows up, her gift for forgiveness is tested and she's left searching for answers. Daniel Beaufort arrives in Nome, longing to start fresh after the gold rush leaves him with only empty pockets, and finds employment at the Powell dairy. Will deceptions from the past tear apart their hopes for a better future?

Endless Mercy by Tracie Peterson & Kimberley Woodhouse, THE TREASURES OF NOME #2
traciepeterson.com; kimberleywoodhouse.com

In early 1900s Montana, Lizzy Brookstone's role as star of an all-female wild west show is rewarding but difficult. However, trials of the heart and a mystery to be solved prove more daunting. As Lizzy and her two friends, runaway Ella and sharpshooter Mary, try to discover how Mary's brother died, all three seek freedom in a world run by men.

When You Are Near by Tracie Peterson
BROOKSTONE BRIDES #1, traciepeterson.com

31901066140486